ADRIAN KENT

Eden Awakening

First published by Kenesis Books 2020

Copyright © 2020 by Adrian Kent

All rights reserved. No part of this publication may be reproduced, stored or transmitted in any form or by any means, electronic, mechanical, photocopying, recording, scanning, or otherwise without written permission from the publisher. It is illegal to copy this book, post it to a website, or distribute it by any other means without permission.

This novel is entirely a work of fiction. The names, characters and incidents portrayed in it are the work of the author's imagination. Any resemblance to actual persons, living or dead, events or localities is entirely coincidental.

Adrian Kent asserts the moral right to be identified as the author of this work.

First edition

ISBN: 978-1-8381444-1-8

This book was professionally typeset on Reedsy. Find out more at reedsy.com

Contents

Chapter 1	1
Chapter 2	11
Chapter 3	24
Chapter 4	36
Chapter 5	45
Chapter 6	56
Chapter 7	68
Chapter 8	76
Chapter 9	86
Chapter 10	94
Chapter 11	107
Chapter 12	116
Chapter 13	128
Chapter 14	136
Chapter 15	147
Chapter 16	155
Chapter 17	164
Chapter 18	179
Chapter 19	190
Chapter 20	202
Chapter 21	211
Chapter 22	219
Chapter 23	233
Chapter 24	244
Chapter 25	253
Chapter 26	266

Chapter 27

Chapter 1

Rye Braden opened his eyes and gazed across at the holographic clock, another sleepless night, and still, only 04:00 am. He swung his legs over the bed and stood up, rubbing his unshaven face as he headed for the kitchen and verbally initiated the coffee machine. Immediately, the coffee maker spurred into life and produced a fresh cup of black coffee which Rye took and sipped before placing it on the side. He sat in the kitchen in the darkness and gathered his thoughts before heading to the shower room.

'Lights,' spoke Rye, and the lights flicked on as he entered the shower room.

The shower jumped into life as he stepped inside the small cubicle, Rye closed his eyes and tilted his face up to the spray, washing the drowsiness from his face as steam wisped around the heavy stream of hot water. Rye stood six feet tall with a hardened physique honed from many years in the military, the tattoo on his right shoulder identified him as a past member of the elite Pathfinder Patrols, a specialist unit tasked with high-level offensive operations. Rye had served ten years in this specialist unit. After he had left in 2050, he started work as a private military contractor for various high paying clients such as ArmorCorp and other private military organisations.

The water stopped and the drying system powered into action with a verbal command from Rye, once he was dry, he stepped back into the living quarters and got dressed choosing his standard choice of black jeans and a dark long-sleeved top. It was still only 05:00 am so Rye switched on the holographic television and scrolled through the channels until he got to the News channel, walking over to the kitchen Rye listened intently to the female news reporter.

'As you can see behind me. Emergency crews are still battling the fire at the United Continents London office after what is reported to have been a large explosion taking place at 02:00 am this morning. Nothing further is known about the incident at present, but the United Continents investigators are on scene.'

The camera scanned across the building showing the raging inferno and wreckage which was once the proud and historical home of the United Continents in London.

At the same time, Rye's residential intercom system sounded into life, 'CALL COMING IN. Si Morgan. Accept or Deny.'

'Accept,' Rye said.

'Rye, where have you been? I've been trying to get hold of you. Have you heard the news about the United Continents London office?' his old friend said.

'Yes, I've just seen the news. What happened? Who's involved?' Rye asked as he sipped at his coffee.

'I am pretty sure it was the FACR. Are you available to meet? We've been summoned,' Si said urgently.

'ArmorCorp offices in twenty minutes? See you there,' Rye swiped the air to end the call and finished getting dressed.

The FACR was the Faction Against Continent Rule, a well organised and supported terrorist organisation spanning across the globe. They had groups on every continent and were an underground organisation causing widespread panic through terrorist activities such as bombings, shootings and kidnappings. They were a highly trained terrorist organisation although they referred to their selves as freedom fighters, as did many terrorist related organisations spanning recent history.

Rye took the airlift down to the ground floor and walked with purpose over to the shuttle carrier. Since 2037 no vehicles except those belonging to the United Continents and those with permission were allowed within city limits. Due to the massive levels of congestion and pollution, motor vehicles were becoming far less, even though all vehicles were now pollution free due to being powered by either hydrogen fuel cells or electric. Any transport throughout the inner cities was now either via foot or government-funded shuttle carriers which ran 24hrs a day and enabled the passenger to choose their route using the network of multiple tunnels situated fifty metres above street level. Each transport tube was made of transparent polymers which were ideal from a construction and security perspective. It was clear that the planet and the cities on Earth could not realistically cope with the continued increase in motor vehicles and so changes had been needed. Vehicles powered by fossil fuels had been banned from production since 2025 after the rate of damage to the climate had increased rapidly. Any remaining vehicles using fossil fuel had been banned entirely by 2035. As Rye lived within the city limits of London; he either used his electric motorbike or public transport to make his way around the city.

Rye entered his destination into the control panel, and the

shuttle moved off gracefully although at speed.

'Destination arrival,' the speaker informed Rye some fourteen minutes later.

It was still dark outside as Rye left the shuttle and walked east along the quiet streets to the meeting place where he had arranged to meet Si Morgan. Rye was dressed mostly in black with a simple black jacket with the collar up to keep out the early morning cold. Rye also carried his sidearm under his coat in the form of a high-velocity Sig C20. The weapon was a combination of magnetic and electric charges able to deliver an array of shots from low power stun through to lethal killer shots. Rye always wore his sidearm as this was a legal right for those that were ex-military who were working as Private Military Contractors. The only other personnel to carry firearms were the United Continents. However, there was a large black market of weapons available with no data on numbers or variety held by terrorists or even private citizens for that matter. Rye approached the office building and swiped his access card across the access terminal, the glass doors slid open, and Rye stepped into the non-descript foyer. He took the stairs to the first floor where a security officer sat behind a desk, the officer, although friendly, maintained his hawklike gaze of Rye as he produced his right hand to the desktop scanner.

'Good morning Mr Braden,' the guard said as the biometric code was accepted, and a holographic image along with the relevant data came into view.

'Morning, is Morgan in yet?' Rye replied, looking at his watch.

'Yes, he is in the operations room.'

The steel doors to the first floor offices slid open to reveal a semi-chaotic scene you would not have associated with the calmness and quietness of the rest of the building. Intelligence officers were darting back and forth holding documents whilst men in suits stood in corners quietly talking. There were also a few private military contractors within the offices, how they carried their selves, calm, serious and with a high level of confidence was unmistakable. A private military contractor or PMC was mainly drawn from specialist units within the military after leaving their service. They commanded large sums of money to complete the often dirty duties of the United Continents or other organisations that could afford such human resources. Rye, as with Si Morgan, had come from the Pathfinder Patrols; this was the most respected and most challenging unit to join anywhere in the world. Rye never thought that he would end up as a PMC. Still, there weren't too many uses in the world for the skills that he had amassed over the years except for security, being a weapons specialist was no use without weapons, or being a skilled sniper without having a target to shoot was equally pointless. Rye accepted who he was and was comfortable with what he was doing. However, he did attempt to ensure that he was not dragged into any unethical missions. He had partaken in these far too many times in the past and his days of killing innocents were over.

Rye knew where he was going and walked along the corridor; passing people focused on their own business. He stopped at office B1 and used his identity card again to gain access, Rye stepped into the room and scanned from left to right taking in the faces present. Out of the five men stood in the room, he knew three of them with one of those being Si Morgan, an old colleague from the Pathfinder Patrols who now worked for ArmorCorp as an operations manager. Si was happy with this role as he was a family man now and not getting any younger, he still saw a fair amount of action and due to his experience and respect gained he was also the first choice for various high-end missions. The other two familiar faces were from the senior management team of ArmorCorp, Felix Danner and Robin Cope. Both men were ex-military officers and had joined ArmorCorp straight from the service after being headhunted by the company; they now acted as leading figures within the private company. They were often found rubbing shoulders with high profile ministers and business owners.

'Rye, thanks for coming,' said Si Morgan as he walked over to meet him. Although Si was forty-seven and much senior to Rye, he was still an exemplary example of a man. His short but stocky frame brimmed with muscle earned over many years of hard physical effort and his closely cropped black hair matched the hardened glaze of his dark eyes and muscled jaw.

'Not a problem,' Rye replied.

'You already know Felix and Robin from the company, and this is Senior Officer Baudin and Senior Officer Fabre from the United Continents Paris office,' Si pointed to the two men, and they nodded slightly to Rye. Even though Rye worked alongside the United Continents at times, he was not overly trusting of them or their methods, and he had heard various stories about the Paris office from ethnic cleansing raids through to genetic manipulation. Rye nodded his head to the two newcomers; they were dressed in dark suits with shoes that were just that a little too shiny for his liking and he instantly knew that there would be no love lost between each

CHAPTER 1

of them.

'As you may be aware the London office of the United Continents was targeted this morning at 02.10 am, the method used was that of a reactive fission bomb which took out half of the United Continents main building,' Si informed the people in the room.

'It is reported that twenty-three people were killed within the building and six injured,' he said as he flicked through the images of the aftermath.

'Do we have confirmation of who it was?' Rye asked, taking a seat at the large glass table.

'We believe it was the Faction Against Continent Rule, although this has not been confirmed, we have agents on the ground trying to gain intelligence as we speak,' Felix replied.

Si interjected, 'That's why we need you Rye, to gather intelligence on the ground.'

'Where do our Paris counterparts come into the equation?' Rye asked, looking towards the two men stood in the corner of the room watching each of the United Continents men intently.

'Mr Braden, we are here only to observe and to establish whether there are any links between this recent bombing and recent attacks in Paris, that is all,' said Jean Fabre.

'So, this is a joint operation between ArmorCorp and the United Continents? Who has field command if so?' said Rye wanting to understand the politics right from the start as he knew that these joint missions could sometimes be more trouble than they were worth. He knew that the United Continents always got ArmorCorp involved for two reasons. Firstly because ArmorCorp had the best personnel in the world that could deal with any situation and secondly because there were specific jobs that the United Continents didn't want to get their hands dirty with. Rye believed he already knew that the latter would be evident in this task.

'You are correct Mr Braden; this is a United Continents mission although using ArmorCorp personnel to execute the mission successfully. We feel that you and your counterparts have the necessary skill sets needed for this type of task,' Senior Officer Fabre said removing an A4 sized image from his bag on the table.

He walked toward Rye and handed him the photo, 'This is Michael Juno, a high-level member of the Faction Against Continent Rule and this is who we would like you to pick up for questioning.'

Rye looked at the photograph in his hand and took in the features of the person staring back at him. Black hair fell across the mans face from a side parting. He had narrow eyes and a straight nose with strong cheekbones. Rye could tell the man was well-groomed, and he had a particular look about him, a seriousness that Rye had seen many times in men like this. Rye memorised the man's face and set the photograph down on the table.

'I assume we have a full briefing pack for this mission?' said Rye as turned his gaze back to the two United Continents officers.

At this point, Si Morgan interjected, 'Yes, you and your team will be fully briefed. You have full support from ArmorCorp. Michael Juno is here in London.'

Rye shot a glance at his old friend; this would mean a swift response as if their intel was correct, then they had him in their back garden and time was critical.

'When do we need to be ready?' Rye asked.

CHAPTER 1

'You and your team need to be briefed and located at Northolt airfield by 5:00 pm, you will then be on standby waiting for intelligence to identify the optimum time to take your target,' Si informed him.

Northolt had been an old Royal Air Force airfield in the past. It had always been linked to special operations, mainly because it was a relatively small and nondescript airbase. It was also conveniently located just six miles north of Heathrow airport, so it was close to the city of London.

This kind of fastball wasn't an issue for Rye or his team as they were used to it. Throughout his years as a member of the elite Pathfinder Patrols, he had been at the tip of the spear and ready to mobilise at short notice. Being with ArmorCorp was no different in that respect, the only differences were that he was now on better pay and he was now classed as a civilian. Pretty much everything else had remained the same. He still had access to the very best equipment and weapons; he was still at the forefront of special operations and still fighting the war on terror. He also worked with those that he had known from his military days as most of these now worked for ArmorCorp or similar organisations. There were not many other civilian roles that people like Rye could fit in. Those that did choose a different career path struggled with the lack of excitement and danger that their new career offered and so they either struggled with life or reverted to private military roles.

'Remember Mr Braden; we need Juno alive for questioning,' said Fabre.

'Understood, we will certainly try our best,' Rye said with just a hint of sarcasm.

He knew that these missions did not always go as planned

and people died, and he was adamant that Michael Juno would die before any of his men were put at risk.

In the four years Rye had worked in the private military sector, he felt he had learnt as much as could be known in terms of how it all worked. Those with the necessary skills of war now worked for the same people they had when they served, companies like ArmorCorp were run by ex-military officers from elite units who were now motivated more by financial gain than loyalty. Operators like himself were lost between the blur of their military past and the role of a mercenary. They worked for the government and other high paying clients, meaning that he and his fellows were no more than mercenaries for hire. Rye knew this, but he chose to dismiss it like most of his counterparts did, he didn't revel in being classed as a gun for hire. He had initially left the military as he felt that his service was being abused for political gain as opposed to fighting right and wrong, the only thing that had now changed was that he was getting paid more, much more. But unlike his superiors, money didn't motivate Rye.

'I get to pick my team?' Rye queried.

'Yes, of course, a six-man team including yourself.'

'Ok, my team will be ready for a briefing at the location, any updates, please communicate these as and when,' Rye finished as he walked toward the door shaking the hand of Si Morgan as he left.

Chapter 2

The shuttle prepared for docking, onboard were various personnel from the United Continents Sky Zone project including engineers, surveyors and high-level officials. The shuttle eased itself into the docking port with the skill and precision of the experienced pilot at the controls. Once in position, the thump of the magnetic clamps sounded on the hull of the aircraft. The airlock hissed as the pressure stabilised between the shuttle and the floating city, which was Sky Zone One.

As the shuttle doors opened, a small squad of United Continents soldiers stood on the central docking bay of Sky Zone One headed by a tall, black-haired male with a sharp nose. He wore the usual United Continents uniform consisting of beige trousers and buttoned beige jacket with short collar. By the insignia on his jacket, it was clear that the man was a commissioned officer.

'Mr Leman, welcome to Sky Zone One,' the man in uniform said to the first person off the shuttle.

'Major Kahn, I assume everything is in order and that the final inspection is ready to be conducted,' the newly arrived visitor replied. Mr Leman was dressed in a black suit and held a briefcase in his left hand; he was in his late fifties with striking grey hair and an athletic build belying his age.

'Everything is in order and ready for your inspection,' Major Khan spoke as he ushered for his guest to enter the newly constructed corridor. 'I will escort you to the main control room to meet the other inspection teams whilst my men take your equipment.'

Major Khan turned to his squad and nodded, and they set off into the shuttle to retrieve the equipment boxes. The docking corridor connected to the main hub of Sky Zone One using a strengthened security access portal which could only be opened by someone that had submitted their biometric signature, this had to be in the form of both a thumbprint and retina scan. On the inside of the secure portal stood two heavily armed security officers dressed in a similar uniform to Major Kahn except their uniforms were all black. They wore black berets showing the cap badge of the Commando Elite, which was a specialist global fighting force belonging to the United Continents.

Since the Earth had become increasingly overpopulated, it had forced global leaders to search hard for alternative options of habitation. There were only three possible options that could facilitate human life away from the Earths surface, firstly to expand civilisation into space, including other planets like Mars. However, this type of lifestyle had not proved to be welcomed by all due to the prison-like conditions this type of environment would offer. Secondly, to build cities on the Earths oceans although the initial productions in the early 2030s had not been very successful and it became clear that nature could not be trusted when it came to taming the oceans to provide habitation. This only left the skies, and for the last ten years preparations had been made to build the Sky Zone network, this consisted of floating cities across the globe for every continent. Each Sky Zone was capable of housing nearly two million fortunate people and their families. Family units as of 2040 were now limited to two children in total; this helped to keep the population down although it had been seen as too little too late in some peoples view. Since there were now only five continents, then the Sky Zone project would only help ten million people escape the cluttered surface. In reality, this would be a pin drop in the ocean, considering the population of the Earth now stood at approximately twelve billion. But then again, those ten million souls would be the fortunate ones, those that had the wealth and connections even to be considered for the Sky Zone project. The main reason why there were global protests against the United Continents and specifically the Sky Zone project, was because it seemed the rich would be saved, and the poor were left to rot on the surface.

Major Kahn and his guests arrived at the central control room; the two guards on the door were dressed in the same uniform as the earlier Commando Elite soldiers. The first guard nodded to Major Kahn and stepped aside as the large steel door slid open to reveal a large circular room which was full of various United Continents personnel. The outer ring of computers and work stations were manned by men and woman who were focusing on the flashing lights of the terminals in front of them. The experienced operators manipulated holographic images projecting from some of the terminals. In the centre of the room was a smaller circle of workstations which were staffed by more operators with various holographic screens in view and with the person situated at that station either inputting data via the keyboard or physically manipulating the holographic screens with their hands.

Within this inner circle of computers was a raised dais with one senior officer sat overlooking and coordinating those seated around him, he wore the insignia and rank of a Captain and was the principal control officer for this particular Sky Zone station.

The entire room was a hive of activity with noises and lights you would expect from a control room of this size, especially one that controlled the daily operation of a miniature floating city. Major Kahn walked over to the far side where a group of men and woman stood around one of the stations. They were dressed in civilian clothes similar to that of the recent visitors. They were intently watching the holographic screen and listening to the operator as he provided information on the monitoring and system checks involved with Sky Zone One's life support system.

'As you can see, the system and sensors are continually checking the various life support systems to ensure air supply, climate and basic life support systems are functioning correctly,' he said as he used his hand to rotate each of the levels into view.

'As we are ten thousand metres above sea level, we have to ensure that each of the sectors is correctly pressurised,' he turned to the listeners and asked if there were any more questions, which there were none.

'Ladies and Gentlemen,' Major Kahn addressed the crowd stood around the station.

'Please meet Mr Leman, he will be leading the final inspection for Sky Zone One and will issue you all with your final duties,' Major Kahn turned to Mr Leman, 'All yours, sir.'

CHAPTER 2

Major Kahn turned and left the inspection team to their duties under the control of Mr Leman. This was the final inspection before Sky Zone One becoming the home to over two million people, including affluent families, politicians and anyone else that was fortunate enough to pass the rigorous medical screening and financial requirements. The Sky Zone project had been heralded as the future of Earth. For this reason, the success of the project came with stringent guidelines which had caused much backlash and deep hatred by those not fortunate to have been accepted and those that believed this type of solution was unjust.

To have been accepted on to the Sky Zone project, potential citizens had to be able to meet the guidelines which included an in-depth health check of each person which was only passable if that person had no current illness or any history of disease. This was to ensure that the environment on the floating city remained sickness free. The fundamental aim of these floating environments was to begin again in terms of creating pollution and biological neutral zones.

The second requirement was that those selected were solvent enough to finance the rest of their days on Sky Zone and also that of their family members, this was the main limiting factor for many citizens and meant that only a small percentage of the population would ever be considered. This alienated many people who would never have the opportunity to better their lifestyles and that of their families. This in itself had increased the compassion towards terrorist groups like the Faction Against Continent Rule and also the smaller yet still potent Rebel Alliance. The latter being a group that frequently attacked large corporations with the reasoning of being against the apparent divide between the poor communities and the rich. The Rebel Alliance were also against the overwhelming profits and control that some of the select corporate organisations held, in addition to certain parts of the government within the United Continents itself.

The final requirement of becoming a resident of Sky Zone One was that every individual accepted for the project would have to allow for a control chip to be inserted into their neural pathways. These days it was a relatively painless procedure and allowed for signals to be intercepted and interrogated by Sky Zone One and its controllers. The main concerns for those that were to undertake the procedure were related to the intrusiveness of having the chip inserted and the fact that from that point on, they would be monitored twenty-four hours per day. Over the years, the term 'Human Rights' had been heavily diluted, and this was mainly due to the authorities removing the red tape protecting individuals. It was felt that human rights and other governing factors to protect individuals and corporations which spread like wildfire throughout the 21st century were protecting criminals and terrorists alike. So in 2030, any legislation centred around human rights and data protection was heavily reduced and edited in favour of law enforcement and the criminal justice system.

Major Kahn followed the myriad of corridors until he came to a large metal double access point, across the door the words read 'RESTRICTED AREA - G1'.

Major Kahn pressed his right thumb against the protruding control panel and at the same time lowered his head to the optical scanner and placed his right eye against the housing; there were three high pitched beeps before the plates of the access point whirred into action. The access point consisted of two layers of strengthened graphene, which was a material that possessed feather-like weight but steel-like strength. This strength to weight ratio assisted in the ability of these floating cities to remain in orbit. The first protective layer of the access point slid open horizontally to reveal the second layer, which then slid open vertically from the centre.

The sharp-nosed officer stepped through the portal, and both layers slid shut immediately the moment he was clear of the portal's sensors, once through he found himself in a smaller corridor than found on the rest of Sky Zone One and one which was much darker. The secure passage was more of a defence mechanism if an unauthorised person managed to bypass the double layer security portal, biometric sensors positioned along the twenty-metre corridor recorded and cross-referenced data held on the security system. If that person was found to be unauthorised, then the mechanism would release a grid of lasers which would crisscross the entire width and height of the corridor from end to end. Anyone caught within the beams of the laser would be sliced to pieces at every intersecting point, this level of security and defence was required for what lay behind the final security portal at the end of the corridor.

Major Kahn accessed the final door before entering the restricted area identified as G1; a guard stood to attention as he entered, 'Good afternoon sir,' he spoke as Major Khan passed him. Inside the secure area known as G1 was a multitude of work stations which sat individuals although this time they donned full facial helmets with black uniforms. The helmets ensured that complete focus was maintained on the information being sent directly to each operator via the control chips that were soon to be implanted into each of the soon to be residents of Sky Zone One. As with the main control centre, this room also had a raised dais in the middle with a small bald man sitting on the rotating chair found at its centre.

Major Kahn approached the balding man, 'Captain Conrad, how are the tests going?'

'Brilliantly, we are currently sifting through data of two hundred thousand test chips. The system and operators are holding up well, so monitoring two million should not be an issue,' the smaller man replied, shifting in the seat that was constructed for a larger frame than his.

'Good, how are the Unicom's doing?'

'They are fine; the experiment is going well.'

Conrad slid off the sizeable black chair. He walked to the side of the control room and placed his eye in front of the retinal scanner. The door slid upwards from the ground and once open, Conrad and Major Kahn stepped into the cavernous room.

The room was dimly lit, although they could still make out the far walls. Major Kahn estimated the size of the room to be approximately four thousand square metres, roughly half the size of the old football pitches that were laid with grass back in the late 2040s. The room was relatively quiet except for the whir and bleeping of the computer systems located around the walls of the room.

In the centre of the room was a circle of computer terminals approximately twenty metres in diameter with a slightly raised centre, from this centre a light blue orb was projected which continually changed in appearance and shade, as if it was alive. The sphere itself was around five meters in diameter, and Major Khan struggled to divert his gaze from the orb, it gave off a calming sensation the longer he stared into it.

CHAPTER 2

As Major Khan walked towards the centre of the room, he saw four people laid in reclined chairs. Each chair was evenly spaced around the circle of machines, with each person wearing some form of a head cradle with three large cables protruding from it. Each cable then connected back to the main computer terminal. Major Khan knew that these cables via the cradle inserted directly into the three main parts of the human brain, the cerebrum, cerebellum and lastly the brainstem. This meant that the human brain could be linked with the powerful computers and the artificial intelligence that had been designed to manage each of the Sky Zone projects. The brain of each of the human Unicoms could interact with the artificial intelligence and police it in a way which had never been attempted before. This would take the optimum attributes from both machine and human and fuse them together to create the ultimate artificial intelligence system. Utilising the precision and raw processing speed that computers offer with the creativity, energy efficiency and consciousness of the human mind, providing the ultimate hybrid of human and machine intelligence.

The real power would come from the computers that powered the artificial intelligence that had been named 'HIAS' which stood for Human Integrated Artificial System, or 'H' for short as most people that was involved with the daily running came to call it. The human brains of the Unicoms merely managed the power and ensured that any computer-based decisions were ethical and in the interests of humankind. They were still testing this form of integration. However, tests had proved encouraging and meant that many people felt more comfortable about using such a powerful artificial intelligence for such a pioneering concept, as Sky Zone was.

Due to past problems with the progression of standalone artificial intelligence where over the last ten years there had been some very concerning incidents, where there was evidence that 'AI' may grow too powerful if left to its own devices. Since then, artificial intelligence had now been confined to non-military roles only and over the years had been replaced by computer power integrated with human minds like that of the Unicom's used on Sky Zone One. Some still refer to this as artificial intelligence, except one with more of a human conscious instead of a merely black and white view of the real world.

Each of the Unicom's were volunteers and knew precisely what they were getting themselves into although Major Khan had come to realise that those that had volunteered were quite different to the rest of the crew and they also kept themselves to themselves. Some of the team were afraid of the Unicoms as they even looked unearthly with their pale skin and white hair, with white hair being a side effect of being 'plugged in' so many times. There were twelve Unicoms on board which were broken down into three shifts, each shift being connected for eight hours at a time.

'God be with you,' Major Kahn said silently as he turned away in disgust, he wouldn't care for a life lived like that.

'Not god, me, I will be with them,' Conrad retorted with a dry smile appearing on his thin lips.

Major Kahn didn't like the small, skinny wretch of a man named Conrad; he knew that the other man took too much enjoyment from this top-secret project, and this sickened him. Major Kahn was by no means a weak man, although what lay in this room was anything but humane and did not sit well with him, even if they were volunteers.

CHAPTER 2

He stopped at one of the Unicorn's and a flash of recognition registered with him for an instant.

'Major, we must go as not to contaminate the Unicorns,' Conrad echoed across the room.

'Major, please!' he insisted.

The Major turned towards Conrad and then back to the Unicorn, unsure where the recognition came from, he turned on his heel and walked towards the access door. Once at the door, he took one last look back before stepping through into the control room.

'Mr Leman, how is your work going, all to plan I hope?' spoke Major Khan.

'Very well, Major, I can see that all the processes and procedures are being adhered to and that everything is running smoothly.'

'I trust you have gained enough information to satisfy the signing off of the station?'

'I am still waiting for the other team's final reports, and then all should be well, I understand there is pressure to start populating the station?'

'Yes, for the test subjects that is, and this is still an important aspect of the initial testing of the station. We have two thousand families who will be the first onboard. They will form the basis of the final tests before the official population begins,' said Major Khan thinking of the families that would be pre-selected and their thoughts on being the test subjects so to speak.

The prize of relocating to Sky Zone One would be a massive honour to those families, the station itself was a state-of-the-art artificial living environment which could only be described as a paradise. Still, if you broke it down, then it was just a type of prison, the irony in its existence was laughable. The magnitude of the ship was hard to comprehend even for himself. Residential apartments were equally spaced amongst green areas hosting many plants and trees relocated from across the planet below them. Futuristic buildings and clean-living spaces provided a serene and pleasant backdrop for living out a person's natural days. The air quality was like nothing experienced for the last twenty years, with this air being pulled from the cleaner altitude above and purified by gigantic filters before being circulated to all parts of the ship. There were also beaches where residents could relax and take in the heat of the artificial sun projected on the glass ceiling, oblivious to the chaos ten thousand metres below them. Every detail had been thought of, and no expense had been spared meaning that once a person set foot on this floating utopia, then it would be very rare for them ever to have to leave. Compared to the surface of the Earth, Sky Zone One offered the ultimate sterile environment to the fortunate families and persons living on it. They would soon be calling this place home and a place to forget the struggles, disease and overpopulation of the planet.

It was getting late now so Major Khan invited Mr Leman and his team to join him on a final tour of one of the sectors of the station, and the area that they would rest up for the evening before their flight back to the surface in the morning.

'I trust you and your team will be comfortable this evening in these guest quarters?' asked the Major.

'Yes, these are more than adequate for our needs, and I may just feel like staying for good,' replied Mr Leman with a cheerful laugh.

Major Khan ignored this comment and left Mr Leman and

his team to their own devices and as he strolled back through the brightly lit corridors, his mind returned to the room where the Unicorns were, and in particular to one of them.

Chapter 3

Rye stepped off the landing shuttle and walked across to the hangar; he wore a black combat suit with tactical body armour consisting of chest harness, protective sleeves and lightweight ballistic helmet which he held in his left hand. In his right hand, he had his G12 sonic rifle which could deliver a lethal shot up to two thousand four hundred metres away or rapid-fire bursts effective up to six hundred meters.

Rye was thinking about the mission he was close to executing; they had received intelligence that a high profile Faction Against Continent Rule member was in London at a known destination. This particular target was known as Michael Juno. He was a French citizen understood to be attending a covert meeting with other London based FACR members. Rye and his team were tasked with capturing this target, concerning the recent attacks on United Continents buildings and the staff that lost their lives in this attack.

Walking towards the hangar where the other team members were waiting, Rye strolled confidently across the airstrip. He approached his team ready to give them their orders for the mission; he looked at each of the five men who were dressed in the same tactical gear as himself although they were holding a variety of weapons each preferred by the men holding them.

CHAPTER 3

'Gents,' he said with a commanding tone whilst looking at each of the men intently. He set up a miniature projector which he would use to provide a visual brief to his men, the projector displayed a floating image of a lean-faced man with long black shoulder-length hair and supporting a short beard.

'This is our main target, Michael Juno,' Rye spoke as he swiped to the next image showing the target talking to a mixed-race female with her hair pulled back in a ponytail.

Rye eyed each of his men directly as he swiped to the next image, 'This is a side image of our target, speaking with another suspected FACR member although for some reason we have no information on this female. You will have Michael Juno's profile image sent to your IPC's so that you can identify the target.'

IPC's or Interactive Personal Computers were active military-grade personal computers which were generally integrated into combat helmets and had a retractable lens which provided the visual interface to the system. The IPC allowed the wearer to physically identify the target by using facial recognition software installed in the design. As the wearer looks in the direction of the target, the integrated computer cross-references the facial makeup of that person with a database of potential terrorists or other criminal orientated persons and to identify matches.

Rye manipulated the projection, and a holographic interpretation of the location appeared.

'This high-rise tower block is where we will find our target, specifically on the top floor in the penthouse. We will approach from the air and fast rope to the roof of the building, we will then split into teams and gain entry. We must use surprise and speed on this mission so make sure you digest your briefing packs, so we are not messing about on the ground,' Rye said as he knew that they usually would have a little more time to go through a rehearsal but sometimes time constraints made this impossible.

'Is the target known to be operating alone?' asked a burly, heavily tanned member known as Guy.

'He is renowned for operating alone although on this occasion there may be numerous people inside the apartment, intelligence has noted at least two further hostiles, but there could be more,' Rye replied.

'Be warned; this guy is an experienced operator. If you find yourself in a situation, then strike first as he certainly won't hesitate.'

Rye shutdown the holographic projector and packed it away whilst he continued to speak to the other five men.

'You should have the full intelligence packet sent to your IPC's, so please digest this. In terms of doing your job, then you are all competent operators, so I do not need to go over the basics. However, I must stress the experience of this FACR member, it is a dangerous mission, so make sure you have your wits about you and you are switched on throughout. Make sure those responsible for entry methods understand what security measures we are dealing with.'

Rye turned to the group stood in front of him, he knew they were experienced soldiers and the best of the best, this didn't stop the seed of uncertainty taking hold in the back of his mind though.

'Sort your admin out, we leave in twenty minutes,' he addressed the group one final time. He had to report to the control aircraft to finalise his plans and movement orders. He strolled over to the large double propped helicopter which had technicians completing their safety checks. The aircraft was a specially designed state of the art airborne control centre as used many times by ArmorCorp, the aircraft would hover high above the area where the mission was taking place and in doing so would provide a vital command link to the men on the ground.

Rye stepped into the aircraft where the commanding officer was busy instructing the other two members of the team to carry out their pre-deployment checks, the short, slim male was known as Leroy Jenkins, and Rye had worked with him before. Rye knew him to be a competent and quick-thinking individual who had served in military intelligence before joining ArmorCorp some ten years earlier.

'Rye, good to see you, my old friend,' Leroy smiled as he spoke.

'Hello Leroy, all sorted my end.'

Rye handed some paperwork to the blonde male sat to his right who busily started inputting data into one of the many IT systems on the aircraft.

'Good, I will have direct comms with you at all times, and obviously, we will be watching from above,' Leroy nodded over to the screens situated in front of the second man.

'Stay safe, my friend,' Leroy said as he issued more instructions to his team.

Soon after and once the raiding team were organised, the two aircraft took off in the direction of the capital. The mission was to track down Michael Juno and secure him by any means necessary for questioning to take place. The mission was not going to be an easy one, and Rye hoped that his target had not been tipped off although this was unlikely in all reality. As the two aircraft got closer to London, they split up with the command aircraft gaining height to remain hidden and to provide a technical overwatch of the assault aircraft.

Rye looked out over the city as the aircraft skimmed close to the tops of the many skyscrapers found there, it was 04.21 am, and most of the city was still sleeping.

'Five minutes,' stated the pilot on the onboard communicator.

'Roger, five minutes,' Rye repeated as he held up five fingers to the rest of his team.

The inside of the aircraft was blacked out as was the outside of the helicopter; each team member wore their assault helmets with built-in night vision and communication sets. The dispatcher shifted over to the side loading door and opened it, the cold air from the early morning spilled into the aircraft combined with the slight whir of the dampened rotor blades powering the aircraft.

The team were planning to exit the aircraft by fast-roping on to the roof of the building where the target was believed to be. They would then make their way in teams to the floor where intelligence placed Michael Juno. Each team member, including Rye, readied their selves at the door of the aircraft, they stood in pairs ready to slide down the ropes that would be released when the aircraft was directly above the target building. Two additional assault officers would also support them on jetpacks. These would provide external aerial cover with each person wearing three small hydrogen-fuelled thrusters, one worn on each arm and one on the back.

The aircraft steadied above one of the large executive accommodation buildings found in the high-profile area of the capital, named the 'El Paradiso' by those not fortunate to reside there. The blades of the aircraft were spinning at speed although the noise was dampened considerably due to the technology used, the only way someone would have known the aircraft was there was by physically looking up at it. As the aircraft steadied, the men heard the dispatcher on their IPC's.

'GO, GO, GO!' came the command.

The first pair grabbed the rope and with blistering speed dropped down and out of sight into the darkness below them. Without even a pause, the next team went until the aircraft was empty except for the pilot and the dispatcher. All the black-clad men had landed gracefully and with a sense of urgency that was born from years of training and live operations. Without a word and with only hand signals now and then, the team made their way to their designated positions, this was a tight-knit team Rye thought to himself as he joined one of the pairs by the roof access point. The first man placed a tactical x-ray device against the door. He examined the small screen; the device was used by many specialist government and military units and would provide the user with a grey scaled image of what was behind the door or wall. This was achieved by using radar-based technology that would seep through the existing barrier and send signals which would bounce back of any physical matter.

'All clear,' said the man.

'Team 1 moving forward' said Rye on his comms system.

'Team 2, roger.'

'Team 3, roger.'

The second man in Rye's team placed a small electronic charge against the door; this would cause a rapid pulse of electricity that would bypass the locking system for the door to then be pushed open. The charge was soundless except for the apparent sound of the lock disengaging, and the team entered the small corridor. They knew exactly where they were going and swiftly made their way to the far end of the hall, and without hesitation took their positions.

By this time, the other two teams commanded by Guy and Tom had positioned their selves as per the assault plan. The second team were poised above the balcony secured by abseil lines, and these were ready to drop on the command, their role would be to assault the only other access point at the same time as Rye and his team. The third team commanded by Tom were providing cover, and protective surveillance for the rest of their team members, and they would be the eyes and ears for the team throughout the assault.

'Team 2 and 3 confirm your position,' spoke Rye.

'Team 2 in position,' confirmed Guy.

'Team 3 in position,' replied Tom.

'Attack Attack' came the response from Rye as the second set of mini charges detonated on the door of the room where Rye and his team had positioned their selves, the door fell open as the charges destroyed the seal around the heavily secured door. At the same time, the third team had swung from their positions above the balcony and penetrated the window of the 130th floor of the El Paradiso building.

The next few seconds were a mixture of flashes and rapid movement as the two teams expertly manoeuvred around the rooms inside the location. The main room where the meeting was taking place was fitted with sparse furniture, including a large square metal table, with four people sat around it. Their surprise was evident although their reactions were responsive as they reached for weapons that were concealed about them. Rye entered the large room first and scanned for the immediate threat, the nearest person to him, which was a large man dressed in an ill-fitting suit had already levelled his weapon at Rye. Without thought and delay, Rye shot twice at the man's head and had already moved forward before the man's body had dropped to the floor. At the same time, the second team had entered the room and were scanning for their target using their IPC for face recognition, a second hostile had been shot in the chest and was writhing on the floor just as a second shot took him clean between the eyes and killing him instantly. There was only one more hostile, and the target Michael Juno left now, although the third hostile had thrown his weapon to the floor and raised his hands in surrender. Two of the second team had immediately taken him to the floor and secured him with restraints, Michael Juno in the confusion and shock of the attack had moved into a secondary room with Rye and one other following him.

'There's no-way-out Michael,' shouted Rye, 'Step forward with your hands raised!'

There was no response from inside the room, Rye and the second officer had taken up positions just outside, and they knew from the building plans that there was no other way out from this room.

'Gas it,' Rye commanded to his man.

'Gas Gas Gas,' replied the officer as he threw a small cylinder-shaped grenade into the room.

The gas grenade was capable of contaminating a room or area. Once the gas had been breathed in, then that person would be immediately put to sleep for a minimum of one hour. There was no delay in the effect so all team members once they had heard the warning had initiated their helmet fitted breathers which were sufficient enough to filter the air around them adequately to stop the gas affecting them.

'3, 2, 1, GO,' Rye commanded, Tom and his second man proceeded into the room.

As they entered, weapons at the ready, they made their way through the gas towards the lone figure lying on the floor. They approached with their weapons trained on the motionless figure who was now face down on the ground. Whilst Tom covered the motionless figure with his gun, his teammate came from the side and kicked the lone figure in the back to gain a response, there was none, so the officer knelt next to the figure and started to roll him over for Tom to check that no booby traps or weapons were present. As he began to roll the body, he could see that it was Michael Juno, although he also noticed that he was wearing some form of a miniature respirator. Tom also picked up on this, but before any of them could react, it was too late.

There was a searing white flash which caused both men to instantly throw their hands up to the eyes to shield them from the burning light, as they did Michael Juno brought his weapon up immediately and shot them both in the head with single shots. He then grabbed the four remaining gas canisters which were attached to the assault vest of Tom and released two as he walked towards the door.

'You kill me, and you learn nothing,' he shouted through the smoke.

He moved forward with a bold stride until his silhouette could be seen filling the doorway that Rye and his men had their guns trained on. Rye caught site of Juno's eyes and knew that the man was not going to surrender, furthermore he knew that he would not hold back.

CHAPTER 3

'Stay still Juno, there's nowhere to go, so drop your weapon!' shouted Rye.

Rye had not envisaged that this was the way it would turn out and the fact that he had lost two men angered him.

'Drop your weapon, Juno. Now!' Rye stated in an even more harsh tone.

Michael Juno was an impressive figure silhouetted against the door frame with wisps of smoke and gas fading about him; he still held his handgun in his right hand. He looked across the room where most of the officers were taking cover staring back and waiting for Rye's command, he looked back to Rye, and a hideous grin started to spread across his lips as he raised his weapon.

Rye reacted instantly and shot twice in quick succession, both shots finding their targets of Michael Juno's knees. The tall man buckled instantly and cried out as a black-clad figure which Rye saw to be Guy moved so quickly that it was like a blur in the corner of his eye, Guy promptly kicked out with his right foot and knocked the hand weapon from the grasp of Juno. The gun skittered across the floor before coming to rest some five metres away, by this time Guy had grabbed Juno and secured his hands using trillium laser cuffs. Trillium had been engineered from a mixture of titanium and steel and took the best attributes from both metals. The cuffs appeared to be a single bar until it was placed against an offender's wrists and then a physical laser beam contoured the wrists and held them tight. The amount of pressure applied to the restraints could be varied in an instant, and this made them ideal in terms of control and restraint of a prisoner.

'Charlie One, this is Tango One. Juno is under our control. Two men down,' spoke Rye as he helped Guy drag Juno, so he was lying face down.

'Charlie One, sending pick up, figures five from the rooftop,' came the reply over the comms.

'Confirmed, five minutes,' replied Rye as he walked into the second room where his two colleagues lay still.

'Let's get to the roof now,' commanded Rye.

The group, including Michael Juno was led out of the apartment with one of the officers checking the route as they went. The lead man made his way to the rooftop checking left and right, as they made it to the roof, the aircraft they were brought in was just about to land. The lead men took up defensive positions while the rest of the group boarded the aircraft, Michael Juno was lifted and pushed into the rear of the aircraft where he was attached to a guard rail and with an officer sat either side of him and a medic to tend to his wounds. Once Rye and the main team were on board, Guy and one other stayed on the rooftop to await the second pick up for the bodies of the colleagues left in the apartment. Once everyone was accounted for, the aircraft took off vertically with a massive surge of power and headed back to base.

'Two men Rye, simple operation and we have two deceased operators!' barked Felix Danner as he stalked back and forth in his office.

Rye started to speak, but Si Morgan interjected first as he knew that Rye was about to say something that would have been detrimental to himself.

'With all due respect Felix, Juno is one of the most dangerous men out there, and we now have him in custody!'

'We have still lost two good men on this mission though haven't we,' came the response from the suited ArmorCorp man.

CHAPTER 3

'Do you think I don't know this? Do you think I'm happy with the situation as these were my men under my command,' Rye stated, fist clenched and ready to create some damage to Felix Danner.

'Rye, we understand, and I am sorry about your men as I'm sure that Felix is too!' remarked Robin Cope who stood in the corner of the room.

Si Morgan walked over to the monitor on the wall which showed the containment cell that Juno was currently held in, 'I think we all need to calm down and get back on mission, more importantly, to try and bleed some information from our prisoner Mr Juno.'

'Yes ok, we currently have interrogators on their way. They will be in first with him, and they will use any means necessary to gain information from our notorious Mr Juno,' stated Felix as he pressed the intercom button on his desk and queried where the interrogation team were.

Rye pressed his lips at this as he would have given anything to be present in that room with Michael Juno.

Chapter 4

Since 2032 the United Continents had forged its dominance on the world, especially after the fall of the European Union some years earlier. After many gritty years of world conflicts, many of the different countries were forced to join together to safeguard the civilian populations against the dramatic rise in global terrorism that had plagued many cities and countries. The primary aim of the United Continents was to join forces with a view of oppressing those that demanded that the rest of the world followed their ideologies and way of life, this involved the perverted religious fundamentalists which started to grow beyond restraint in early 2000. By the year 2025, such groups had grown in number. They were able to force their way like a plague into many countries, recruiting through propaganda those individuals that wanted to be part of something larger and that had been blinded by the ill-fated concept of a particular religion and it's exaggerated ideology. In addition to this other non-religious groups started to rise out of the shadows, one of these was to be the Factionists who later formed into the highly sophisticated Faction Against Continent Rule or FARC for short. In the early days, they were a small group ranging from ex-military personnel through to people that had been wronged in one way or the other by their government. It was not until the United Continents was formed that the FARC developed into a highly sophisticated network of more than capable terrorists and was by this time a significant threat to the world.

When global powers push governments and countries together, there will always be high levels of friction from those opposed to being bullied or coerced into new ways of life. It was evident that something had to shift to combat the global rise in terrorism, which was becoming an uncontrollable cancer. The United Continents offered a chance of peace and reduced attacks through the unity of many nations; it was also formed to rid the world of corruption although as with other cancers this can be difficult to remove altogether.

What was clear was that the implementation of the United Continents was rapid once the mainstream of countries had signed up, having this unity spread using the leaders of those countries. They believed in a united front to protect the globe. This also meant trying to bring an end to other threats, including global warming, diminishing resources and other prominent global concerns. By 2032, the world had forged in terms of countries becoming more interlinked with their continents and those countries on each continent becoming ruled by one specific leader, who was the President of that continent and all the states and populations within. These remaining continents included Eurasia, the Americas, Africa and Australia, meaning that Eurasia was now the most extensive and most governing of the United Continents despite being the most complicated. Antarctica had become a waste ground and not inhabited by man anymore, mainly due to the effects of global warming and the loss of the polar ice caps.

The United Continents had become the global response to preserving the Earth and had been hailed in the early days as the saviour of the planet. This was mainly through the binding of countries and their leaders. There wasn't one area on the planet by now that didn't have some form of United Continent rule, and the United Continents ensured that their laws, regulations and policies were adhered to by every single person on the planet. The United Continents were ruled by leading figures from across the globe with the higher echelon consisting of each of the four continents having their own President. Every President had four Secretary Generals under their power, which led to each Secretary-General having four Field Marshalls under their direct control. These Field Marshalls each being responsible for the four areas of current warfare, Land, Sea, Air and Space. The ruling individual over the United Continents was the Commander General; this was now the highest rank on the planet with even the remainder of the worlds royal families being under this one person's rule. The current Commander General was an ex-military high-ranking officer from Eurasia, named Pierce Davenport. He was a no-nonsense straight talker that was adept at thinking dynamically and revered for his direct action; this split the population of the planet into either favouring him or loathing him.

The United Continents were responsible for most if not every element of the planets functioning; this included governing the citizens of each continent, passing laws, policing of the continents including use of military force where necessary and general rulership over the billions of humans living on the planet. They had made significant progress in terms of preserving the Earth. However, this had come at some, unfortunately, unavoidable cost; this included strict laws governing childbirth whereby only married persons were able to give birth or raise children from donors, and each marriage was limited to two children. The use of natural resources on the plant was heavily restricted to ensure their longevity. Advancements in alternative power technology were heavily funded, to release the burden form the natural resources which by 2030 were becoming less and less. Mans addiction to war was also crushed through the rise of the United Continents. The world had seen many changes and most of which were for the better, even though there were still visible differences in all areas of humanity in terms of wealth versus poverty. World hunger had been overcome by 2042 due to the efforts of the United Continents and its humanitarian projects. However, this did not alleviate poverty as such but did ensure that men, woman and children did not starve to death through lack of aid reaching them as opposed to earlier in the century.

Some would say that the United Continents ruled with an iron fist meaning that they dealt with any opposition in a quick and sometimes brutal way, this was achieved due to the might of the military assets now commanded by them. It was also partly due to the abrupt nature of the current Commander General and his staff. In particular, some of the Field Marshalls under his command. This had been one of the success factors of the United Continents once it had gained enough support and power, amalgamating the soldiers and assets of the different countries now under United Continent rule.

The United Continents was also a valued defence against the rise in epidemics and pandemics which had been causing significant concern since the increase in pandemics in 2020 which had taken the lives of millions of people, showing total disregard for life and the human population. The rate at which the virus had spread across the globe had shocked even the most mighty of governments. So every effort from that point on had gone into protecting against the ongoing virus and any new viruses that materialised. As time moved on, then it was clear that private pharmaceutical companies were playing god with vaccines, holding the population to ransom and being selective with who received vaccinations first. This forced a change in the way the pharmaceutical industry was run, and the companies that operated in this space were absorbed by the United Continents although at very healthy selling prices. Even though the rich got more prosperous from the sales of these companies, it meant that medicines and vaccines were made equally available to everyone. It was refreshing to see that when it came to disease and cures that the United Continents did not discriminate or promote profit over wellbeing.

Another area of scientific medicine and one which was heavily criticised was that of genetic mutation experimentation, despite the advancements in this scientific area, there were still many people that did not agree with this type of human testing. It was true that genetic mutation had helped alleviate some of the worst diseases for humans. However, it was rumoured that gene mutation was also being used in top-secret experiments. Still, nothing could be proved.

One such project was named the 'Eden' project, and although so secret that civilians were never aware of it, there were still those in government and high-ranking positions that had heard whispers of what the United Continents was conducting and were not supportive. Due to the different secrecy levels within the United Continents, then it was difficult for anyone to either confirm or disprove that something like Eden was taking place unless of course, they were part of the project.

Genetic mutation has been historically linked to testing on animals and crops and frowned upon concerning testing on humans. However, there are many diseases and deaths which are caused by natural mutations such as cystic fibrosis, sickle cell anaemia and even various cancers. The United Continents and their scientific teams had made leaps and bounds in terms of eradicating most of these genetic disorders. They were being heralded by many as heroes. However, it didn't take long for scientists to use these advancements in knowledge to learn how to manipulate the human body. This led to enhancing individuals, and this is where the Eden project began. One single scientist hid away in an underground laboratory seeking out the holy grail of human capability, and he had found it.

Oliver Randall was a small individual who looked much younger than his already young twenty-six years; he had lank black hair cut short which exposed most of his face and large almond eyes set above a small rounded nose. Oliver was a typical scientist, passionate about his work and thus spent most of his time learning and understanding genetic biology. He had majored from one of the leading science universities based in Paris, and he was one of the youngest to graduate with a PhD in genetics and modular medicine at only twenty-two. From here he was headhunted by one of the scientific teams at the United Continents. For the last four years, he excelled within the world of genetics specialising in genetic mutation. Oliver was awkward around most people and especially large crowds; he was more at home alone in his lab doing what he loved best. An orphaned child with no siblings for support, he had found it difficult growing up in one of the cities orphanages as these were generally filled with more streetwise kids. They believed Oliver to be the weak link and so targeted him for verbal and physical abuse. It was not that Oliver wasn't affected by the bullying, as it did affect him. However, he knew deep down that someday he would rise much higher than these back-street scrappers, and that gave him the resolve to continue through the daily and sometimes agonising attacks on him.

Oliver had dedicated every waking hour to his research and by doing so, had neglected any form of personal life. With his parent's dead, there was no one in his life anymore that he cared for or even communicated with outside of his work. This level of focus is what had made him so knowledgeable in the subject of genetic mutation and how he had found ways in which to nurture genetic mutations that could alter human subjects in ways in which were previously thought to have been impossible. His research had been noticed by his seniors and especially for one specific purpose, that being warfare. The military leaders had seen this as a valued use for Oliver's research. The United Continents believed that his research could be used to enhance various aspects of a soldier which in turn would further improve the capability and sometimes brutality of the United Continents military. This project had been named Eden and was classified at the highest level within the United Continents with only a select few senior officers and researchers being aware of it.

The aim of project Eden was simple, to enhance the physical and mental capabilities of a specific group of soldiers to improve combat effectiveness. This included enhanced strength through muscle fibre manipulation, skeletal system strengthening, vision enhancement for greater focal coverage and low light capability, faster reactions through modification of the cerebellum and other areas of genetic engineering. The effects of such interaction with the human body would create what many people would call a super soldier who would be stronger, faster and more dynamic than any other human on the planet. Oliver's research had opened the pandora's box of warfare, making Oliver one of the most powerful scientists on the planet.

The secrecy of the project had been unprecedented with only a select few knowing of its existence, let alone the full details of the project. This was mainly because some thought that it would be frowned upon and break ethical boundaries, and they would be right. Even though the United Continents had brought many benefits to the world through unification, there was a thin line between unifying the world and creating a dictatorship which has genetically mutated super soldiers in its arsenal. The United Continents was starting to overstep that line and unconsciously replace the unwanted powers that they had removed for the very same reasons that they were now being found guilty of, an ironic cycle of blinkered leadership. However good or different a new leadership thought they were, they always seemed to nose dive into the same methods and governance that governments, leaders and powers before them slipped into.

Members of elite military units had volunteered for the Eden project, without understanding the real risks involved. The boundaries of the physical body had been pushed far beyond what was ever attempted before and with some disastrous effects where the candidate could not take the adaptations to the body and mind. These such cases were left with severe mental or physical disabilities and hence retired from the military, albeit with a substantial financial payout.

Those that did survive underwent unbelievable changes which even surpassed the scientist's expectations, all except Oliver Randall's expectations as he was always trying to push harder with each experiment. There was no public applause for what he was achieving as the entire project was unknown to the public and even to most of the United Continents, he didn't care though. The respect of those not in his field of expertise meant nothing at all to him, only the praise of those that he respected was needed. However, he knew that would never happen as he doubted that anyone outside of this covert circle would know about what was being achieved.

Oliver believed that he was probably the most influential person within the United Continents, playing god with his test subjects and getting results. He bathed in the power this gave him and revelled in his success. Of course, there were other scientists involved, but after proving himself time after time, Oliver himself ran the science element of the experiments, and no one got in his way.

Chapter 5

Rye didn't get back to his apartment until late in the evening after the mission that had been so bittersweet; they had captured Michael Juno, the notorious FACR terrorist. The bitterness element came from the fact that they had lost two operatives on that mission, both killed at the hands of Michael Juno. Rye entered his apartment and immediately sensed a presence within the place. He quietly pushed the front door closed and slid out his Sig C20 firearm. He stood statue-still, eyes scanning the darkness and listened for any sign of movement; there was none. He moved with stealth and precision, and as he moved into the lounge, he had his pistol gripped tight into his body ready to shoot, and when he saw the still figure sat in the corner of the room in darkness, he instantly knew who it was.

Ruby Monroe sat there motionless, her figure only just recognisable against the dark backdrop of the room, as the lights of the living room came into life her smile broadened across her face.

'Hello Rye,' she spoke softly.

'Ruby, I wasn't expecting you to be here,' Rye replied, scanning the rest of the room as he spoke.

'Yes, I can see that by your entrance!' she said as she stood up and walked towards him.

She wore a knee-length cream dress with long black boots, her dark shoulder-length hair was worn down and complimented her tanned skin. Ruby Monroe was thirty-one years of age, and there was no argument about her attractiveness. Her large brown eyes and chiselled nose complimented her slim face and appealing features. Standing at just under six foot, her body was that of someone that took pride in their appearance and was lean and athletic. As she approached Rye, she slid her arms around his muscular body and pressed her head against his solid chest.

'I hear that you had a busy day today,' she said softly, and with evident compassion.

Regardless of the frustration and disappointment, Rye was feeling, he loved Ruby and longed for her attention.

'Yes,' he said, pulling her in tight to him.

'Do you want to talk about it?' she asked.

'Maybe later, right now, I want to take you to bed!'

With that, he lifted Ruby from the floor and carried her into the bedroom before slowly lowering her to the bed.

Rye opened his eyes as morning light crept into the room, Ruby was still sleeping next to him, one leg draped over his and her head buried in his chest. Rye carefully slid out from under her and swung his legs off the bed. He sat there for a few seconds before standing and walking into the kitchen. He made himself a cup of coffee and switched on the news channel as he checked his messages, scanning through them as he came to one from his friend Si Morgan. The message was an update on Michael Juno stating that they still had not made any progress through the interrogation that had been taking place since they had arrested Juno the day before. Even

CHAPTER 5

with all the modern techniques involved with interrogation which for the last twenty-four hours had made no effect, Rye still believed that he could get Michael Juno to talk. He just needed ten minutes in the same room as him. Rye was still smarting from the loss of his two colleagues, made even more unbearable for the fact that Rye was the officer in command for that particular mission.

As Rye flicked off the news, he felt Ruby approach from behind and place her arms around him.

'Good morning, handsome,' she purred.

'Are you ready for that chat now?' she said as she kissed the back of his neck.

Ruby Monroe had been with Rye Braden for three years and in that time had grown accustomed to his work as a private military contractor. She even understood why he did what he did, and that included having a level of respect and pride in what he had achieved throughout his years in the military and other areas of his life. Ruby understood professionalism, and she understood what pushed Rye emotionally and mentally. She probably understood more than any other person as not only was she his partner but she was also a psychologist and one that had consulted for various parts of the United Continents in the past. Like Rye, Ruby excelled at her profession and had gained recognition swiftly as a leading psychologist. Her passion and dedication to her work meant that most of her time was involved with one project or another. This meant that she did not get to see Rye as much as she liked, although deep down, they both knew that they were okay with this.

'I lost two men yesterday, two good men at that!' Rye spoke as he twisted around to face her, slowly brushing her brown silken locks out of her eyes.

'I'm so sorry to hear that Rye, I am,' she responded, looking directly into his eyes.

'The good news is that we caught the man we were after, the man we believe is linked to the recent bombing of the United Continents London office.'

'Where is he now?' she enquired without hesitation.

'He is being held in an undisclosed location and undergoing interrogation as we speak. There are a lot of people and agencies interested in what he has to say, for obvious reasons,' Rye said.

'Your team know the risks Rye, as do you and so you can't put the blame on yourself,' she said as she poured herself a coffee.

'I know that, but it was still my command, so I have to take some responsibility for what happened.'

'I need to get back to the office this morning; you want to walk with me,' Rye said as he walked towards the bathroom.

'Yes, as I have to be somewhere too, but only if I can join you in the shower!' she mused joyfully.

'Stupid question!' he replied as he stripped down and entered the shower.

Both Rye and Ruby were dressed now and had decided to walk most of the way to where they both needed to be, Rye needing to chase up the progress on Michael Juno and Ruby attending one of her private appointments. The morning was crisp although the sun was trying to make an appearance, the streets were relatively quiet as the rush hour had passed and most people preferred to take public transport these days as opposed to walking. They continued side by side past the mostly residential apartment blocks that spanned

CHAPTER 5

the long streets on the outskirts of the city centre; vehicular traffic was barely present this close to the city due to the restrictions brought in many years ago to reduce pollution and congestion. It made for a much brighter and pleasing environment without the noise and smog that came from the twenty-first century congestion. As they were walking along chatting to one another, Rye felt his highly trained second sense telling him that something wasn't quite right. Instantly he had an awareness that someone on foot was following them. Due to his job, Rye was exceptionally experienced in anti-surveillance measures and knew how to detect, avoid and manipulate surveillance being undertaken on himself. For now, he continued, as usual, talking with Ruby and continuing along the pristine city street.

As they turned the corner, Rye immediately noted a silver van parked up on the same side as he and Ruby were walking. It wasn't that it was an unacceptable reason for the van being there, it was more Rye's intuition that told him something seemed out of place. Although the streets were quiet, they had now caught up with a handful of people walking about unaware of what was potentially unravelling before them. People without any form of security or military experience did tend to be slightly more ignorant of their surroundings compared to those that had to be aware due to their jobs.

As they approached the silver van, Rye was able to check window reflections to now see that two men were walking behind him and Ruby. He could also hear their footsteps becoming quicker.

Twenty metres to the van now, Rye surveyed his surroundings again.

Fifteen metres, there were limited escape routes where they

were currently situated. If it was an attack, then Rye's options were becoming remarkably limited.

Ten metres, Rye did have his Sig C20 firearm beneath his jacket sat snugly in his covert holster. This gave him confidence in his response if it came to that, albeit it was seemingly looking like this situation unfolding in front of him was intentional.

Five metres from the van, Rye heard the footsteps behind him gaining even more speed and being much closer than he would have liked and with that he reached out for Ruby with his left arm and pulled her across his front and towards the wall of the residential apartment block on his right. At the same time, he had drawn his firearm, swivelled around and dropped to one knee just as one of the men had fired his weapon at him. Rye knew that if he had not fallen to one knee, then the shot would have found its target.

Rye released a controlled shot and instantly dropped the first male, with surprising speed honed from years in the military he had loosed another fatal shot at the second man before he even had the chance to remove his weapon from his jacket. Two targets down Rye thought to himself, but even as that thought had crossed his mind, Rye heard the door of the silver van slide open but by the time he had swirled back around three men had dived on him. Two burly men grabbed his arms, and the third grabbed him from behind in a chokehold. Ruby had only just recovered from being flung against the wall by Rye, and she sat up on her knees holding her head as she observed what was happening to her partner right in front of her eyes. Rye had his gun ripped from his hand, and his attacker's grip became stronger by the second as they attempted to drag him towards the open door of the waiting van. Rye knew he was stronger and fitter than the average person, although he also knew that these three men that were holding him were not your average person.

Rye could feel his mind going hazy from the lack of oxygen due to being held in a chokehold, he was feeling desperate for the first time in a long time, and he didn't like the feeling. With that, Rye pushed his mind into focus and assessed the situation in an instant, by this time one of the men had stepped into the van and had started pulling Rye in whilst the other two continued to push. As the man climbed into the van, he released one of his arms on Rye to grab hold of the van to help himself inside. As he did that Rye flexed his arm and with one massive effort, he pulled the man across his body and into the path of the second man holding his left arm. They smashed into each other but only the male who had one arm on Rye released, but this was enough for Rye to react further.

With his right arm, he slammed his fist into the back of the head of the man he had just ripped from the back of the van. There was a sickening crack as Rye's fist contacted with bone, this also forced the man's head forward at unbelievable speed and directly into the face of the man holding his left arm. Both men had now released Rye's arms and were crashing to the floor just to the left of where Rye was standing. In that instant and with effortless speed, Rye placed both of his feet on the side of the van and pushed with all his might. The effect was that both Rye and the last man holding him in a chokehold went flying back at least five metres from the van with Rye landing on top of his attacker, who by this time had released his grip on Rye's neck. Rye instantly smashed his right elbow into the man's ribs and another crunching crack could be heard, Rye rolled over onto one knee, the man he had just elbowed was reeling in pain. Rye focused his attention on the other two assailants who by now had climbed back to their feet and were approaching fast, one holding a knife.

The first man with the knife lunged at Rye with incredible speed although Rye was much quicker and managed to dodge the lunge and at the same time clothesline the man at throat level with the top part of his hand. The impact physically took the man off his feet and onto his back with a loud thump. The second man was about to draw his weapon when Rye grabbed the front of the man's jacket with his left hand, pulled him close and as he did, he punched him twice in quick succession, once in the head and once in the throat. The man flew back under the force and lay still, his body motionless as soon as he hit the floor. The other man that he had also knocked to the floor was holding his throat and struggling to breathe. Rye ignored him and knelt next to the man that had just had his ribs broken by Rye's recent elbow; he pressed one of his knees into the man's chest which caused a loud groan from the man.

'Who sent you?' Rye said through clenched teeth. The man continued to groan and writhe under pressure exerted by Rye's knee.

'Who sent you?!' Rye said louder as he applied more pressure to the man's chest.

'Damn you!' came the response through blood-spattered words.

'One last opportunity to tell me,' Rye threatened although he knew this man was professional and that it would take much more to get him to speak.

By this time sirens could be heard in the background and Rye knew that the authorities were on route, he looked over at Ruby who was now standing up with tears in her eyes and

CHAPTER 5

visibly shaking. As he did so, a United Continents drone hovered above them; its camera and weapon systems pointed directly at the group below. Even with facial recognition Rye knew not to make any sudden or erratic movements when a drone was present as mistakes were easily made. He also didn't want to take his chances with the drone in case it didn't recognize him as a private military contractor, plus the fact that he didn't know who these other men were as they could be equally as bona fide as himself.

'Don't move,' he said to Ruby as he raised his arms to show that he was no threat.

Drones had been utilized as law enforcement first responders since 2030 once the technology had been advanced enough to facilitate autonomous flight and increased flying time. By deploying thousands of drones to patrol the skies above the streets meant that big brother could keep an eye on most of civilization and at the same time offer a rapid response to any criminal incidents taking place. This was in addition to CCTV covering every street, square and open space available; it was scarce not to be observed these days by one kind of camera or another. Human rights activists and most of the public had been fighting the big brother syndrome since the early 2000s although it had been inevitable that surveillance would continue to spread.

The men that had attacked Rye were also slightly hesitant now that the drone was on-site, although one of the men, the man that had his ribs broken by Rye's elbow seemed keen not to be arrested. He stumbled to his feet, clearly in pain although still very mobile. He walked towards the open door of the silver van even with warnings being issued from the drone which had now been taken control of by a human law enforcement controller.

'STOP!' came the stern voice from the drones onboard tannoy as it repositioned itself in a better position now that the man had moved.

Rye could hear the sirens of the United Continents law enforcement response vehicles getting louder; they would be here in minutes if not seconds.

By this time the male had leant into the rear of the van and was now coming back into view, but this time he was holding what looked like a rocket launcher. He barely had time to swing the weapon round in an arc before the drone let loose with a volley of lethal shots directly to the man's centre mass. Rye could see that he aimed to shoot the drone out of the sky, but this had been a pathetic attempt as once the man had been recognized as hostile then the drone had initiated its counter attack.

United Continents vehicles arrived on scene swarming the area, firearms at the ready. Fortunately, they had been briefed on their way and knew who to arrest and who was friendly.

The scene was carnage with one dead hostile and three other wounded prisoners, blood covered the pavement where the opportunistic man had nearly been cut in half by the drone.

As the surviving aggressors had been bundled into different vehicles, another vehicle came to collect Rye and Ruby and take them to the station for a debriefing as questions needed answering. Rye messaged Si Morgan to inform him what had happened and to meet him at the station where they were headed.

Ruby Monroe gripped Rye's hand in the back of the vehicle; she was clearly still shaken by what she had just witnessed.

'I've never witnessed violence like that before, I wasn't naïve to what you do but never have I seen that level of raw violence and especially from you,' she said with a shaky tone.

Rye released her hand and placed his arm around her shoulder and pulled her in close and kissed the top of her head, more to try and alleviate any shock that she may be experiencing.

'I've never seen strength like that either and the speed that you reacted; I didn't think that was possible!' she said in a bemused tone as she stared up at him.

The vehicle they were in was speeding along to the nearest station, buildings were flashing by, and Rye could see people going about their everyday lives oblivious to the carnage that had just occurred a few streets away.

'Rye, you must know that how you took those men down was not natural don't you?' she inquired tentatively, by this time she had sat up and away from Rye as she spoke.

'It's the training,' Rye responded, 'Its how I react when someone attacks me,' he replied, facing forward.

Deep down Rye knew that there was something different about him, and this incident had just proved that. He had known for some time that he was stronger than other people, his reactions were sharper, thinking about it even his vision and hearing were more acute than anyone he knew.

Rye stared out of the window and tried to remember if he had always been like this or whether there had been some kind of change in him at some point. Either way, maybe it was time to start asking some questions.

Chapter 6

Sylvia DeMarco stepped off the private jet at King Khalid International airport, where a blacked-out SUV was waiting on the tarmac. As she walked towards the waiting vehicle, an Arab man dressed in a black suit, white shirt and dark blue tie approached her.

'Good afternoon Miss DeMarco,' he said with perfect English.

'Good afternoon Ahmed.'

Sylvia DeMarco was an attractive woman with striking features, at forty years of age she was ageing better than most woman, being mixed race she had naturally golden skin, brown curly locks and a toned and slender body. Her day to day job was in property with her having an impressive portfolio across the globe from luxury flats in the Middle East through to corporate office buildings in the heart of London. This multitude of properties also ensured that she was able to assist her more secretive counterparts. These being high ranking members of the Faction Against Continent Rule terrorist organization as Sylvia DeMarco was also the main conduit for this opposition group against United Continent rule.

Her lavish lifestyle was part-funded by the Elders who were

a secretive collection of influential people from before the rise of the United Continents. These discreet individuals funded organisations like the FACR because they were not pleased with the restricting landscape that the United Continents created and this meant restrictions on what they could get away with themselves, compared to an era before United Continents rule. No one outside of the Elders circle knew their identity, and they ensured that this anonymity was maintained through the strictest measures possible. As long as Sylvia DeMarco did their bidding, then she would be protected by the Elders, and she could continue being one of the richest women on the planet. Although she felt confident that she was safe dealing with them, she also knew not to anger them as she could easily be replaced as everyone outside the Elders inner circle was expendable.

Sylvia spoke softly as she scanned through her mobile device, 'I would like to go to the penthouse to freshen up before my meeting please.'

'Of course,' replied Ahmed as he eased the powerful yet silent electric SUV away from the runway and out of the airport towards Riyadh.

The penthouse was located in the downtown area of the city. Riyadh was one of the wealthiest cities on the planet and a city which the United Continents didn't have much of a hold which meant that those trying to avoid the United Continents for one reason or another could do so quite easily. This was why Riyadh was an excellent location for Sylvia DeMarco as her movements and activities were much less restricted compared to other major cities, and the activity that Sylvia was involved with demanded zero awareness from outsiders.

Since the death of her parents when she was just thirteen

years of age, she had never felt any form of belonging or connection with one singular place. This was probably the reason for building such a lucrative empire which allowed her to have multiple residences across the globe. Each one an extension of her global reach and more importantly, the reach of the Elders who relied heavily on the mobility and access that Sylvia brought their organisation. Since her parents were killed in a United Continents air strike in 2027 in Milan, she had more reason than most to act against United Continents rule. However, combined with the generous financial backing of the Elders, then it made it all so much easier to oppose them. She had grown accustomed to her affluent lifestyle. She was by no means prepared to go back to the hardship of her earlier years after losing her parents, the time before she was saved from the countless foster homes and disinterested pretend families. Those families that had taken her in mainly for the financial incentives involved with fostering. She would never forget the man that had saved her from the vicious cycle that was her life back then, this man being Rupert Everson.

Sylvia had been boarding at one of the leading boarding schools in Italy when she was requested into the principles office and informed of the terrible news about her parents. A United Continents airstrike had not been as on target as it should have been. It had taken out an adjacent building to where the intended target had been, which had been a recurring problem with United Continents airstrikes. The building, which was a hotel had been destroyed with most of the occupants being killed, including both of Sylvia's parents.

'I am sorry for your loss Sylvia,' came the muted sound from the principal.

The words echoed around the room but didn't hold any

CHAPTER 6

meaning, her gaze was drawn to the large window of the principal's office and the grey skies beyond it, this was the day when she knew that her life would never be quite the same again.

Sylvia arrived at the affluent yet remarkably indistinct tower block where her penthouse apartment was located, the well-dressed concierge exited the building and opened the door of the SUV. She elegantly slid out of the vehicle. Inside the building was an array of luxurious furniture, artwork and décor. The main reception desk was staffed by a tall and slender male receptionist with a nose that seemed to absorb most of his face.

'Good afternoon Miss DeMarco, I trust you are well?' came the well-spoken words from the man behind the reception desk.

'Hello Luiz, I am fine, thank you. It's good to be back.'

The penthouse suite came with a private elevator, which only certain people could access for security reasons, using biometric data including retinal scan and voice scan. Sylvia entered the elevator, and the security system automatically scanned her retina whilst she instructed the elevator to take her to the top floor of the building. Once inside the penthouse, the grand designs were unmistakable with elaborate marble flooring, high ornate ceilings and elegant furniture throughout the apartment.

Sylvia enjoyed her luxurious life, although she had never taken it for granted. She knew it could all be ripped away in an instant as was the case after she had lost her parents in the unjustified United Continents airstrike. In that instant, she had lost everything dear to her. This included her inheritance due to the after actions of the United Continents legal team. They had made attempts to cover up various details of the incident and won the legal case after Sylvia's team had expended most of her inheritance fighting them.

She had been too young to understand the consequences of such a cover-up and the complexities surrounding the incident. It was as she grew into maturity that she understood the depths that the United Continents had gone to attempt to distance themselves from the attack that had killed not just her parents, but also many other innocent civilians. Once Sylvia was at an age to understand, the deep-rooted anger and resentment soon set in and ate away at her once innocent child-like character. She had a hidden side to her life now, hidden from most people. She longed for retribution for the murder of her parents and the life she once had.

Sylvia had been nurtured over the years to direct her pain and anger towards the likes of the United Continents and those who serve under the far-reaching control of this organisation. There were many against the United Continents, including political, terrorist and paramilitary groups. Each with their gripe against who the United Continents were and what they stood for. Many believed that they had merely replaced the corrupt governments they had removed, with an even deeper corruptness but on a much grander scale.

Sylvia was due to meet some of the Elders that evening, and it had been some time since they had last met, Rupert Everson was in town visiting a close colleague, so it was an ideal time for the three of them to meet up.

It was 7:00 pm and the heat of the day was still evident outside, inside the temperature was a cool twenty degrees thanks to the air conditioning cooling every part of the building. Sylvia stripped off her clothes from the day. She gracefully moved about the apartment, finally entering the elegant bathroom with its classic roll top bath situated in the middle of the room surrounded by ornate marble furniture. Sylvia ran the hot water for the bath as whisps of steam rose throughout the room. She stared at herself in the mirror. Sometimes she didn't recognize the person looking back at her. She had changed so much since her childhood, especially after her innocence had been ripped away from her all those years ago. She had become more and more calculated and driven to ensure that her plans came to fruition.

She switched the taps of the bath off and stepped into the deep warm water before effortlessly lowering herself so that the water line covered all of her body except her breasts and face, with the water lapping close to her exposed nipples. She laid still for a moment contemplating the evenings planned meeting. Rupert Everson had a varied past from working within the United Continents through to setting up a radical group named Deliberate Action, which was a far-right political group. The second person who would be joining them was Muhammad Al-Mutawa. He was fifty-four and was linked to one of the previous Royal families and now a recognized global businessman. However, Sylvia knew a different side to Muhammad, that of being part of the secretive group named the Elders.

Sylvia dried herself in front of the full height mirror using the luxurious cotton towels; she pressed the towel lightly against her body as she stared once again in the mirror. She had come so far, and now the end was in sight, the downfall of the people and organisation that had affected her so much all those years ago.

Sylvia had already organised her dress for this evening, a

long black cocktail dress with a low cut back and made of the finest silk you could find. A diamond necklace sat around her long feminine neck with her hair tied up away from her face. She would be turning heads this evening, and she enjoyed the power that the feminine shape could command from the male and sometimes female population.

The meeting was being held at one of the finest restaurants in Riyadh. Muhammad Al-Mutawa himself owned it, so privacy was guaranteed whilst they discussed the evening's agenda. As she stepped from her apartment building, her driver opened the door to the blacked-out SUV, and she casually climbed into the rear seat. The vehicle silently powered off to their destination, the roads were relatively quiet at this time of night, and the city lights sparkled in the humid evening air as the vehicle silently glided through the streets of the city.

As her vehicle pulled up at the restaurant, a tall, well-built man stepped from the front door and approached the SUV; he then waited for the vehicle to be unlocked before opening the door for its occupant. Sylvia slid her legs from the vehicle, her silk dress parting slightly to show her long, tanned and well-toned legs. Once out of the vehicle, she made her way to the entrance and was met by another gentleman wearing an immaculate dark suit covering a muscular build. He nodded at her before ushering her to follow him into a waiting elevator. She didn't hesitate as she knew these men were part of the location's security team. The elevator swiftly rose to the top floor of the restaurant, which she knew to be the private member's bar, which was always the preferred location for any Elder business in this part of the world.

The door to the elevator opened and her escort ushered her

into the grand room which sprawled out before her. There were various seating areas in the middle of the room, with the main bar was set against the opposite wall, with a row of stools aligning the bar. The décor was tasteful and expensive, grand chandeliers hung from the ceiling and everywhere you looked was crystal in one form or another.

In the far left of the room was a raised area with a large table and twelve chairs spread around it, just before the raised area stood another security guard in an equally well-tailored black suit. Behind him and sitting at one of the corners of the large glass table were two men, Sylvia recognized both of them immediately as Rupert Everson and Muhammad Al-Mutawa. She proceeded towards them, and the security guard stepped aside to allow her on to the raised area, as she did, both men stood to greet her.

'Sylvia, I can't tell you enough how good it is to see you each time,' spoke Rupert in a soft English accent as he placed his arms around her and pulled her close.

Sylvia smiled, 'Thank you, Rupert, it is always too long between seeing you I find.'

She then turned to Muhammad and smiled whilst she extended her hand.

'Muhammad, thank you for setting this meeting up to discuss our new plans,' she spoke as he took her hand in his.

'It is my pleasure as always Sylvia. Your unrelenting focus drives us all towards our final objective.'

They all sat around the table and Muhammad gestured for the waiter to approach already holding what appeared to be a bottle of red wine.

'A special occasion deserves a special treat, Domaine de la Romanee, one of my favourites.'

Muhammad tested the wine that the waiter had poured into his glass. He nodded in approval and gestured to the waiter to pour for his guests.

'Thank you,' replied Sylvia, and she tasted the wine and relaxed.

Once the pleasantries were over, Muhammad made sure that any staff had vacated the room so that any conversation was private. He knew the room was continually swept for listening devices and other forms of technical surveillance. This particular room also had ongoing countermeasures to identify and deny any technical surveillance being installed by guests or visitors.

'Let us begin,' stated Muhammad with a serious edge to his voice.

Muhammad was of average height and a few pounds overweight which for his age was not uncommon amongst many men. Regardless of his build, he had a face and demeanour of someone that you wouldn't cross and more importantly, someone that wouldn't tolerate being crossed.

'I want to start our discussions with the Faction Against Continent Rule. They are beginning to get above their station. They seem to have slipped their collar and becoming somewhat annoying,' he was looking at Rupert Everson now as he knew that Rupert had the strongest link to the Faction Against Continent Rule's leaders.

'I agree with Muhammad, the recent attack on the United Continents London office was not as agreed and their methods were excessive, to say the least,' replied Rupert as he took a swallow of his drink.

'We should let them off the leash more often, results happen if we do!' spoke Sylvia looking Muhammad directly in the eyes.

It was clear to both men that Sylvia DeMarco had approved the method of attack on the United Continents building, and she savoured the chaos that it had brought to the vile opposers.

'We welcome attacks Sylvia, but we need to keep control of the FACR otherwise they will spiral out of control, they need to remember who funds their activities,' said Muhammad.

'We have a very tender hold on them if I am honest and the opportunity to cause us issues could be high. I will speak with them and remind them not to bite the hand that feeds them,' Rupert said as he nodded slightly at Muhammad.

Sylvia finished her wine and placed the glass on the table, 'Ok, well I will leave it to you two to get hold of our terrorist friends. On another note, we failed to reclaim any evidence from the London office during the attack, so we are no closer to understanding any more about the Sky Zone One project.'

'That is not good,' replied Muhammad, 'We need to know facts and fast, with this information being passed on to Gabriel in the FACR.'

'I know the FACR are conducting their own lines of enquiry, I think they are keen to prove their worth in intelligence gathering although I believe their tactics are much more direct than ours, which does concern me,' Rupert said looking from one to the other.

'Well we need to be kept abreast of their intentions, this is exactly what I mean. They seem to think they can run off and do what they like without passing it by us; it won't be tolerated much longer!' said Muhammad.

Sylvia looked at Rupert with a disturbing look before addressing her gaze to Muhammad, 'What if they get the desired results though? Does it matter how they do it?'

'Yes, it does matter. If they bring unwanted attention to the Elders and our mission, then it does matter!'

Tensions were rising now, and it was clear that Muhammad was not happy with the rogue attitude of the FACR and Sylvia assumed that the Elders were starting to lose control over them and that this would bring additional problems to the Elders and their cause.

The Elders were still more powerful than any terrorist organization and so were not to be dismissed by anyone. Their power came from the Elders themselves. Powerful characters throughout the world were combining their wealth, power and contacts to be one of the most secretive forces on the planet. Sylvia did not doubt that if Muhammad lost total respect in the FACR, then he would do his utmost to remedy that and if there were no remedy, then he would delete them from history.

'We need to send a message to the FACR and remind them that this is our cause and our resources that fund it, I will not have them jeopardizing everything that has been accomplished so far.'

'I agree but let me speak with them first, as you said I have the best link with them, and if I can't get them to come into line then it would be difficult for anyone else too.'

'Agreed, speak to your contacts and get them to listen. If they do not, then we will have to think of another way to educate them,' Muhammad replied.

'On another note, I hear mutterings about someone in the United Continents sniffing around the Eden project, there are fears that someone may be trying to find out what this is and who was in charge of the project. I am concerned that attention is being generated in our direction and jeopardises the mission to restart the project. If someone is asking questions, then they need to be stopped immediately. I believe the person is a hired gun working for AmorCorp so could be very dangerous. He is located in London. Sylvia, I would like you to look into this as I believe you have the biggest network in London. I want you to find out any information and if even a scent that this man is looking into Eden, then I want him dealt with,' Muhammad concluded.

'Yes, of course, leave it with me, and I will head to London in the next day or two,' replied Sylvia.

They carried on the rest of the evening, discussing certain aspects of Elders business. However, the focus remained on three main things, their mission, resurrecting the Eden project and further details of the mercenary asking too many questions.

Chapter 7

As Sky Zone One had passed its final inspections, it was time to start populating this extraordinary project using the fortunate people that had been pre-selected. To say this was going to be a major operation was an understatement and one that Major Kahn would have to oversee as part of his duties. These duties included the security of the facility and its two million occupants, meaning that his responsibilities blended into welfare, legal issues and duty of care. He was not phased by this as there was an exceptional team behind him, including his second in command Captain Nick Hughes, with whom he had served together since joining the military and had explicitly chosen Nick to be his right-hand man.

Captain Nick Hughes was a giant of a man with model looks and well-kept blonde hair cut short to his head. In addition to his good looks, he was one of the smartest men that Major Kahn had ever come across and one that could have done so much more than serving in the military although it was the only thing he ever wanted to do.

So much talent and he risks his life in the military when he could be earning a fortune in one of the big cities, Major Khan thought to himself.

A lot was riding on the success of Sky Zone One, and Major

CHAPTER 7

Khan felt this pressure every day and had done for the last couple of years. Other Sky Zones were being built and would be deployed across the globe in the same capacity as Sky Zone One. Never in the history of humanity had anything come close to the scale of this project

Major Kahn had overseen the design and build of Sky Zone One and had ensured his advice and guidance was taken onboard. This would ensure that the required levels of security were implemented from the start. The secrecy of this project had been paramount, only those with the highest level of clearance were included in the design, build and ongoing operation of Sky Zone One.

'Major Kahn,' came a familiar voice from behind.

Major Kahn turned to see Captain Nick Hughes approaching from one of the landing docks on the lower terminal of the floating city.

'Nick, I thought you were heading to the surface for some leave before the mass exodus began?' Major Kahn spoke as he shook Nicks's hand and patted him on the shoulder with the other hand.

'I am boss. I just wanted to check some last-minute security protocols. I'm then heading to surface at 3:00 pm.'

'Good, as you've worked meticulously hard on this project and I will be forever grateful.'

'Are you not taking leave then?' enquired the burly officer.

'No, I've vested as much in this as you and so want to ensure everything remains in place before onboarding starts,' replied Major Khan as he looked back down the corridor in the direction that he was going.

'Plus, I have nothing of interest on the surface anymore, unfortunately,' he added.

Major Khan shook his Captains hand and gave him a wry smile before walking off.

'See you soon, Captain!' he spoke as he waved his right hand in the air dismissively.

Major Khan walked back to his cabin and pressed his palm against the biometric reader to the side of the door, the door whizzed open, and he stepped into his large but minimalistic living cabin. He walked towards a side table where a half-drunk bottle of Scottish Whisky sat, he poured a big shot into the glass tumbler and walked back towards one of the soft leather chairs located in the living area of the cabin. He sat down and brought the glass level with his eyes and studied the golden liquid. He then took a large mouthful before placing the glass on the small side table next to him. He closed his eyes and let the memories flood back into his vision. He could see the explosions, hear the screams as the chaos unfolded in his mind.

Major Khan suddenly came back to the present as an incoming call came in.

'Major Khan here,' he stated as he rubbed his chin.

'Major, we have a report of a minor glitch on the central computer system. It has rectified itself now, but I wanted you to be aware,' said the controller on the other end of the call.

'Ok, thank you. I will be there soon,' replied Major Khan.

He walked into the bathroom and splashed water on his face to wake himself up. He then stared into the mirror for a minute before towelling his face and changing his shirt. He then headed out the door to the main control room to see what the concern was with the computer system, these days most things relied on a computer of some sort and unlike the start of the century, cyber-crimes were more or less minimal these days. It was highly unlikely that the Sky Zone system could be hacked, so any problem was most likely to be to do with the system itself.

Major Khan arrived at the main control room in just under seven minutes and placed his right thumb on the access device whilst looking into the retinal scanner, he heard the security locks release, and the access door opened. As most people had gone to the surface for leave, there was only a small contingent left on Sky Zone One. This included a security team, engineers, controllers and other people that Sky Zone needed to run, just enough to keep the floating city in the Troposphere.

'Jackson, run back the log to the time of the glitch please,' commanded Major Khan as he walked over to where a tall thin United Continents officer was sat in front of a console made up of a large screen and not much else.

'Yes sir,' replied Jackson as he used his fingers to manipulate the screen.

'Quick as you can Jackson, no time to waste,' Major Khan added, the effect of minimal sleep making him snappier than usual.

Jackson wriggled in his seat as he tried to bring up the glitch that had been identified earlier.

'Here it is sir, you can see that a security alert was logged at 1:10 pm but was so brief that it did not activate any further automated security response.'

'Should we be worried then?' asked Major Khan genuinely.

'The system seems fine now, and it's very doubtful that any external threat could have caused this change,' said Jackson as he continued to manipulate the screen.

'Doubtful isn't a word that I want to hear, if not done already get the system technicians to conduct a full scan of the system as soon as possible!'

'Yes, sir, immediately.'

Major Khan walked over to another controller whose sole responsibility was to monitor the Unicoms to ensure that they were functioning correctly.

'Is everything ok with the Unicoms,' Major Khan enquired.

'Yes, all checks in order, sir,' she replied.

Since the late 2030's the integration of technology and humans had become more widespread and accepted. However, the use of an example like the Unicom integration had caused a massive uproar from many human rights organisations. Even though every Unicom utilised throughout the Sky Zone projects had volunteered for whatever reason they had decided to remove themselves from everyday life and become part of an integrated yet virtual existence. People from all backgrounds volunteered to be part of this project although mainly it was those that had nothing else to live for, those that were lost and those that struggled to find a place in the modern world around them.

There were people with other reasons, of course, some just wanted to feel part of a higher consciousness believing that becoming a Unicom would provide a god-like existence. Others wanted to serve their continent and be part of something meaningful, saviours of the planet. Whatever their reasons, it was no real existence. Major Khan couldn't think of anything worse.

'Give me a life support status for the Unicoms,' spoke Major Khan as he took his eyes away from the monitor.

'All life systems in order Major Khan,' said the softly spoken female operator he knew to be Private Sarah Ashford; he knew this as he had got to know her intimately during the build of Sky Zone One. This was something that he hated himself for, tarnishing the most distinguished career by sleeping with someone under his command, and a private rank at that.

'Thank you Private,' he said without directly looking at her, although he yearned to see her beautiful face framed by her shoulder-length blonde hair. He would be seeing her tonight, so that was more than enough to keep him going through the day, he had surprised himself at how much he had enjoyed the company of this attractive yet younger female. His professionalism had been worn down by this energetic, engaging and carefree individual.

'Major Khan, we have completed a full diagnostic of the systems and found no malware or hidden threats, sir,' said the first operator as he sent the full report to Major Khans personal computer.

'Ok, I want you to monitor the system over the next twenty-four hours with full scans every two hours,' Major Khan replied.

'But that will...' started the operator until Major Khan held up his hand and stopped the operator from saying any more.

'Just do it and send me the full scan report every two hours.'

The Major was not one to take any risks especially as he had invested so much time and energy into the security and safety of Sky Zone One, to have any incidents this far into the project would not be good at all.

He left the room and made his way around the floating city checking all was in order as he did so, visiting different departments from engineering through to communications. He did this often as he felt that this was the best way to understand the progress on the ship and to familiarize himself with as many staff as possible, he had got to know most of the crew on a personal level although still keeping his seniority in place. It was getting late by the time he returned to his sleeping quarters although he was still alert as he knew there would be someone waiting for him in his cabin. Private Sarah Ashford had made her way to his cabin, ensuring that nobody saw her enter her superior officers personal quarters. Their relationship had been a secret for over a year, and it was in everyone's interest that it remained a secret. Otherwise, there would be severe consequences for both of them.

Major Khan arrived at his cabin, and before entering, he placed the palm of his right hand against the door and paused briefly before he entered. He did this to mentally prepare himself for what was about to happen, as Private Sarah Ashford was much younger and much more energetic than him, probably more energetic than most people.

He entered the cabin and immediately heard the shower running, a small smile sprang across his lips as he made his way towards the bathroom, removing his clothes as he went. As he approached, he saw the shape of her body through the misted glass of the shower screen and instantly, he started to get aroused. Her body was tight, not muscular but toned all over; her blonde bob framed her attractive face and feminine features. He could clearly see the sides of her pert breasts and rounded bottom as she pressed both her hands up against the back of the shower wall, waiting in anticipation for him to walk up behind her.

Her lips curled in excitement as she felt him press up hard against her back, feeling his excitement pressing into the small of her back, his large hands wrapping around the front of her body to cradle her ample breasts.

CHAPTER 7

'You took your time,' she purred, 'I was starting to think you were going to be held up with work. Are you happy that the glitch is just a glitch?'

'I am, although I will monitor the situation to make sure. Anyway, less chit chat and more action,' he said, spinning her around to face him.

Chapter 8

It was a cold night. The stars were fully visible as the lone figure walked across the desolate compound square, he looked up at the sky as he crossed the open area and gritted his teeth and thought about what he was about to do. As he approached the other side of the compound he arrived at a large steel door where a heavyset guard stood outside smoking, the second male was dressed in dark clothing similar to that of the new arrival. He was a lot taller than the lone figure and held an assault rifle in his left hand whilst he used his other hand to hold the cigarette. As the lone figure got closer, the guard flicked the cigarette away and opened the steel door before stepping out of the way.

The lone figure entered the dimly lit windowless room and immediately saw his intended victim, a hooded man was sat naked on a chair in the middle of the room. Flex cord tying him tightly to the metal chair, with the chair being screwed to the floor.

The lone figure walked straight up to the hooded man and removed his hood and then stepped back. Light flooded in where seconds ago it had been total darkness, making the man screw his eyes shut. As the man squinted, he could barely make out the shape of a person stood in front of him, and as

CHAPTER 8

his eyes adjusted to the light, he could see it was a man. The man stood just over six feet he guessed, slim but muscular build with a shaved head and a stare that could penetrate even the hardiest of people.

The man stood stationary, just staring into the eyes of the man strapped to the metal chair, watching him move about nervously as he took in his new surroundings.

'My name is Gabriel Durand, I am part of the group named Faction Against Continent Rule, and I am here to gain information from you,' Gabriel said calmly. He circled the man tied to the chair in the middle of the windowless room.

'What information?!' said the naked man, the fear more than evident in his voice, 'I'm just an engineer, what do you want with me?'

The man was now trying to frantically loosen the flex cord holding him down, fear spreading throughout his body.

Gabriel watched him intently, absorbing the fear from this helpless figure, feeling excited by the power he now held over this person.

'Yes, you are only an engineer, but you are an engineer on the mighty Sky Zone One,' Gabriel said, staring the man in the eyes, not trying to hide his contempt.

'This means you hold a lot of valuable information that is important to us. Unfortunately, this does not bode well for you!' Gabriel said as he pulled a six-inch knife from a sheath attached to his belt.

Gabriel pressed the cold metal blade against the neck of the man tied to the chair, drawing the tip of the knife down the neck onto the chest. The man tried to force his body away from the blade, but the flex cord holding him down was well tied, and the man was going nowhere.

'There is no use in struggling or holding back information, regardless of how long it takes we will retrieve the information we need,' said Gabriel.

He pressed the tip of the blade harder into the man's chest until the sharp end pierced the skin of the man's pectoral muscle.

The man called out in pain, 'Stop, please!'

Gabriel ignored him.

'I will ask you some questions, depending on the level of response will depend if I am satisfied or not,' continued Gabriel as he now knelt in front of his captive with a wicked grimace etched across his face.

The man was clearly in fear for his life now; tears started to run down his dirty face. He was shaking his head in denial of the situation he now found himself in.

'Firstly, how many docking ports are on Sky Zone One?' said Gabriel calmly.

'What?! I'm confused, why have you got me here torturing me over this?'

The naked man was looking frantically around the room for answers or some magical escape route. It didn't materialize.

'Just answer the question.'

'Forty!' the man blurted out, 'There are forty docking bays on Sky Zone One.'

Gabriel tapped the blade of the knife in his palm and smiled to himself. He smiled as he already knew the answer to the question as previous intelligence had informed him of the fact.

Gabriel and the Faction Against Continent Rule had been gathering various intelligence on Sky Zone One ever since it had become public knowledge to start to move those fortunate enough to pass the rigorous standards into the skies above the surface. The FACR had plans for Sky Zone One and had been slowly increasing their means of gathering intelligence to ensure that they had the information they needed. However, at the same time were careful not to draw attention to their activities and not to raise suspicion.

'Ok, now let's dig a little deeper,' replied Gabriel, 'I need to know details about the security systems and also the security team on board, I know that you are aware of the security systems and so it is in your best interest to comply.'

Gabriel had changed the tone of his voice, now it was sterner, and his mannerisms had become more intense, darkness had entered the room.

'I'm just an engineer. I don't know about the security,' replied the man.

Gabriel strode purposefully up to him, and as he neared he smashed the butt of the knife on the centre of his nose, the instant crunch confirmed that he had just broken the man's nose and the blood that burst from the now disfigured mass of broken bone also suggested the same.

The man screamed out in pain, a visible look of shock now spreading over his face. The prisoner knew he was in a lousy situation, although now it had gotten much more severe and any hope he may have had now dissipated before his watering eyes.

'Stop, please stop. I beg you,' screamed the man.

'Tell me what I want to know, and the pain will stop. Tell me how big the security team is on Sky Zone One?' Gabriel continued.

Although the man was in pain and feared for his life, he was also aware of the risk to so many people if he released any sensitive security information about Sky Zone One.

'I don't know!' he lied.

Gabriel moved with impressive swiftness as he stepped forward and swung the blade down so that the tip pierced the right thigh of the captive man, followed by at least four inches of the metal blade.

The man paused slightly before letting out an unholy scream, spit and dribble falling from his open mouth.

Gabriel left the knife in the man's thigh for a few seconds before swiftly pulling it free and stepping back.

'I have all the time in the world, and I expect all my questions to be answered promptly and truthfully. I will leave you to think for now, but I will be back later, and I will expect answers!' spoke Gabriel as he wiped the blade of the knife on his trousers, before spinning on his heel and casually walking from the room.

'Check on him in fifteen minutes to assess the blood loss, patch him up if needed but keep him alive,' Gabriel said to the guard on the other side of the door, before setting off back across the compound and into another room.

As Gabriel entered the room, he was met by a wave of electronic noise and activity, with four lines of tables lined up end to end, with every table housing some form of monitor or computer of some kind. This room was much different from the scant room that he had just left. Each desk had at least one person sat in front of it working away, with various other people walking back and forth across the room. At the far end of the room was a massive screen which was connected to one of the computer systems, this seemed to be the primary operations screen and in the centre of the screen was what looked like technical plans for a large ship of some kind.

CHAPTER 8

Gabriel walked up to a small group stood in the corner of the room, and as he approached, a balding man in his fifties who was slightly overweight turned to greet him.

'Was our guest helpful?' said the balding figure.

'He will come around, trust me.'

A second person joined the conversation, a tall female with short brown hair and a prominent burn scar on the right side of her face.

'We need this information,' she said sharply.

Gabriel turned to her and noticed her gaze was unflinching under his scrutiny. He knew Teresa to be a resilient and robust member of their organisation who once set on her objective, would see it through with unwavering ferocity. She, like many others, had lost loved ones through the wrongdoing of the United Continents with her daughter being killed in a building assault which led to a ferocious fire in her apartment building, killing her daughter and scarring her mentally and physically.

Gabriel maintained her icy stare, 'We will get the information we need, he is currently contemplating his options!'

He returned his gaze to the other man, whom he knew to be Boris Atanassov. Boris was the current operations officer of the organisation and was a wise and intelligent man with a talent for playing the long strategic game.

'Walk with me, Boris, please,' spoke Gabriel as he headed towards the other side of the room where there was a row of small offices.

Once they were inside one of the offices, Gabriel closed the door and held out his hand to offer Boris a chair at the table in the centre of the room. Boris accepted, and they both sat facing each other, Gabriel placed his hands on the desk and began to brief the operations officer on his recent activity including the approach to drawing information from the detained engineer from Sky Zone One.

The Faction Against Continent Rule became established in the year 2040 after the United Continents had powered its way to being the ruling force of the world, engaging and directing their will since inception in 2032. The FACR now believed to number five thousand members across the globe, was the main antagonist against the United Continents. They used terrorist tactics to disrupt, subdue and destroy United Continents assets and operations. They had secret locations in every country and had built up an alarming infrastructure consisting of administration staff, operational officers and many supporters, regardless of some of the bloody tactics they used in their methods.

In the beginning, they were directed by the Elders, although more recently they had started to resent the Elders and act on their own whims. To begin with, they were solely funded by the Elders, which gave the Elders some level of control over them. However, over the years, they had increased their income streams from various illegal activity and were slowly breaking free from the iron grip of the Elders.

'I am impressed with your progress Gabriel,' stated Boris.

'Thank you, everything is coming into play with regards to our future intentions, and this will be the single most important activity of our organisation.'

Gabriel Durand had joined the FACR at the tender age of eighteen. However, he was not so tender at that age after surviving a life of broken homes and internal solidarity, with the latter making him much more mindful and intelligent than many his age. He would never have wished his upbringing on anyone, the constant moving from home to home, the foster

CHAPTER 8

families that were more interested in the monthly cheque than him, and the current shunning of his peers due to not being good enough for them. All after being abused as a child by not just one parent but both. Now, twenty-nine, the last eleven years had flown by in a blur of carnage and internal progression, and he was now one of the highest-ranking officers in the organisation.

His desire to get to the top of this organisation was born from an unwavering need to be part of something bigger, something that had meaning. He had been shunned by society and had finally found his feet all those years ago in an organisation that defied standardisation and dictatorship. An organisation that had allowed him to soar, that organisation being the Faction Against Continent Rule.

'We need to have as much intelligence as possible for this plan to work or even come close to working,' spoke Boris, 'We can't do this halfheartedly, and we cant do this unprepared.'

'I know, if anyone knows this then I do! I have lived and breathed this plan for so long, every waking minute has been focused around this upcoming attack.'

'You need to move faster on the engineer and also on the informants we have, especially those that are part of the Sky Zone project.'

'I agree and I will, the Sky Zone officer is delivering excellent intelligence although we need to be careful in case he changes his mind and brings it all crashing down on our heads. The last thing we need is for our activities and efforts to get picked up by the United Continents and Sky Zone security.'

'Well you need to bleed him for more information and then dispose of him but make sure he doesn't go missing too soon and raise the alarm,' said Boris with a hint of concern.

This entire plan was now at a stage where the line between success and failure was minuscule. They had worked hard to ensure that anyone outside this tight circle had identified no part of this plan.

'Don't worry its all in hand, the engineer we have won't take much to break. With our team going up to Sky Zone One soon and in addition to those that have previously infiltrated this project then we are very close.'

'I do worry Gabriel; it is my job to worry. It is also my job to keep the Elders happy, and currently, this is becoming more difficult due to your apparent distrust in them.'

'Ignore the Elders, they are becoming less necessary in our plight, and once we have completed our next mission, then I doubt we will need them at all.'

'You're wrong Gabriel, even to think like that puts us all in danger. Do you think you can detach from the Elders like that? They helped achieve all this, without them then the Faction would be little more than a back street anarchy group.'

Suddenly Gabriel turned on the shorter man grabbing his shirt in his right hand and pushing him hard against the wall. His face bore down on Boris's with a wave of deep anger emanating from his eyes, 'Do not question my intentions!'

Although shorter Boris was not a meek individual and although shocked at his associate's response, he was not afraid.

'I suggest you take your hands off me now before you regret it.'

His tone was calm, although it held enough menace that Gabriel slowly released his grip. Boris adjusted his shirt and stared back at Gabriel, thinking the stress was getting too much for him, or the power was going to his head too fast. To dismiss the Elders like that was foolish and put them all at risk, he had to keep an eye on Gabriel and the situation.

This was the last thing we need, Boris thought to himself, and with that, he left the room.

Gabriel stared down at his clenched fists, unsure where that anger had come from, he needed to get back on mission. He inhaled deeply, clenched his teeth and then let his anger dissipate with his outgoing breath. I will deal with the Elders later; for now, I need more answers from our guest.

Chapter 9

Rye Braden walked from the United Continents station with Ruby Monroe by his side. Si Morgan was already waiting at the bottom of the steps, ready to greet them.

'Let's get you two home,' Si said as he directed them to the waiting vehicle outside the building.

'That sounds like a plan mate,' replied Rye as he placed his arm around Ruby's shoulder and guided her to the car.

Rye could tell that Ruby was still shaken by what had happened and that it would take a lot for her to come to terms with it, not just the attack but how Rye had dealt with it. He also needed to find the truth behind why he was so much different than most; he always had an idea that he was stronger and faster than most, but now he wanted answers. This particular incident had unleashed something extra for some reason, and he was going to do all he could to find the truth behind his superior abilities.

The three of them travelled in silence as Si expertly navigated the electric vehicle through the streets of London, arriving at Rye's building forty minutes later. He pulled up to the kerb and jumped out of the car and went straight to Ruby's door and opened it like a chauffeur would for their client.

'Thank you,' said Ruby as she forced a smile from her pale

CHAPTER 9

face, her eyes were sunken and dark and Si could see her confidence had been knocked.

Si turned to Rye and gave him a short nod, 'Go and get yourselves sorted mate and ring me when you're ready to talk.'

Rye escorted Ruby into the building taking the elevator to the eighth floor where his apartment was, the hall light flicked on as he entered the apartment and he guided Ruby into the lounge. Rye voice-activated the coffee machine and made Ruby a strong black coffee, just how she liked it.

'You need some rest,' Rye said sympathetically, as he placed the cup of hot coffee on the table in front of her.

'I know.'

'You know I'm going to find the truth about why I'm different, don't you?'

He sat down next to her on the couch and placed his muscular arm around her shoulder.

'Yes, I know. I can help you if you need me to?' she said softly.

She loved Rye and always had, it was just that now she knew there was another side to him, and if she was honest, it scared her.

'You should stay here for a couple of nights,' Rye said as he rubbed her back.

'I will stay tonight, but then I need to get away. Especially if you are going looking for trouble.'

'Where will you go?'

'I have friends outside the city. It will be much safer.'

She turned to him now looking directly into his eyes.

'I love you, Rye, but this has shocked me. I don't want to lose you, but you need to do what you need to do, and I need some time,' she laid her head against his chest.

'I know,' he replied as he held her close and thought about what he needed to do.

The next morning Rye woke early and made sure he didn't wake Ruby as he knew that she needed the rest. He made his way quietly into the kitchen and started about making some fresh coffee and breakfast. He didn't put on the news as he didn't want to disturb Ruby in the next room. Instead, he scrolled through the messages on his mobile device, ignoring the ones that weren't so important and marking those that he would come back to once he had woken up a bit more.

He messaged Si Morgan to see if he could meet him later that morning at a café not far from where his apartment was located, this being a usual casual meeting point for the two, mainly because it made the best coffee in London. Instantly, Si responded with a time, which Rye confirmed before placing his mobile device on the kitchen counter. He could always rely on Si Morgan, and he had been a rock for Rye ever since he had met him all those years ago when he had joined the Pathfinder Patrols.

Rye poured fresh steaming coffee and scraped the scrambled eggs from the pan on the hob onto a plate, adding salt and pepper to them. He then sat at the kitchen table to eat his breakfast whilst he thought through what his plan of attack was today. He had to find answers, but he knew that they would not be forthcoming and that he would have to push some buttons to get them. He tried to think where he would even begin on this journey to find whether he was different and what exactly made him different. Since the incident yesterday, he had been feeling much more energetic than usual and also feeling very confident, he had always been a confident

CHAPTER 9

person, but something was different today.

Rye placed his empty dishes on the side and checked on Ruby before jumping in the shower. As the water ran off his body, his mind flashed back to his time in the Pathfinder Patrols and in particular a period just after finishing his advanced training package where he learnt all his tradecraft and advanced military tactics. He was trying to remember the transition from training to becoming operational and joining his squadron. However, it was a little hazy, and Rye couldn't think if it was due to how long ago it occurred or that it was hazy for another reason.

The time was now coming up to 8:00 am, and Ruby hadn't even stirred, Rye slipped into the bedroom and took some clothes out of the wardrobe and went back into the living room where he dressed in his usual black jeans, dark technical top and assault boots. He always liked to dress in clothes that would be fitting for any kind of incident that may arise, and he had the feeling that they would undoubtedly rise before the day was out. Rye wasn't meeting Si Morgan until 10:00 am so still had a couple of hours to burn, so he started looking back through his military records which were held securely on the cloud. He was trying to trace back his career from when he first joined the military as an infantryman back in 2036 at the tender age of sixteen. He had spent four hard years being a foot soldier which meant serving through the early stages of the United Continent take over. These first years had seen some of the heaviest fighting across the globe as those against the United Continents fought hard to deny the take-over, this included everyone from civilian personnel through to foreign governments and their military forces who were the last to be absorbed by the United Continents.

He remembered his first day at the infantry training regiment and the gruelling thirty weeks of physical training, basic military tactics and countless exercises in the cold and wet. He remembered graduating at just seventeen and that being one of the proudest moments of his life, before being shipped to his new infantry regiment. This is where he had to start from the bottom of the pile all over again until he had proved himself as a competent soldier. He had always known hardship from a young age, and this had better prepared him for his life as a warrior, fighting battles was all he knew, and now he had to fight another battle, this time a personal one.

By the time Rye had finished drilling over his past it was nearly 9:00 am and Ruby had now woken up although was still in bed, so Rye went into the bedroom and sat on the bed next to her.

'How are you feeling,' he said.

'Better, much better,' she replied as she rolled over to face him.

'I'm still going to go away for a few days, just to clear my mind,' she said softly.

Rye smiled, he loved Ruby, but he also knew she'd had a big shock yesterday. He cursed himself inside, what the hell was happening to him and who were the men that attacked him.

'That's fine, it will do you good and will give me some time to figure out what's going on.'

'I'm going to jump in the shower and then get going,' she said as she stood up, she was naked, but neither of them felt any passion this morning, so she walked out of the room to the bathroom and closed the door behind her.

Twenty minutes later, Ruby and Rye were saying their goodbyes as she hugged him tightly as they paused in the

CHAPTER 9

reception area of Ryes apartment building.

'I will see you soon and be careful Rye.'

It was nearly 10:00 am now, so Rye set off to meet Si Morgan at the café close to where he currently was, the sun was shining brightly now, and this made Rye feel optimistic about what he needed to do.

Rye entered the café and knew precisely where Si would be sat as they always went for one of the booths along the far wall; this provided a little privacy for their discussions. As he thought, Si Morgan was sat in the furthest booth and with the café being relatively quiet.

'Thanks for coming Si,' said Rye as he sat down opposite his old friend and mentor.

'No problem, always here to help a mate in trouble,' replied Si as he raised his hand to get the attention of the waiter buzzing about.

'What's going on then Rye, seems to be pretty heavy whatever it is?'

Si spoke in a hushed voice as he added sugar to the newly arrived coffees.

'I have no idea who the attackers were, or why they focused on me, the only thing I can think of is that they are related to Michael Juno?' replied Rye.

'Well, the authorities have had no joy with the men they picked up, and I doubt they will by the looks of them. They are British though so if linked to Juno then they are probably part of a criminal outfit, or the alternative is that they are part of something else entirely?'

'Whatever it was, was well planned. But that's not my only reason for asking you here,' Rye said as he sipped his coffee, 'Have you ever noticed anything different about me Si?'

Si Morgan looked at Rye, he had always known there was something special about Rye, and that was no secret. Rye had been one of the best recruits he had seen walking through the doors of the Pathfinder patrols, and Si had seen many come through. Si had just taken this as being natural, with Rye being fitter and stronger than most soldiers he had seen over the years.

'I've always known you've had skills mate, why do you ask?' asked Si.

'Because the attack yesterday was different, it was like something had been released. I can't explain it properly, but I feel different as if I've become aware that I can do more than I thought I could?'

Rye held up his hands and stared at them intently as if he was analysing them like he would a new weapon system.

'It's like something took over and to be fair I took four guys down with ease, but that feeling is still with me today, something has happened and I need to know what. It's like I now have a better understanding of my abilities, meaning that something has changed in me recently or I have just become aware of something that changed in me some time ago. Either way, I feel different.'

'Ok, you're talking about physical or mental changes?'

'Both, my physical strength is off the scale, but its more than that. My senses seem more acute, hearing, sight and general awareness.'

Si placed his elbow on the table and extended his hand to Rye, 'Show me then.'

Rye looked at his friend with bemusement, 'An arm wrestle? Hardly a scientific test, but if you insist.'

Rye grabbed his friend's hand and set his elbow on the table in front of him. He knew Si was stronger than himself as always had been, so maybe this was a good test.

'On three,' spoke Si smiling confidently at the man opposite him.

'One, two, three.'

Si instantly applied pressure and tried to force Rye's arm to the table, but there was zero movement or give from Rye. He asserted more pressure and moved his entire body into the action, still no give from his friend who looked as though he wasn't putting any effort in at all.

'Ok, my turn now,' Rye said as he forced his arm against that of Si's and quickly forced the back of his hand to the table surface.

'That's insane,' responded his friend clearly in awe.

'That's just one benefit; everything has changed; my senses have been awoken. But I don't know when this happened or why these feelings were suppressed, I need some answers, and at present, my instinct tells me that someone inside the United Continents knows something.'

Chapter 10

Oliver Randall was sitting in his tiny bedsit staring at the cheap framed copy of a classic seventeenth-century painting entitled 'The Alchemist', his mind wandering from thought to thought, but mainly reverting to his time under the Eden project where he had lead one of the leading human genetics programs in history.

His bedsit was minimal with one couch, a desk littered with computers and technology, and a small kitchen area in the far corner. There was also a tiny bathroom adjoining this main room with a door for privacy. Oliver was not a materialistic person, and he valued knowledge much more than mere objects. He had worked hard his entire life to get to the top of his industry and had been one of the greatest minds in terms of genetic manipulation.

That was before the Eden project had been closed down in 2042 by unknown people within the United Continents, not much information had been given, and the entire research, documentation and records had been removed from existence, or at least Oliver believed they had been. Even the test subjects had disappeared, all were now just memories to the select few that had been involved in the project.

Oliver Randall rubbed his eyes and looked around the grim

CHAPTER 10

bedsit; this was his life now since the Eden project had been taken from him. All the effort and pioneering moments he had vested in this project, all for it to be ripped away, it had been twelve years now since the project had been shut down. Oliver was now thirty-eight years of age, and the years had not been good to him, he looked haggard and had lost the spark that he once possessed. His hair was long and greasy, he even hosted a straggly beard, the only thing that was the same was his large almond eyes, but even these were duller than they had been in his prime.

The day that the Eden project had been taken away from him was the day that he lost his motivation for science and the day where his life would never be the same again. Since that day, he had gone from one unmeaningful job to another, and never quite getting the same level of interest or excitement as the Eden project had given him. He was the one that had found the answer to the questions they had sought, the one that made the project successful. He had found a way to modify and enhance the capabilities of the human body; he had opened pandora's box to the human gene pool.

Oliver walked to the sink in the kitchen and ran the tap, he picked up a glass from the work surface and filled the glass before taking a long gulp of water. He walked over to the only window in the small bedsit and stared out at the gloomy wet night, he could hear the noise of the city outside, but he felt detached from the real world, everything was a blur to him these days. As he stared out of the window, his mind went back to the day he had started at the United Continents under the watchful eye of Dr James Cook. Dr Cook being Oliver's mentor in the early stages of the project. However, it wouldn't be long before Oliver superseded Dr Cook due to his natural talent and knowledge in the area of genetic mutation.

He had learnt quickly how to modify the human body with a view of enhancing the natural limitations found within the human race, unlocking the code that generally placed limits on us as humans. Sure, some people trained hard and practised mental positivity training, but these were still nowhere near the strength, power and capability of those test subjects under the Eden project. Oliver had been able to manipulate muscle fibres to make them much more substantial than they were before. This included manipulating a person's skeletal system using a solution called Xeren II, which was surgically injected into the skeletal system and due to its ingredients was able to harden the bones and joints without limiting flexibility. Oliver himself had created this solution. He had also pioneered other genetic engineering with the test subjects having faster reactions through modification of their cerebellum. This being the receiver from the bodies sensory systems, the spinal cord and other areas of the brain, in turn regulating motor movements of the body. The final aspects of the Eden project enhanced the sight and hearing of all those involved ensuring that their sensory capability was sharper and more acute than any other person on the planet.

All this work had been conducted in secret with only a handful of people knowing the actual depth of the work being carried out, those test subjects that were involved were all volunteers. However, realistically they were not aware of how violating the procedures were going to be. The experiments were not all successful, with some casualties being subjected to some severe side effects. Some became paralysed from adverse reactions to Xeren II; others lost their sight after the delicate micro-surgery had gone wrong. There was always going to be risks with this type of pioneering genetic manipulation as there was with any advanced surgery. Many had been seriously affected by the treatment and some that hadn't passed the stringent physical and psychological assessments. In the end, only thirty-two test subjects made a successful recovery from the testing out of the initial one hundred.

Oliver walked back to the small sofa and sat down, throwing his head back, he stared at the ceiling thinking back to the actual day when the strangers had entered and told everyone to stop their work. Several armed guards were providing support to a small group of suit-wearing individuals. The new group were senior members with the United Continents from a variety of departments including legal, ethics and operations. The main person had stepped forward, introducing himself as Mr Clarkson, as he passed over a warrant signed by one of the four Secretary Generals with authorisation from the current President. Oliver had read through the warrant and could see there was no point arguing with what the newcomers were doing. It was more the shock of how and why this was happening.

'This is preposterous,' Oliver had said as he had frantically tried to recover his storage drives from his desk which had all the vital information stored securely on them.

'Everyone, please stay exactly where you are and do not touch anything,' said the lead person from the newcomers, who had earlier identified himself as Mr Clarkson.

'Your work here is now done,' he continued as he urged his armed officers to distribute themselves around the room to stop anyone from interacting with their desks or computers.

Oliver remembered how his protests had amassed to nothing and how each of them had then been escorted to individual office rooms where they were formally told about what was happening. They had been informed what they must and must not do, especially in line with the very intense non-disclosure forms and official secrets act each of them had signed and agreed.

He remembered the sinking feeling of not being able to do anything, at that precise moment in time he was not even able to speak with his boss. This group had just stopped everything that was happening and even took charge of the remaining thirty-two test subjects who were currently housed in comfortable but minimal secure quarters. This meant Oliver had no idea what had happened to these men and woman that had been genetically enhanced.

'Surely they wouldn't have killed them to keep this secret from reaching the outside?' Oliver thought to himself, 'Maybe they employed them in a specialist kill squad?' He was guessing now as he had no idea what happened to these thirty-two genetically enhanced test subjects.

It was getting late now, and Oliver was starting to feel tired although he knew he wouldn't be able to sleep as he had trouble sleeping these days, the past haunted him, and it seemed there was nothing he could do to right the wrongs of his past. He knew two of his old scientific team from the Eden project had mysteriously gone missing after trying to go public with the details about what had occurred under the United Continents Eden project. He didn't know if they were dead or buried somewhere, whatever had happened to them he didn't want it to happen to him, so he had never said anything to anyone about the project. His vivid imagination about what had happened to his previous colleagues helped him to keep quiet as he had come up with at least a thousand

CHAPTER 10

different brutal endings for them.

Unknown to Oliver, all the test subjects had been detained. Then after careful consideration, their minds had been wiped to precisely remove the memories of what had occurred in terms of what they had witnessed and what they had done to them. This meant that any knowledge of their abilities had also been wiped and this memory suppression meant that they would never realise their full potential. At one point, certain elements within the murkier areas of the United Continents wanted all thirty-two test subjects to be terminated. This had been stopped due to the slim possibility that these superhumans could be of value in the future.

Suddenly, Oliver was brought back to the present by a loud knocking at the front door, followed by the shrill of the door alarm being pressed. This surprised him as he had never had anyone knock at his door before; he didn't know anyone. A few seconds later, another firm knock, this time, Oliver sprang to his feet and slowly approached the door. There was an electronic viewing screen to the right of the door and Oliver could now see two men stood the other side of the door, both dressed in black, and both looked rather large and menacing.

Oliver started to panic; he was frantically trying to think who they could be and why they were banging on his door. He looked around the room, wishing he was not there, but he was always there, becoming more of a hermit as each year passed. Damn it he thought to himself, as he could feel his heart rate quickening, a feeling of complete fear rose from his chest and took hold of him. Again, another hard knock on the door. He had no choice, he had to open the door, or they might force their way through, he was petrified now and sweating profusely.

'What do you want?' Oliver stuttered through the intercom.

'We need to speak with Mr Oliver Randall,' one of the men replied.

'He isn't here,' responded Oliver hoping that his meagre attempt at fooling them would work.

'My patience is running out,' said the man in a stern voice, 'We know it is you and we know you live alone, so open up so that we can inform you of the matter in hand.'

Oliver now placed his back against the door and looked up at the ceiling; there was no other way out of this tiny bedsit. Maybe, just maybe they were there to pass on some information, perhaps these weren't bad men anyway, and it was just his paranoia kicking in.

'We are here on behalf of the United Continents, check my identity card if you must.'

The lead man scanned his identity card against the intercom.

Oliver turned his head to see the credentials flash up on his screen, the person's name came up as Steve Grishaw along with his United Continents service number and at the bottom in green capital letters was the word 'CONFIRMED'. This meant that the ID the man had scanned had been confirmed as genuine, this provided some relief to Oliver although he was still worried.

Reluctantly, Oliver released the locking mechanism on the door and opened it tentatively, peering around at the two men stood in the hallway.

'May we come in?'

Oliver opened the door fully and gestured for them to enter. The bedsit was hardly big enough for the three men, so they all stood.

'We would like you to come in to answer some questions

about a project you headed up some years ago, namely the Eden project,' said the man as he looked at Oliver.

'Eden?' Oliver replied without hiding the surprise in his voice.

'But... I don't know anything about the project anymore. What use would I be?'

Oliver was perplexed now, after twelve years, these two men show up at his door asking about Eden.

'We would like you to come with us, just in case you start to remember. It's imperative!' said the other man now staring at Oliver with hard dark eyes.

It felt like Oliver didn't have any choice, similar to the time when Eden was ripped away from him. He quickly assessed his options, and after a few seconds, he submitted to their request.

'Ok, let me change quickly.'

Oliver scurried off into the bedroom and came out a few minutes later in fresh clothes.

'Ok, I'm ready now,' he muttered as he grabbed his coat from the back of the door.

The two burly men walked either side of the much smaller framed man they had just picked up, they took the elevator to the ground floor and exited the scruffy apartment block. They had a dark people carrier waiting for them at the kerb, the more outspoken man guided Oliver to the rear door and opened it to let him in whilst the other man slipped into the front behind the steering wheel.

Oliver felt his stomach turn, and the feeling of anxiety felt overwhelming, he tried to control his breathing, taking long slow breaths in and out. He was still perturbed by the fact that these two men were here because of the Eden project, after all this time with not even a hint of the project that he had once headed up. He watched as they continued street by street although he wasn't aware of exactly where they were or where they were headed, he just sat back in his seat and closed his eyes.

He felt like they had been driving for hours, but when he looked at his watch they had only been going for just over an hour and a half, but he knew that you could travel pretty far in that time. It was getting dark outside as they pulled up to a set of iron gates which looked to belong to a factory of some kind. A man approached the driver's window, and Oliver heard it lower under its tiny electric motor, he listened to the driver say something but it was muffled. Whatever he had said had made the man return to the gate and open it, as he opened the gates fully, he gestured for the vehicle to drive through. As the vehicle entered the open space beyond the metal gate, it waited for the man to jump into the passenger side before it continued to where the man was pointing.

'Where are we,' enquired Oliver hesitantly.

There was no response; the man sat beside him didn't even look his way.

'You're not from the United Continents are you?!'

Again, no response to his question. His breathing quickened as he struggled to keep his calm.

The vehicle drove around the side of the large factory and then into an open-access point where the metal shutter had been half raised to allow the vehicle in. Once inside, Oliver heard the shutter lower behind them and watched as the light faded in their new surroundings.

The driver exited the vehicle, before opening Oliver's door. 'Out.'

CHAPTER 10

Oliver hesitated.

'Move,' said the man sat beside him.

Oliver grabbed the handrail and stepped out of the car. He tried to take in as much of his surroundings as possible. In his head, he was looking for an escape route, but he knew there was no way out. He even looked towards the two men that had initially picked him up for reassurance as these were now the closest people he had for support, but he quickly got a grip and told himself to stop being pathetic.

'Mr Randall!' came a voice from the darkness directly ahead of him. It was a voice he thought he recognised, he squinted into the darkness to try and confirm who it was.

The mysterious figure continued to walk forward, 'It has been a long time.'

As soon as Oliver heard the voice again, he instantly knew who owned the voice. Then as the man came into view under the dim lighting, he saw a face that he had not seen for twelve years.

'Rupert Everson!'

'Yes, Oliver, it is good to see you again.'

'But you went rogue?' stated Oliver, 'You're not with the United Continents anymore, so you have me here under false pretences.'

'Rogue is a bit harsh Oliver,' Rupert walked up to the man that had been his lead scientist for the highly secret Eden project.

'But I was told that I was being brought to the United Continents, what am I doing here?'

'Well, Oliver, you were the main man behind the Eden project, and I now need your expertise again.'

'For what?' Oliver was getting irritated now as he wanted

answers, but they were not forthcoming.

'I am reopening the Eden project,' came the simple reply.

Oliver stared at his old superior for a moment, trying to register what he had just heard. 'This is ludicrous,' he said to himself, but at the same time, this was what he had yearned for since the project had been ripped away from him twelve years previous.

'I don't understand,' said Oliver as he searched for the truth in Rupert's eyes.

'I am starting up from where we left off, and I want you to be at the forefront of our work, giving you back your true calling.'

'How? We were shut down years ago. We don't have any test subjects or data.'

'We have both,' smiled Rupert, 'My team are picking up the last of the old test subjects as we speak.'

Oliver was trying to piece together what he was being told, so the test subjects must still be alive and held somewhere secret, or another of his theories was that they could have had their minds wiped.

'The subjects are still alive?'

'Yes, and I have copies of all of the data you produced. We have everything we need to restart the project.'

Oliver was amazed, a few hours ago his life was a pathetic comparison to what it had been twelve years earlier. Now, he was stood in front of the man that had been his superior and one of those responsible for the birth of the Eden project and a pioneering force in genetic manipulation for military purposes. But why now?

'I understand you may have many questions and I will answer them in time, all I need for now though is to know

CHAPTER 10

whether you are on board or not?'

Oliver took a moment before answering. He didn't know where he was or who he would be working for. The only thing he did know however was that he would be reunited with his one true love, the thing that had come before all else, his work. He never imagined he would be in a position like this again, to be back in charge of the Eden project. He didn't care who these people were around him; he didn't even care if he never had his freedom again. All he cared about was being back doing what he loved.

'Yes, I'm in,' he said without hesitation.

'Good, follow me, please.'

They walked deeper into the building until they came up to a sizeable double steel door which looked to be much newer than the rest of the building. The double doors were about eight metres in height, and each one was approximately four metres in width, they were huge compared to the men now stood in front of them. Within seconds mechanisms could be heard releasing, and the two doors started to open out towards the men stood in front of them with Rupert Everson stood at the front of the group.

As the doors fully opened, Oliver and the rest of the group stepped inside. The room was gigantic and quite surprising compared to what Oliver thought would be inside. As his eyes scanned the room, he was speechless as he took in the various equipment and furniture that made up this very high-tech looking laboratory. He couldn't entirely take it all in as his eyes darted from one part of the room to the next until his eyes rested on a selection of beds in the centre, most of these beds with people lying on them. He counted approximately thirty beds, although only about two-thirds of them had people on, the rest were empty.

'Are they who I think they are?' Oliver was staring intently at the people lying on the beds.

'Yes, Oliver, they are the original test subjects from the Eden project. Well most of them that is, but I plan to have them all very soon, the ones that are still alive that is.'

Chapter 11

The man was in severe pain now, he had been strapped to the metal chair for hours and tortured repeatedly. There was a pool of blood and sweat below him, and he stank of urine where he had to urinate where he sat. In addition to that, the constant embarrassment of being strapped naked to a chair in the middle of a dark room was enough to break any man.

The door to the room opened and the light from the midday sun flooded into the previously dark and dank place, the man could make out a silhouette entering the room and then it went dark again as the door was slammed shut. As the man's eyes readjusted to the little light in the room, he started to recognise the figure approaching, and instantly his body stiffened whilst his eyes frantically looked for a way out, but there wasn't one.

'Good afternoon, I take it you have had ample time to think about your situation,' spoke Gabriel Durand.

The man could not speak; the fear that gripped him was immense due to the pain that the man stood in front of him had previously inflicted.

'Please, please, no more…' the man was physically crying now, 'I'll tell you everything. Just stop.'

He didn't want to tell these terrorists what they wanted to know, but he just couldn't take any more pain or torture.

'That's very good,' replied Gabriel as he walked back to the door and gave it one knock, 'You may have just saved yourself a lot of pain.'

The guard from outside the door, a large bald figure with hands the size of shovels strode into the room and walked directly to where the captive man was sitting. He walked behind him and roughly started to untie the man's hands and feet, pulling the flex cord like it was a piece of string.

'Stand up,' he said gruffly.

But the man that had been tied to the chair for nearly twenty hours could not stand, he had lost the ability to use his legs, and the pain he was feeling was unbearable as the blood started to flow back into his legs as he tried to stand. He willed himself to move from the chair but instantly fell to the floor and was barely able to use his arms to break his fall.

The guard took two steps towards the collapsed man, bent down and with one arm dragged him to his feet. The crippled man cried out in pain as he was viciously dragged upwards at speed, his legs started to give way again, but the brute of the man holding him kept him upright. The man holding him up started to half walk and half drag him towards the door, and as they stepped out into the bright sunlight, the man flung his hand up to protect his eyes from the glaring sun. His initial thought was where was he, as he couldn't even remember coming to this place, the last thing he remembered was walking to his car ready to return to Sky Zone One after finishing his leave. As he went to unlock the car door, he had felt someone grab him from behind and then darkness.

The captive man's mind was racing now, where were they taking him and what were they going to do to him next. He was managing to hobble a bit now, mainly because the pain of being dragged by this mountain of a human was more painful than the rest of his injuries put together. The painful journey was brief, from the room which he had honestly thought was the place he was going to die. They now stood outside another door, with his guard using his free hand to open the door and then walking them both inside. The room was a stark difference to the one he had just left, there was much more light, and it even smelled differently, more like a hospital room compared to the recent death room he had been held in.

'Wait here,' said the guard as he walked through an adjoining door and out of sight.

The room felt sterile and clean. On the far side, there were three beds which appeared to be hospital beds; they even had an intravenous drip machine next to each of them. There were numerous white cabinets around the room and in one corner a light grey table with four plastic chairs set around it. It appeared to be some form of medical room, but why had they brought him here? His optimism started to return, and he felt a wave of relief wash over him, he wondered what was happening.

Was this part of the United Continents training, he thought to himself. It could not be as he had been tortured beyond belief, maybe if I do tell them what they want to hear, then I will survive this?

His mind was racing as he thought frantically to understand whether this whole situation was real or not. He knew it was real though as the pain his body felt proved that to him, never in his life had he been in so much pain and he just wanted it to stop now. He could hear footsteps approaching from the adjoining room and turned towards the noise nervously, for the last twenty odd hours any noise or movement had resulted in brutal pain.

A woman in her late forties walked into the room wearing blue jeans and a white blouse, but she also had a thin plastic apron on, one that would be worn by a nurse or medical practitioner of some kind.

'Please come to the bed,' she spoke with what he thought was a French accent.

Her dark hair was pulled back in a ponytail, and she wore no make-up, she was much shorter than him although with an athletic and strong figure. He walked over to the bed where she gestured for him to sit, which he did whilst maintaining eye contact with her.

'What are you going to do?' he asked nervously.

'Please, lay back and relax. I need to look at your wounds.'

He could sense that she would not be saying much to him except giving him basic instructions. He lay back on the bed and tried to relax a little although he was still naked so it was challenging to relax completely, whatever she was going to do would ultimately be more painful if he tensed up.

She went to work cleaning and fixing each of his wounds. There were several puncture wounds from where Gabriel had pierced his skin, but the significant injury was the one on his right thigh where Gabriel had viciously stabbed his knife through the muscle. He jolted as she cleaned the wound with some form of an alcohol-based solution; the pain was nearly as bad as that when he was being tortured.

'Keep still. Otherwise, I will ask Raymond to come back in,' she said with irritation in her voice.

He guessed Raymond was the beast that didn't speak much, the thought of this man mountains hands holding him down made him wriggle less.

CHAPTER 11

'What's going to happen to me?' he asked as he lay there tightly holding the sheets that he was laying on as a means of trying to ignore the pain that the lone female was putting him through.

She ignored the question entirely; she didn't even register a look in his direction. As he thought, she was not the person to try and find out what was going on, and he laughed internally at himself for thinking he was safe now. She continued her work for the next forty minutes, and by the time she finished any wound that he did have had been expertly cleaned, stitched and bandaged. She also gave him some painkillers which were now taking effect; he felt relaxed now and was given a disposable gown to put on. He was almost feeling human again.

He must have fallen asleep as he lay on the bed, as voices woke him. He looked around the room and could see that the voices belonged to his torturer Gabriel and the man-mountain which he had presumed had been Raymond. It was the first time he had heard Raymond speak more than a few words and it was clear that he was English, what was an English man doing amongst these French people?

They stopped talking once they were aware that he was awake and turned towards him.

'You're awake,' said Gabriel as he walked over to the bed where the man lay.

'My friend here is going to take you to another room so that you can have some food and drink. We can then have a chat later.'

The larger man of the two ushered for him to get off the bed, he then guided him to the adjoining door and into a room which was full of lockers and benches. They continued through this room to a door on the opposite side. Once through this door, they entered a corridor with doors to the left and right. They continued along the windowless corridor for about fifteen metres before the man rested his hand on his shoulder. The large man called Raymond then opened the door on the left and pushed him through, although it was a gentle push this time.

Inside the room was a rectangle table with two chairs sat each side of the table, other than that the room was empty apart from a hanging light from the ceiling which sat about six feet above the table. On the table there was a plate of food, sandwiches of some kind using thick cut brown bread, next to that was an apple. He immediately sat down and started on the food. There was also a jug of water and two glasses, so he poured water into one of the glasses and drank and ate vigorously.

Twenty minutes later the door to the room opened, and Gabriel walked in, Raymond was still inside the room and remained seated as Gabriel closed the door behind him.

'I see that you have managed to eat,' said Gabriel as he sat down opposite the man dressed in the medical gown.

'Yes,' was all the man could muster, the sight of Gabriel still made him nervous even though the entire situation had seemed to change.

'Good, I hope you can now see that we don't want to hurt you, but we must have answers. The more you help us, the easier it will be for you and the better your chance of walking out of here alive, which is what we all want,' continued Gabriel.

The gowned captive looked at Gabriel and then at Raymond. Could this be possible, he thought, could he make it home to his wife and child?

CHAPTER 11

'I have several questions about Sky Zone One which I need you to answer in as much detail as possible,' said Gabriel as he tapped his fingers on the metal table.

'The more you co-operate, the more reward you get and the more chance you have of getting home. Defy me, and we will revert to the more brutal means of obtaining the information. Understood?'

Gabriel locked eyes with the nervous man sat opposite him.

'Understood,' stuttered the man.

He knew what they were capable of and he guessed he had only witnessed half of it, he wanted this to end, and he wanted to go home so he was going to help them in any way he could.

Gabriel began to ask questions about all manner of things relating to the project named Sky Zone One, from the build progress through to the security and staffing numbers once Sky Zone One was populated with citizens. The questioning went on for hours, and the captive man had to be replenished a couple of times with food and water, as the entire process was very intense even to the point of getting the captive man to draw plans in some instances.

It was getting late now, and darkness had spread across the isolated compound, the moon was in a full state in the evening sky, and the surrounding area was eerily silent with only the sound of nature in the background.

Inside the compound building, Gabriel exited the interview room where they were holding their captive man and carried on along the corridor until he came to a large metal door. Gabriel entered a six-digit number into the access point to the left of the door, and the door slid open straight away, Gabriel stepped into the room beyond and was instantly aware of the activity emanating from the room which was acting as the group's control and planning room. He walked over to one of the smaller briefing rooms where he found Boris Atanassov pouring over a heap of plans spread across a desk. The bald man was intently scrutinizing the plans which Gabriel knew to be secret plans relating to Sky Zone One. The Faction Against Continent Rule had managed to source the technical schematics for Sky Zone One which were vital to their next mission, which was the attack of this floating city. The FACR had been planning this mission for years, and it would be the biggest and most daring attack in history, taking the Sky Zone residents hostage to push their demands on the United Continents and pretty much the entire world.

Gabriel saw Boris looking up at him, and it was clear that he was still annoyed with his recent outburst about the Elders, but he didn't care about that now. He felt excited at the prospect of undertaking such a daring mission, and he would push himself and his team to their limits to execute this mission, his life involved nothing else at present, and his focus was absolute.

'I have confirmed what the schematics and plans have told us, our engineer friend has decided to co-operate fully now and is supplying even more information than I thought possible,' said Gabriel.

'Good, what about the information on the security force on Sky Zone One?' replied Boris as he continued to flip through the documents on the desk.

'We have a good estimate of numbers and organisation of the security forces, albeit he is an engineer so his detailed knowledge of all security aspects would be minimal,' Gabriel said as he poured himself a black coffee from the pot on the table.

'And your military informant, the Captain aboard Sky Zone One?'

'He has identified the chief security officer as a Major Khan who is responsible for the entire security and safety of Sky Zone One. I will task the intelligence cell to find out as much about this person as possible, more importantly, to ascertain if he has any weaknesses. The Captain is still feeding us information and will be joining us very soon ready for the final stages.'

The Captain they were speaking about was part of the Sky Zone One security team and was an essential addition to their plan. This had been a golden nugget for Gabriel and his team and involved a sleeper agent planted by the Elders many years earlier. Now that seed had developed into one of the highest-ranking security officers on Sky Zone One. As much as he had started to hate the Elders, he couldn't disguise his awe at their forward-thinking and planning.

'The time is close,' he said to Boris, 'There is nothing that can stop us now.'

Chapter 12

Rye had been called to the ArmorCorp offices by Si Morgan and been told that it was urgent, so Rye had left his apartment immediately and headed to the office. It was early morning, and although the sun was starting to rise, the chill in the shade was noticeable. It didn't take Rye long to reach his location. The nondescript office building could have housed any corporate business as no tell signs were indicating that this was the home of one of the largest private military contractors on the planet. The only real indication that it belonged to ArmorCorp was the polished brass nameplate on the wall by the main door to the building, and even this was relatively small in comparison to the front of the building, ArmorCorp liked to keep things under the radar and not draw unwanted attention to themselves.

Rye entered the building using his access pass; the reception area was as sterile as any corporate office building in the area. A female receptionist sat behind a large reception desk and nodded as he walked past, from a hidden video screen behind her desk she could see that it was Rye Braden once he had submitted his access card at the front door. There was also facial recognition in action as he had stridden into the reception area, confirming that this person was, in fact,

CHAPTER 12

Rye Braden. The security measures were high at this location, albeit discreet.

Rye made his way to the first floor where a security officer was sat behind a small desk. The officer nodded to him as Rye passed through into the main area of ArmorCorp. As usual, the place was a hive of activity, utterly different to the serene reception area he had just passed through. Rye wasted no time and found the room where Si Morgan was located, along with two other men which he knew one to be Felix Danner but the other one he had not seen before and was of middle eastern origin.

'Rye, great to see you,' spoke Si Morgan as he shook his friend's hand.

'You know Felix already, and this is Tariq Al-Saker who is an intelligence officer for the United Continents based in Saudi Arabia.'

Rye shook both men's hands, he knew Felix Danner to be one of the head sheds at ArmorCorp and whenever he was present meant that a high-risk mission was in the pipeline. The second man he didn't know, he had small eyes set above a large nose with slightly receding hairline. He was dressed in a black suit with no tie, Rye had never come across any staff from Saudi Arabia before, and he had never operated in this country either, despite working in almost every other location on the planet.

They all sat down around the table, and Felix began to explain the reason they had been called in, as he did so, he activated the large screen to assist with his briefing.

'Thank you for coming in at short notice, but we believe this to be a critical issue,' said Felix as he looked at each person sat around the large glass desk.

'The United Continents have requested our assistance in Saudi Arabia. This is concerning another capture mission. This time involving a high-ranking member of the FACR organisation.'

Felix brought up a facial image of an attractive woman in her forties of mixed-race origin. She was pictured getting out of a black SUV.

'This is Sylvia DeMarco, a business-woman with global contacts and someone we now believe to be working with the FACR, more importantly, we believe her to be the main link between the Elders and other terrorist groups,' said Felix.

'The Elders?' queried Si Morgan.

'Yes, they are a group that we have never been able to gather much information on, even the United Continents are in the dark as to who they are and what their objectives are,' replied Felix Danner.

'There are many stories about the Elders, they are like ghosts,' spoke Tariq for the first time with a strong middle eastern accent, 'But we are now learning more about their organisation. Capturing Sylvia DeMarco will help us to identify exactly who the Elders are.'

'That's right. After many months of surveillance and intercepting communications, we believe Sylvia DeMarco to be the go-between for these two groups. We also believe her main business activities which include property are more of a front or at the very least funded by the Elders,' interjected Felix, 'Tariq here is heading the operation in the middle east. His team are currently observing Miss DeMarco whilst she is in Saudi Arabia.'

The screen image changed to that of a large tower block which Felix identified as an apartment building where Sylvia

CHAPTER 12

DeMarco owned a penthouse apartment. The next slide was of a stylish restaurant which Felix identified as a place of interest due to following Sylvia to this location.

Felix looked around the room, 'The interesting link that we have uncovered is that we have identified a known person seen entering and leaving the restaurant at similar times to Sylvia DeMarco, this is interesting as this person was identified as Rupert Everson. Everson is a person of interest as the United Continents had previously employed him under the banner of the Special Warfare Cadre. This was in addition to other special projects with one such project rumoured to involve genetic manipulation, none of these rumours ever being confirmed as accurate though.

'We do not have much time before Miss DeMarco leaves Riyadh for her next location, she is not in each place for very long, and hence this makes it difficult to monitor her movements and activity,' continued Felix.

'As the United Continents have gathered enough evidence on this person, they now want to pick her up, and this is where you come in. We are to provide a capture squad who will travel to Riyadh and pick Miss DeMarco up and then transport her to a safe house located in Safaga in Egypt.'

Felix locked eyes with Si Morgan as if to make him absorb his next sentence.

'This is a priority call from the United Continents so whatever you need will be supplied, I trust you can formulate a plan of attack?'

'Yes, we can formulate a plan once we have spoken more with Tariq and his team,' said Si as he looked at Tariq and then at Rye.

'Rye, you will be the team leader for this, so let me know

who you want for this task. It will be a six-man team including Tariq,' Si followed up.

Rye looked at his old friend with a cautious look. He didn't like taking unknown people on missions, especially one as sensitive and dangerous as this. His mind drifted back to the last capture mission, where his team suffered fatalities after trying to capture Michael Juno. He clenched his jaw as he reran the mission in his head; he was damn sure that he wasn't going to lose any more men under his command.

'Rye, this is your mission, and I respect that. I will just be coming along to make sure all goes well,' said Tariq smiling briefly.

Felix turned the monitor off and turned back to the group, 'We want you to be in Egypt tonight ready for final checks, so time is of the essence, you can brief your team mid-flight, and we will make every resource available to you.'

Rye would have to wait on his personal mission to find answers about why he was different, for now, he had to focus on the new task and started running through the type and level of equipment he may need to execute such a mission overseas. He did not doubt that they could get across and back without being detected, that was probably the easy part and the responsibility of the pilot anyway. His job was to plan and execute the capture of Sylvia DeMarco. This meant synchronising his execution with the intelligence from Tariq's team currently on the ground.

Si Morgan would be coming on this mission and this pleased Rye, it would be good to have him nearby albeit Si would be in the control aircraft monitoring from a distance. Rye believed that the best option would be a similar approach to the Michael Juno task whereby the team would enter from above, especially if the target lived in the penthouse. This would involve the silent approach that the CK-150 attack helicopters provided, enabling them to get close enough to then fast rope to the roof. From there, each team member would have their exact instructions and would execute them with speed and agility whilst Rye and Tariq stood back ready to enter once the penthouse had been breached. For this mission, Rye and his team relied heavily on the intelligence fed through from Tariq's unit on the ground, this concerned Rye as had never worked with this intelligence team. Still, he knew the intelligence services of the United Continents were well trained.

The flight which would take them to undisclosed airfield base in Safaga was scheduled for 1:00 pm. This meant Rye and his team had an hour and a half to get their equipment sorted. They would only need to take their personal assault kit on this flight, and everything else would be there waiting for them when they landed. Their personal assault kit would consist of ballistic body armour, a lightweight ballistic helmet and personal weapon systems. There would be a tactical link between each team member and control. Rye's personal weapon systems consisted of G12 sonic assault rifle and Sig C20 sidearm. Any additional weapon systems he could pick up once in-country as there was always an armourer close by.

Rye had picked some of the team from the last mission, these being Guy and another veteran named Jimmy. The other two members were relatively new to ArmorCorp although both Si Morgan and Guy had personally vouched for them, so that was good enough for Rye. The final member of the team was Tariq which was the unknown risk for Rye. Still, he didn't really have an option on this one as it was a United Continents mission and Tariq was the intelligence officer heading up this particular mission. Rye didn't like it, and he would be keeping an eye on Tariq Al-Saker.

'Thirty minutes until we land at Safaga,' said the Pilot over the communication system.

Rye acknowledged the warning, and through his communication system, he requested the pilot to check to make sure their ongoing transport was prepared and ready. The pilot responded within seconds to acknowledge that the CK-130 attack helicopter was ready and waiting.

Rye could see that his team were getting ready for the swift switch over from their transport plane to the CK-130, ready to cross the Red Sea and travel the thirteen hundred kilometres to Riyadh. The CK-130 attack helicopter could travel close to six hundred kilometres per hour and had a range of more than two thousand kilometres due to the hybrid fuel cell engine. It housed some of the most up to date and deadliest weapons of any attack aircraft on the planet. Hopefully, we won't need to test the weapon systems today, thought Rye as he ran the plan through his mind again.

As they touched down in the small-government airfield in Safaga, Rye could see the awaiting CK-130 with its sleek yet muscular lines glinting in the early morning sun. Rye and his team exited the transport plane and made their way to a nearby hangar which had its doors wide open, and a small group of men stood around a table and monitor. Rye gestured to his team to wait over in the corner of the hangar and recheck their equipment, whilst he strode confidently over to the group of men. Si Morgan accompanied him as he was still the mission leader due to outranking Rye and this meant that he would also be the main communication channel between the planned snatch activity on the ground and the keen interest from the United Continents and his employer, ArmorCorp.

'I trust you have an update for us?' spoke Si Morgan as he approached the group.

The closest person turned as he heard Si speak, he was a tall Arabian man with long shoulder-length dark brown hair and piercing eyes.

'Yes, we have an update for you.'

The man introduced himself as Manaf and that he was the country station manager in Saudi Arabia. He spoke with a stern and authoritative tone. Manaf shook hands with Si Morgan and Rye Braden before he began his briefing of what had occurred during the time that Rye and his team had been in the air. There had been no real change to the routine and activity of Sylvia DeMarco, and it was agreed that the surveillance team in place would observe through the day and then for an evening snatch to be arranged, this meant Rye's team had a few hours to rest and regroup.

Rye briefed his team and then set up a personal area in one corner of the aircraft hangar and laid down and waited for the mission to begin, his mind went back to his own personal issues and how he was going to find out the truth about who he was and what made him different. As his mind drifted back, he tried to piece together all his years in the military and construct a timeline without any breaks or missing memories. The one part of his life that always came up as grey was the time just after he had passed selection to join the Pathfinder patrols, for some reason this transition was blurry.

At that point, Si Morgan came over and sat on a metal box beside Rye.

'I've just had an interesting chat with Felix Danner about

the job,' said Si as he cautiously looked around the hangar to make sure no one else was in earshot.

'He has dug deeper into Rupert Everson. They have found out that he was dismissed rather sharpish from the United Continents due to being involved in genetic enhancements on humans.'

At this, Rye sat upright and urged his friend to continue, his curiosity getting the better of him.

'There's not much more to tell at this stage except that he was kicked out of the United Continents after heading up the Special Warfare Cadre which was a secretive department within the United Continents that designed and tested new weapon systems,' Si continued.

Si knew Rye had to find out what was going on within himself, deep down he also wanted to know why Rye was so unique, 'ArmorCorp is looking into this more, but I thought you'd want to know.'

Interesting thought Rye as he deciphered what Si Morgan had just told him. Was genetic mutation what made him stronger? Was genetic mutation what had been done to him. Surely, he would have known if something like that had happened to him, he thought to himself.

'Have you ever come across this genetic mutation before?' asked Rye.

'Only what I've seen and heard on the news mate, but that's on animals and plants, not bloody humans!' replied Si as he stood up.

'If I hear any more then I'll let you know asap, but remember this may not be linked,' Si warned as he stepped away.

'Thanks mate, appreciate it,' responded Rye.

I need to know more about this and especially about Rupert

CHAPTER 12

Everson, he thought to himself.

With that Rye got his gear prepared and walked over to the makeshift briefing table where Manaf and Tariq Al-Saker stood talking, they stopped as Rye approached.

'Any further updates?' queried Rye as he reached the table.

'Our surveillance team has been on Miss DeMarco all day and no movement from her apartment,' confirmed Tariq.

'If there is still no movement from her by 8:00 pm then we recommend moving in,' interjected Manaf in his usual authoritative tone.

'We have a staging area forty kilometres from the target building which we have secured. This will allow you to react quickly to any changes,' Manaf continued as he manipulated the monitor in front of him to show a large area just south of Riyadh.

'Ok, I will get the team together to leave in thirty minutes,' replied Rye.

Thirty minutes later, Rye and his team were on the CK-130 with the rotors turning slowly. The pilot confirmed they had the green light and the thrusters flared into life propelling the attack helicopter two hundred metres into the air, Rye could feel the power of the machine as it rose. Seconds later the aircraft threw its occupants back into their seats as it set off for its next destination, the holding area forty kilometres south of Riyadh. Although the primary power source for the CK-130 was delivered by fuel cells and thruster engines, the rotors provided additional power and manoeuvrability to the aircraft.

'We're now entering Saudi airspace and will be at the holding area soon,' said the pilot over the aircraft's communication system.

Rye looked out of the window scanning the horizon as the sun started to disappear behind it, casting an orange hue over the barren land beneath them.

Rye had communicated the attack plan to the rest of his team via his Interactive Personal Computer, and he could now see that each team member was carefully scrutinizing their own IPC's. Any questions could be raised later once they reached their destination.

The communication system sparked into life once more, 'Holding area in figures three zero.' That was quick thought Rye. These CK-130's were impressive aircraft he said to himself.

'Do you have communication with the control bird?' responded Rye over the radio. The control bird was the second CK-130 which was to be used as command and control aircraft, Si and a small team of operators were aboard this second aircraft.

'Yes,' came the simple response from the pilot.

'They are on our six, you need me to patch you through?' added the pilot.

'No, all good,' confirmed Rye.

As the two aircraft touched down in the holding area, wisps of dry sand were thrown around like small sandstorms until the silent thrashing of the main propellors came to a halt and then all was quiet. As this was an unknown location to Rye, he had told his men to be acutely aware of the absence of the normal and the presence of the abnormal.

Both teams made their way over to one of the buildings surrounding the mini airfield, and once inside they placed their equipment down in order so that when the call to action came, they would be ready without confusion.

CHAPTER 12

Rye checked the time, 6:30 pm, they had made good time from Safaga to this location.

'We could get the call to move at any time, make sure you are ready to move when the call comes in.'

Rye walked over to the centre table where Si Morgan, Tariq and Manaf were scrutinising electronic mapping on a portable tablet.

As Rye got closer, he could see that it was a live feed from one of the surveillance drones showing a view of the targets tower block from above.

Si Morgan turned to him, 'There has been no activity, she has been holed up in her apartment all day.'

'Ok, well let's get in there and get this done,' Rye said.

'I agree, no point waiting any longer.'

Manaf looked at the two ArmorCorp men and spoke up, 'I also agree so please ready your equipment and prepare your team.'

Rye strode off with Tariq on his tail and verbally briefed the other members of the team, the men moved with a calm but confident manner as they loaded weapons and rechecked equipment. Rye was confident that this mission would result in a much better outcome than the last mission, especially now he felt more energised and focused than he ever had before.

Chapter 13

Private Sarah Ashford stretched out and rolled on to her side. The bedsheet was hardly covering her body as she propped her head up on one arm. It was 6:00 am, and she could hear her love interest moving about in the small kitchen.

'Smells good,' she purred.

'You're awake,' came the voice of Major Khan from the tiny kitchen.

He walked back through to the bedroom, wearing just a towel around his waist and sat down on the double bed next to her.

'Well, with all that clattering about, it was hard not to be awake,' she mused mockingly.

'Sorry about that but I guessed that you would be hungry after last night!'

'I am hungry, but not for food!'

She pushed herself up on her knees and snuggled in behind him, kissing the side of his face whilst her hands wandered over his chest.

'Ha, well food will have to do for now as it's a big day today. You know it's onboarding day.'

She sighed loudly, 'Ok, but I want you back tonight, Major!'

With that, she stood up from the bed showing off her naked

body and making sure that her man noticed her walk into the bathroom by looking back just as she disappeared out of sight.

Major Khan walked back into the kitchen and finished making the breakfast he had been cooking, he placed the two plates on to the small table and took a sip of his black coffee. His mind checked all the things that he had to do today before the first shuttles arrived with the new citizens of Sky Zone One. Finally, all his and his team's hard work had come to fruition with the onboarding of the first Sky Zone project.

Sarah was dressed now and joined him at the table, she was wearing her Sky Zone uniform, and he thought she looked very young sat there in front of him, it didn't matter though as he had fallen for this blonde bombshell and yearned more for her company each day. He never thought that he would love another person since he had lost his wife and little girl, he had been devoid of all feeling and that's why the Sky Zone project had been such an attractive offer to him.

Major Khan had been happy rising through the ranks of the United Continents when he had met his wife. She had made him appreciate more than what the military had taught him and had given a different perspective of life. He had married Monica within a year and not long after she had informed him that she was pregnant with their first child, everything was perfect in his life. They had settled in Denmark where they lived an enviable life, him a rising star within the United Continents and Monica as a primary school teacher where their daughter had just started school at the age of four.

He was away a lot with his role as a commissioned officer in the renowned Commando Elite who were at the forefront of the United Continents military efforts. This meant he could be deployed anywhere on the planet and at short notice. He loved his military career but loved his wife and child more, and this was why he was prepared to give up the excitement and adventure of the Commando Elite and focus more on his personal life.

'Right, my duty starts in fifteen minutes, so I'm off,' said Private Sarah Ashford as she stood from the kitchen table.

'Yes, of course.'

'Are you ok?' she asked, 'You seem distant?'

'I'm fine, just running through what needs to be done today,' he lied.

She kissed him and left the cabin, as the door closed his mind went back to his wife and daughter and in particular the day they were ripped away from him by the terrorist group called the Rebel Alliance. The day they were caught up in an attack whilst visiting London, the Rebel Alliance had staged an attack on a corporate building in the heart of the financial capital. In the worst of luck and the smallest window of opportunity, they had all been in the wrong place at the wrong time. They had been caught in the explosion set off by members of the Rebel Alliance.

The blast had utterly ripped through the immediate area, glass windows imploded with shards flying everywhere, brick and mortar acted as lethal missiles ripping through human tissue and dust and debris clouded the area. Major Khan could hear people wailing, multiple alarms sounding although the background noise was eerily silent with only these specific ghostly sounds being heard. He remembered being on the floor, and the seconds it took to realise what had happened, as the dust settled he could see his wife and daughter a few metres away, their motionless bodies covered in dust and debris.

He had called out their names, screamed them in fact. He

CHAPTER 13

had got to his knees and tried to stand but fell immediately. He had then crawled to them, an absolute fear in his mind. They were both face down, still motionless. He had grabbed his wife by the shoulders and rolled her over. That moment would remain with him for the rest of his life; her limp body and lifeless eyes staring up at him. In that instant, he knew she was gone, and his body started shuddering uncontrollably as his gaze wandered over to his daughter Evy, her tiny body face down in the rubble. His hands shook as he reached for her, her name struggling to form on his lips, his stomach feeling like it was being ripped from his body. He picked her limp body from the ground and held her in his arms. Her face seemed so angelic even amidst the chaos surrounding them.

His mind flashed back to the present as his intercom sounded; he was physically shaking from his recollection of the past. The intercom was still ringing, so he answered it; it was the duty operations officer.

'Sir, we have been informed of the time of the first shuttle arrival,' spoke the operations officer.

'What time?'

'First shuttles to arrive at 11:00 am sir.'

'Ok, I am on my way to the main control room.'

Major Khan focused on the present now; this was probably one of the most notable times in history. The onboarding of Sky Zone One, the first habitable mega-ship and valid response to decaying earth. With a further three Sky Zones following, this was the real test for a solution that was the most realistic and practical way of continuing life on earth until other options became more realistic. This meant that everything relied on Sky Zone One being a success, and Major Khan was at the forefront of ensuring this happened. He had put everything he had into this project, simply because at the time he had nothing else to live for and the Sky Zone project had kept him going since the death of his beloved wife and daughter.

It didn't take Major Khan long to reach the central control room for Sky Zone One and once through the security he was hit by the buzz of activity occurring around him.

'Sir, we have started running the system review and zero failures,' said the duty operations officer.

'Good, let me know if any failures do arise.'

Major Khan continued checking with each control officer spaced around the large room as he wanted feedback on every system on the ship. This included life support, security, welfare, communications, and every other department you could think of that would be needed to operate a miniature floating city. Major Khan also checked that all staff were back from their ground leave to ensure that the ship was fully crewed during the onboarding process.

'We have two personnel not accounted for sir,' said one of the control officers.

'Who?'

'Captain Nick Hughes and a senior engineer named Karl Roberts.'

'Have we gone through the follow-up procedure?'

'Yes sir, we have reached out to all persons listed on each man's file. We have also deployed security staff to their home addresses.'

Major Khan was concerned at this news, not just for the safety and welfare of his staff but also for the security risk that this posed. His role was ultimately the safety and security of all staff and guests on Sky Zone One and not knowing where

CHAPTER 13

two staff members were was a concern indeed.

'I want a full report from the commander on the ground as soon as he has any information,' ordered Major Khan.

He had only seen his friend Nick Hughes a few days ago, and all seemed well with the younger officer. Where the bloody hell are you, he thought. He made his way to his office so that he could try Captain Nick Hughes on his secure line. He needed to know where he was and whether he was ok. The secure communication system rang but could not connect with his friend's mobile device; he tried again before closing his secure line.

He brought up the personal file for Karl Roberts, who was the engineer that was also missing. He could see that this person was married with a son and that he had an exemplary career with no red flags and no reason why he would be missing.

An incoming call for him came in. It was the operations officer, presumably with an update.

'Yes,' answered Major Khan with limited patience.

'Sir, we have made contact with Engineer Karl Roberts wife.'

'Continue.'

'She has not seen him for two days now, and the last she heard from him was a message stating that he had returned to work and would not be able to communicate with her until he had finished his work.'

'Really? Did she not think that was odd,' replied Major Khan.

'She did sir, but she also knew the secrecy and importance of Sky Zone One so didn't raise the alarm.'

Major Khan felt his heart sink at this point, this was serious and something that had to be escalated.

'I want a Level One response sent to the United Continents

immediately, I will also contact Field Marshall Russell myself,' stated Major Khan as he disconnected from the call.

A 'Level One' response was the highest message possible. It would detail all that was occurring, the fact that a senior Sky Zone One officer and an engineer were missing may well justify stopping the onboarding process.

Major Khan composed himself, it was now 9:25 am and time was running out before the first shuttles arrived from the surface. He brought up the contact for Field Marshall Russell and tapped connect. He needed to escalate this to the very top.

'Major Khan,' came the powerful voice from the silver-haired officer on the screen in front of where Major Khan was sitting.

'Sir, thank you for taking my call so quickly.'

'Well Major, I have just received your Level One response on my desk!'

'I thought you should be made aware immediately sir, we have two key members missing, and we are moments away from receiving our first guests,' Major Khan said hesitantly.

'We have dispatched a team to search for both men, this includes tracing their last electronic footprints. Face recognition has also been activated across all United Continents areas,' responded the senior officer.

Major Khan knew that it would be near impossible for these two men to escape the United Continents trace, with there being too much coverage and too many ways to locate people of interest. Unless they or someone else tried hard to bypass the multitude of CCTV, face recognition and other dominant surveillance measures that the United Continents had in place across the globe.

CHAPTER 13

'Sir, my concern is if their absence is linked and the risk to Sky Zone One.'

'At this point, we continue with the onboarding. I am providing you with five hundred extra soldiers to reinforce and support the onboarding process,' said Field Marshall Russell.

'Yes sir, thank you.'

'I do not need your thanks, Major, I need you to secure Sky Zone One,' the reply was dry and unforgiving.

'Of course, I understand.'

The Major finished the call with his superior and let out a long sigh. He had dealt with every problem that the Sky Zone project had come up against over the years and now at the final hurdle, it could be in jeopardy. It was also clear that no one wanted to be responsible for the stopping of the onboarding however risky the situation was.

He decided to return to the control room and monitor the situation from there, in addition to managing every other aspect of the onboarding process. With the ground-based investigation teams from the United Continents searching for the two missing men then Major Khan could concentrate more on the present situation as he knew that those hunting the missing men would not leave any stone unturned.

As he reached the control room, he was approached by the operations officer.

'Sir, we have five personnel cruisers approaching?'

'Yes, we have been given extra soldiers to secure Sky Zone One, in case those missing have created a security breach,' replied the Major.

'We are not delaying the onboarding?'

'No, we are not!'

Chapter 14

The two aircraft had their engines running and their main rotors circling slowly, in anticipation for the imminent mission where Rye Braden would lead his assault team into Riyadh to secure Sylvia DeMarco.

Rye ordered his five-man team into the helicopter as Si Morgan and the control team did the same in the other aircraft, as Rye stepped in he indicated to the pilot to take off. The two attack helicopters rose into the early evening sky with little or no sound, merely a whooshing from the main rotor. As they climbed, they headed east towards the city of Riyadh, gaining a healthy altitude to avoid being compromised. When they arrived at the target building, both aircraft would then drop to one thousand metres where the command helicopter would remain whilst the primary assault helicopter with Rye and his team would hover down to the roof and commence the assault.

Rye was in constant communication with Si Morgan as he and his team dropped to just above the rooftop to Sylvia DeMarco's tower block. Once in position two ropes were dropped from either side of the now open cargo doors with both just hitting the floor of the rooftop. Rye gave the command to his team, and in a well-rehearsed drill, they exited

CHAPTER 14

the hovering aircraft with three men each side and with only a few seconds between each member of the team. Rye hit the ground last after observing his team successfully fast rope from the attack helicopter. There was still just enough light to operate with the human eye, although each member did also have enhanced night vision capability.

In fluid movements, Rye and his team moved swiftly to their pre-determined assault positions on the roof. Rye had decided to keep close to Tariq, and so they were committed as a two-man team, and this meant that Rye could keep a close eye on their new team member. There was no way that he was going to have any more bad missions, and this meant controlling every stage of this assault.

'Team 1 in position, status check team 2 and 3?' said Rye over the assault team's communication link.

'Team 2 in position.'

'Team 3 in position.'

With all teams in position, Rye confirmed all was clear from the control helicopter hovering just out of sight above them.

'Area clear, no movement,' confirmed Si Morgan as he observed the screens showing what the image intensifying cameras attached to the control helicopter were viewing.

With that, Rye gave the command, and his men sprang into action. Team two, led by Guy, were responsible for breaching the rooftop access point. This also meant disabling any electronic security measures that may be in place which would alert someone to their presence.

'We're in,' came the simple response from Guy.

'Roger that, all teams proceed,' replied Rye as he started moving to the now open rooftop door.

Team three would secure the rooftop, and top landing whilst

the other two teams entered and searched out their target. As far as any intelligence was concerned, Sylvia DeMarco was still alone in her penthouse apartment although had been for some time.

The rooftop access point was the easiest way to approach the penthouse without being seen. It would mean that the assault would be entirely from above, and this limited the chance of being compromised during the assault. Once through the rooftop access door, the two teams would make their way down a narrow staircase to a second door which opened out into the main external corridor of the penthouse apartment which was where the lift was located.

The team carefully bypassed any security alarms and prepared to disengage the door locks when Rye placed his hand on Guy's shoulder, which made Guy freeze immediately. Rye twisted his head as if hearing some movement on the other side of the locked door, he was not sure how he could hear the activity, but he could. He heard the elevator doors opening, and then footsteps walking from left to right and he pictured in his mind two people walking from the elevator towards the main door of the apartment.

'Wait,' came the hushed command from Rye over the radio.

Rye listened further and heard a single knock on the door before the door being opened. Shortly after he heard the same door close, who were these new arrivals, he thought to himself.

'Zero Alpha, at least two people have exited the elevator and are now inside the target apartment,' spoke Rye over the radio.

'Alpha One, do you have eyes on?' came the immediate response from Si Morgan.

'Negative, I heard them before we breached the door.'

CHAPTER 14

'Confirm "Heard Them"?'

'Yes, I heard them exit the elevator and walk to the apartment, knock and then enter.'

'Roger that,' came the confused response from Si Morgan acting as Zero Alpha.

'We now have the target and possibly two-plus persons inside the apartment,' updated Rye.

'Wait out,' came the reply from the control helicopter above.

Si Morgan got on the secure radio and contacted Manaf, who was monitoring the operation from the holding area back on the ground.

'Manaf, we have unknown persons that have entered the target apartment? Why have your surveillance team not picked this up?'

Manaf responded immediately, 'Let me look into this now and get back to you.'

Si Morgan lowered the radio handset and cursed to himself, how did these new arrivals not get noticed entering the elevator. A split second later and they would have been compromised once they had breached the second door.

Moments later Manaf was on the radio to Si, 'We have an operative with a visual on the elevator door, and there has been no movement at ground level, they must have come from a different floor?'

'The elevator is a private elevator for the penthouse use only, if it can be accessed from different floors then we have seriously missed something!' replied Si Morgan in a stern voice.

'Alpha One, we have no visual or description of anyone using the elevator,' said Si.

Rye and his team were still in the stairwell leading from the rooftop, 'Roger that, do we continue with the assault?'

Si Morgan thought with speed and made the decision, 'Yes, proceed with the assault.'

The decision was to proceed, and Rye and his team would need to be prepared for a hostile situation unfolding, especially if these new arrivals were armed. Rye didn't like this new situation, but he and his team were professional enough to deal with most if not any problem that arose from these missions.

Rye with his hand still on Guy's shoulder now squeezed it to indicate to Guy to proceed with breaching the door locks. Guy immediately activated the electronic charge, which defused the locking mechanism with a click.

'Secondary door breached,' Rye informed those listening on the radio.

Team one and two moved from the maintenance area into the luxurious surroundings of the main hallway of the penthouse apartment, with its high ceiling, expensive carpets and classic furniture aligning both sides of the long hallway. There were two security cameras at either end of the hall. However, these had been taken care of by Guy implementing a simple yet effective looping system into the live feed, so anyone observing the camera monitor would only ever see a clear hallway whilst the looping system was in place.

Rye and Tariq remained in a squatting position with weapons trained on the elevator door whilst Guy and one other approached the main access door to the luxury penthouse. The door was a large double door in white with intricate gold trim. The team already knew that the door was reinforced and may also have its own power source making it difficult to bypass. Guy removed a series of high explosive charges from his pack and placed the connected charges on various parts of the door. He then moved back from the door until he was level with Rye.

He looked at Rye and gave a short nod of his head. Rye returned the non-verbal communication and Guy pressed the handheld detonator. There was a bright flash of light as the explosive charge erupted in a flash of debris and smoke, immediately the team could see that the well-placed explosives had done their intended job and left a large hole in the ornate door.

'Go, Go, Go,' came the command from Rye.

Guy and his opposite number crashed through the door with their weapons in their shoulder. They were scanning the immediate area in front of them. The door had opened into a large reception area with a water fountain set in the middle. Smoke was still whipping around the room from the controlled explosion. Guy went left, and his teammate went right, both shouted, 'CLEAR' once they had confirmed their area of responsibility was clear from any danger.

Rye and Tariq were next to enter the room behind Guy's team. Time was of the essence due to the noise that had been made by the forced breach. Rye pushed forward to the next door which again was a large white double door similar to the main entrance they had just blown a hole in.

'Guy, with me,' commanded Rye.

Immediately Guy stepped in behind Rye and placed his hand on his shoulder, Rye took a deep breath and pressed down on the door handle and pushed it open. The door swung open, and this time Rye threw in a thunder flash grenade which erupted in a flash of noise and light. As per their training, Rye stepped in, and right whilst Guy covered the left of the room. They both scanned the room before them, this time, the room was not empty.

Rye saw them first, and he dropped to one knee immediately, his weapon trained on the unknown man that had Sylvia DeMarco by the throat with one hand and with a gun in his other hand pressed against her temple.

'Drop your weapon!' Rye shouted.

The man didn't move and held Rye's stare, the second man also had a weapon, but he had been closer to the thunder flash and was using one hand to clear his eyes. It was now a standoff with both parties not reacting, although each of them knew that the situation was about to change very soon.

'Drop your weapon,' Rye commanded again.

'You lower yours. Otherwise, I will blow her head off her pretty little shoulders!' said the man holding Sylvia in a very thick Arabian accent.

Rye quickly calculated his options which were somewhat limited in this type of situation. As he was about to speak again, he heard a weapon fire and before he knew where it had come from the man holding Sylvia by the throat flew back, but as he did his weapon discharged.

Rye instantly switched his weapon to the second man and with the skills of a trained marksman shot him twice in the head. He watched him drop to the floor before turning his attention back to the first target. Rye sprinted over to Sylvia DeMarco who was now on the floor convulsing, the shot had not penetrated her skull, but Rye could see that the bullet had significantly grazed her head and left an indent where her left temple should be. Her eyes were glazing over, and Rye knew that there had been significant damage to the head, her mouth was drooling now, and although she was speaking her words were not cohesive.

CHAPTER 14

'Where did the shot come from?' shouted Rye.

His question was answered as he turned back to the door they had just come through. He saw Tariq stood there with his weapon in hand scanning the room. Tariq must have taken the shot from the reception room and taken the man by surprise, Rye ignored Tariq and focused his attention on the injured female in front of him whilst Guy checked over the two males who had been shot by Tariq and then Rye.

Rye knelt beside Sylvia DeMarco and lifted her head from the floor, she was shaking all over and although there was no blood Rye knew this was serious.

'Zero Alpha, we have the target, although she is in a bad way,' Rye communicated to Si Morgan.

'You need to exfil as we have picked up chatter on the local radio. Your presence hasn't gone unnoticed, so you need to move now,' replied Si Morgan from the control helicopter.

'Roger that!'

As Rye finished talking on the radio, Sylvia DeMarco gripped his arm.

'I know you,' she said through broken speech.

'Rest up. We're getting you out of here.'

'I know who you are,' she said again.

Rye looked her in the eyes; she must be confused from the head injury he thought.

'You are Rye Braden… You are different…'

'What did you say?' Rye said instantly.

'Project Eden,' she stuttered.

Rye was now intently focused on the person in front of him. The person that was his target for this mission but was now becoming a person of more personal interest.

Sylvia was now falling in, and out of consciousness, not now

Rye thought to himself.

'Stay with me.'

She came too but was now struggling to breathe, the head injury sustained from the misfire must have caused considerable damage as she was fading away faster than Rye could imagine.

'Damn it, stay with me, Sylvia!'

She took in a sharp intake of air, and her eyes opened in shock, she grimaced but turned towards him.

'They are coming... for you,' she battled to say.

'Who, who is coming?'

'Eden... Everson... You are different!'

Her body convulsed and then went rigid, a slow exhale of air left her mouth and then she was still.

'We need to exfil now and ready a crash team,' Rye shouted over to Guy.

'Roger that,' replied Guy as he finished up taking fingerprint and blood samples from the men they had killed.

'Tariq, give me a hand with carrying DeMarco.'

Rye and Tariq picked the lifeless form from the ground and started back to the stairwell to the rooftop.

'What about the two hostiles,' asked Tariq as he hefted the dead weight of the female in his arms.

'We have their DNA and fingerprints. We can try and identify them later.'

'Zero Alpha, we are on route to the rooftop.'

'Roger that Alpha One.'

Rye and Tariq climbed the stairwell and exited on to the roof. They placed the body on the floor of the roof as their helicopter dropped down to a few feet above the flat rooftop. Guy and his team were now also on the top, and each member gave all-round defence whilst the helicopter got into a position for them to enter.

All of a sudden, a burst of fire sounded from a distant rooftop with each shot ploughing into the concrete floor around them.

'Incoming,' came the shout from Guy as he tried to locate where the shots had come from.

More shots smashed into the building around them, high-velocity shots as every contact made the point of impact explode in a shower of rubble.

Rye instantly found the location where the shots were coming from.

'Three hundred metres, east, tower block with masts,' came the immediate response.

As soon as the team had been directed to where the shots were coming from, they returned controlled fire. In addition to this, the control helicopter swooped down and acquired the lone shooter with its pulsar cannon. Fire from above rained down on the hostile shooter as the team on the other rooftop started boarding their helicopter, including hoisting the body of Sylvia DeMarco inside.

Rye was last to board, but as he approached the open door of the aircraft, he heard a sound that made him stop in his tracks, and as he turned he saw a hand-launched rocket flying towards the helicopter from a different rooftop.

'Eagle One, inbound!' Rye screamed into his radio.

In an instant, the pilot forced the helicopter to bank right in an aggressive manner. The rocket skimmed past the underside of the aircraft by centimetres.

Seconds later, more bursts of fire rained down on where Rye was stood, and he could see two attack drones bearing down on him. He looked back towards the helicopter, which was now more than fifteen metres away from the edge of the tower block. Rye didn't have time to contemplate his next actions. Without hesitation, he sprinted towards the edge of the building and launched himself at the open door of the helicopter.

Everything slowed down as he thrashed through the air, even the helicopter rotors felt like they were just ticking over. As his propelled body met the open door of the aircraft, time seemed to speed up again, and he reached out and grabbed the metal fast rope bars located just above the open doorway, once he had a firm hold he ordered the pilot to gain height and get them out of there.

Chapter 15

The room was a hive of activity, men and woman operated their screens with focus and precision whilst large control monitors flashed and lit up, depicting the state of each area of Sky Zone One. The control room buzzed with excitement as everyone who had been part of this epic project knew that all their hard work was about to be realised, once the civilians started to board the giant floating city.

Major Khan stood in the middle of the control centre absorbing the energy created by the constant activity occurring around him, he pinched the top of his nose and used his index finger and thumb to massage his eyes. He had still not heard from his friend Captain Nick Hughes, and the investigative teams on the surface had learnt no more about the disappearance of the senior engineer Karl Roberts.

Stressed was an understatement, he knew this day was coming although he hadn't been quite prepared for it, it seemed. Not only did they have two missing key figures which caused a significant security concern, they now had to facilitate and absorb an extra five hundred security troops which they hadn't expected. In addition to this, the common problems arising from populating a floating city ten thousand metres above the Earth's surface was enough to stress any person out.

'Sir, the first of the shuttles are arriving in fifteen minutes,' spoke the operations officer.

'Ok, tell the greeting party that I am now on route to the main docking area.'

With that Major Khan turned on his heel and walked out of the control room, he had to make a quick stop at his cabin and change his tunic and swap his beret for his parade cap. It was not every day that he got to wear his best uniform. The first guests to arrive at Sky Zone One would be the VIP's including politicians, royalty, senior government officials, wealthy business owners and so on.

The onboarding process was going to last for days as shuttle after shuttle arrived at the forty docking bays on Sky Zone One, a logistical nightmare some would say. Although Major Khan and his team had worked day and night to ensure that the processes in place ran as smoothly as they could, Major Khan ran a tight ship.

'Hello sir,' said a smartly dressed officer as Major Khan arrived at the docking bay.

He had arrived where they would be welcoming the first of their arrivals. The docking bay glistened as the lights danced off the highly polished floor, banners and flags were positioned around the bay whilst personnel hummed around in their finest uniforms waiting for the first landing craft to set down. If Major Khan hadn't been so stressed about the missing men, then he would be revelling more in the abundance of excitement that was in the air.

'Hello, what is the estimated time of arrival?'

'Three minutes sir.'

'Good, let us get into position,' said Major Khan as he

approached the front of the group.

As the seconds ticked down, the air of apprehension grew. Major Khan adjusted his collar and puffed out his chest. He already wanted this day to be over.

'Prepare for docking,' came the voice over the tannoy.

The massive docking bay doors opened up with considerable speed considering the size of them. They mechanically whirred until the door had risen out of sight, followed by a loud click as the door secured itself in place. Even though Sky Zone One was so high, the life support systems ensured that the air pressure, temperature and oxygen levels were maintained even whilst docking doors were open.

Major Khan could now see the large transport ship approaching, as it came closer he could see the two large windows at the front with the two pilots sat in their cockpits. The sun glistened off the thick glass of the cockpit, and Major Khan could see that the pilots had their sun visors down over their faces. As the gigantic transport ship approached, the pilots expertly manoeuvred it so that it was now side on with the docking bay. It hovered there for a moment before starting to move sideways into the docking bay, its side thrusters powering it in the direction of the landing area.

Major Khan marvelled at the elegance of the massive transportation ship and at the finesse the pilots used to land it within what he thought was a relatively tight area. The four large feet of the undercarriage pressed down on the shiny surface of the docking bay floor followed by the sound of pressure being released from the suspension as the ship rested to a halt.

Without instruction, eight of the Commando Elite soldiers marched over to the aircraft's side door and positioned themselves four each side. They were dressed in their finest dress uniforms which were kept for show parades and special occasions. Once they were in position, the locks on the ramp style door could be heard disengaging. The massive ramp door lowered smoothly and at speed, and once it had come to a stop on the floor of the docking bay, Major Khan started to approach.

As he approached he could see two soldiers of the Commando Elite at the front start to lead the passengers off the aircraft in an orderly fashion, Major Khan knew that the first occupants to set foot on Sky Zone One would be the very highest members of society. He adjusted his peaked cap as he approached. Beside him were two further officers of Sky Zone One, these being Lieutenant Rachel Azure who was the media relations officer and then Captain Wayne Emery who was the Communications officer for Sky Zone One.

Once the two Commando Elite escorts stepped on to the docking bay floor, they peeled off and joined their counterparts standing to the left and right of the open door, as they moved out of the way Major Khan noted a small thin man with receding hairline and round spectacles approach them.

'Good morning Major,' came the well-spoken voice.

'May I present to you Lord and Lady Stockwell,' the small man gestured to the two people standing behind him as if to expect some immediate response of awe from the Major and his counterparts.

'Good morning,' came the simple reply from Major Khan although he did bow slightly towards Lady Stockwell.

The first influx of guests to Sky Zone One was kept to two hundred so that the main ceremony and speech could be heard and experienced by all. Once all passengers were off

CHAPTER 15

the aircraft, they were then welcomed with an assortment of drinks whilst they mingled about in their air of superiority.

Superficial self valuers most of them, Major Khan thought to himself.

Major Khan and his team of greeters went through the next few minutes smiling and shaking hands with various dignitaries and people of supposed importance, his jaw starting to ache from forcing a smile. Each of these very excited people had been rich enough or just fortunate enough to know the right people to gain their place on this floating utopia.

One of the people to approach him was a United Continents senator who Major Khan knew to be a hard-hitting, no-nonsense character previously an officer in the Special Forces although before Major Khans time.

'Major Khan, I presume?' came the strong voice from the newcomer.

'Yes, sir.'

'Pleasure to meet you, I've heard only good things about your work on Sky Zone One, and I would personally like to thank you,' the newcomer said as he held out a large hand.

'It's a pleasure, sir.'

'Of course, it is, government work is always a pleasure!'

Senator Bob Mills had served with distinction in the Special Forces for fifteen years gaining various awards for gallantry and exceptional service, on leaving he had been swallowed up by politics where his meritorious service would shine bright amongst the everyday voter. He had finally found his way to becoming a senator with responsibilities including security and resilience, space exploration and alternative energy.

'Anything you want me to add to the speech Major?'

Nothing that could be added openly, Major Khan smiled to

himself.

'No sir, I'm sure you have it covered.'

With that, Senator Bob Mills made his way over to the raised podium and as he did so rehearsed what he was about to say in his mind. He climbed the steps and steadied himself on the stage, taking in all the faces before him.

'Ladies and gentlemen,' his voice boomed across the docking bay with the aid of the microphone and tannoy system.

Instantly, people turned towards him, ready to listen.

'We are here to witness history, the first of many to have the opportunity to better our lives and begin a new chapter, a chapter of hope and salvation.'

A round of applause erupted around the docking bay, and people's heads nodded in agreement with the speaker.

'It is without a doubt that our inclusion in this project is one of privilege and with that comes responsibility, the responsibility to ensure Sky Zone One and those Sky Zones that follow are respected and allowed to prosper,' continued the senator.

The audience were now fully behind the speech, nodding to each other, smiles appearing on their faces at the thought of what they were embarking on.

'It is public knowledge that the surface is struggling due to the rising temperatures, rising sea levels, increased precipitation and rising carbon levels in the atmosphere, these, unfortunately, are just some of the risks we face on the surface.'

The audience flowed with the speech, changing from happy smiles to shaking heads in disappointing acknowledgement.

He knows how to play a crowd, Major Khan thought to himself, and a typical silver-tongued politician.

'Sky Zone One gives us the chance to start over, to create

CHAPTER 15

an environment where our children and grandchildren and their grandchildren can flourish and prosper. A place that mirrors Earth's surface before it became dark and barren, a place of natural beauty,' continued the senator as he bathed in the attention of the audience.

Major Khan eyed the crowd, scanning one face to another. He was still acutely aware that there was an ongoing security risk with the two missing persons.

'May I ask you all to salute the people that have made this happen and the staff that will continue to execute what is a marvel of technology and vision. To Sky Zone One!'

The crowd erupted in applause with cheers filling the enormous space in the docking bay. The nominated press officers scurried about capturing images of this historic event. People turned to each other and shook hands as if they had been instrumental in the success of Sky Zone One. As the noise calmed down, smartly dressed staff in white tunics entered the docking bay and started to escort each of the guests to their new homes upon this floating paradise. The newcomers would start their new life away from the problems of the surface, buying themselves a ticket with a value worth much more than the actual ticket price.

Once the official onboarding celebration had finished, Major Khan went straight to the control room to receive an update on the ongoing security concerns and to monitor the arrivals of the next transport ships which would be carrying many more passengers than the first ship.

Major Khan arrived at the control room, and as soon as he had entered the room, he was bombarded by information from his operations officer, and now it begins, he thought to himself.

He could feel uncertainty in the pit of his stomach growing in intensity, threatening to take control of his mind. He needed a quiet space to clear his mind and focus on the complications that had started arising. With that Major Khan headed for his office which overlooked the control room, this was his very own command and control room where he could monitor everything going on. As he climbed the metal staircase to the access door, his mind reeled with the potential outcomes if his two missing officers had been kidnapped or worse.

As the secure door slid open, he stepped inside, and the door closed behind him with a slight mechanical whir. He had not told any of his seniors about the recent blip in the system, mainly because he had conducted complete scans of the entire computer systems and nothing sinister had been uncovered.

We have the absolute best cybersecurity people trawling the Sky Zone systems and been given an extra five hundred officers of the Commando Elite, he thought. He tried to counter the rising anxiety inside him.

He sat in his chair and closed his eyes; deep breathing had always allowed him to take back control of his thoughts and actions.

He was abruptly brought back to the present with his communication device sounding off, he picked it up from his desk and answered it.

'Sir, you need to see this urgently. It's an update about the missing persons of interest!'

Chapter 16

Gabriel Durand opened the door and entered the room that was now the temporary isolation cell for the man named Karl Roberts, an engineer from Sky Zone One. Even though he had been cleaned up by one of the medical staff, his wounds were still visible, and it was evident that he had been tortured. The room he was now in wasn't a prison cell as such but was secure and had no external windows. It was much better than the place that he had been held previously. At least he wasn't naked, and he wasn't secured to a chair in the middle of a dimly lit cold room anymore.

'I hope you are feeling better?' Gabriel said in a sincere tone.

'Yes, thank you,' replied Karl Roberts. He was still hesitant as this was the man that had tortured him and inflicted so much pain on him just hours before.

'Good, now that we understand each other then we can continue with the questions.'

Gabriel sat on a chair set beside a small metal table. He looked over at the engineer Karl Roberts who was now sat tentatively on the edge of a single bed in the corner of the relatively small room.

'Remember, you're helping yourself by answering these questions. All you should be considering now is yourself;

nothing else should matter.'

'You promise to let me go once I've answered your questions?'

'If you help me, then I will help you, it's as simple as that.'

Karl was aware that this didn't answer his question, although he was also acutely aware that his captor didn't need to answer any questions.

The next two hours continued without a break, question after question about every aspect of Sky Zone One. The questioning was relentless, although conducted in a friendly manner compared to his earlier experiences. Karl felt a shadow over him as every word he was saying was putting his fellow Sky Zone One colleagues in danger, but he had to think of his own welfare now, he had to put his family first, however difficult it was.

'I'm not sure I can tell you anything more,' Karl said hoping that the wave of questions would cease.

'I will tell you when you have satisfied my need. Do not mistake your position as one that can demand anything.'

'I..I...I wasn't demanding, I apologise.'

Gabriel walked towards the door and before he left he turned back to Karl Roberts, 'You're doing well, and I appreciate your efforts. Soon this will all be over.'

Gabriel left the room and closed the door behind him. Karl was left to his thoughts once again; his mind drifted to his wife and his young daughter. He missed their voices and tried hard to imagine what they would say once he was back in front of them, soon he thought to himself, soon.

Gabriel walked back to the main control room to update the rest of the team with the intelligence he had just gained from their now compliant hostage. He had every piece of the puzzle now. He revelled in the satisfaction that the long term plan he had formulated had come to fruition and he would inflict massive disruption on the United Continents and those that supported this tyrannous organisation.

'You appear happy Gabriel,' came the voice of Boris.

'I am, I believe we have everything we need to finalise the planning of the attack of Sky Zone One. I need to write it up and then will present later this evening, make sure all the team leaders are in attendance for 9:00 pm this evening.'

Gabriel went to his office and closed the door. He wanted to make sure he included all the intelligence and details acquired over the last couple of years. His presentation later that evening needed to inspire and build confidence. He wanted every member of the Faction Against Continent Rule to be as confident as he was about taking control of the first Sky Zone. The attack would be the most daring and demanding act of terrorism in the history of civilisation, to take nearly two million people hostage at one time and in one location was pioneering. It had been Gabriel's idea from the outset and was scoffed at initially, especially by the Elders who had laughed at him to his face. Well, they were not laughing now as he had made his dream become a reality achieved through perseverance and dedication to the cause.

He concentrated on the task ahead, and two hours later, he felt he had a presentation that would firstly communicate the daring plan, and secondly how they would implement such a plan. Once he had finished, he felt a wave of tiredness flow through his body; he couldn't remember the last time he had slept or even eaten for that matter. But now wasn't the time to sleep, he looked at his watch, it was 8:25 pm, so he closed his laptop and headed for the makeshift briefing room they had set up.

By the time he had set up the briefing people had started to drift into the room, including Boris and Teresa who were two of the highest-ranking members of the organisation, other attendees were operational members of various kinds. One particular person was Constantin Holm, who was one of Gabriel's military commanders. He was a veteran of the Kommando Spezialkräfte which was the German Special Forces unit which was active until the United Continents took over. Constantin was a monster of a man with strength and speed that belied his age, at fifty-six he was one of the more senior faces within the organization and so most people looked toward him for guidance, including Gabriel.

'Welcome everyone. Once you are seated, we will begin the briefing.'

The secure door was now closed, and the room numbered approximately twenty people, all having critical functions within the Faction Against Continent Rule. Someone had arranged the seating around a small table in the middle of the room where Gabriel had his laptop set up, beaming out of the integrated projector was a blueprint for what appeared to be a vast ship with many levels.

'As we all know, we have now come to the final stage of our plan. The plan to take control of Sky Zone One and its occupants, by any means necessary.'

Gabriel circled the large projection, making sure to make eye contact with all those sitting in the room.

'We are on the verge of making history, we are the closest anyone has come, and anyone will ever come to bringing the United Continents to its knees. This will be a turning point in history where the tyranny and control that the United

Continents has had over the planet will come to an end.'

He was working the group in the room now, although this wasn't a sales pitch he realized as all those in the room had their reasons to want to take down the United Continents.

'Our plan centres around three main points; these include the planning stage where we have used various sources and methods to gather information on the Sky Zone project. Secondly, the infiltrators that we have within the United Continents and this includes actually on board the ship. Finally, the attack which incorporates all aspects of this planning and execution.'

He continued speaking through the basis of the plan and mentioning those people associated with each layer of the plan.

'For the attack itself, we will have five teams, each with approximately forty fighters. Constantin, Teresa and I will lead three of the teams, and then we have two further leaders who will lead the rest of the teams.'

He searched the room for any sign of disagreement, although none came. He continued, 'We also have various people on board Sky Zone One as residents and crew who have been feeding us inside information for some time. Their identities are being kept hidden for now until we start the attack. They have been preparing for our arrival and will continue to support us during the attack.'

'How many in total will we have on Sky Zone One that will be involved in the fighting?' asked a dark-haired man.

'By the time that Sky Zone One is at full capacity, then there will be fifteen who will be assisting us in various ways, but all will be fighting for us when it comes to it. It doesn't sound much, but the work they are doing will greatly assist us.'

The briefing continued and as time went on Gabriel became more confident that the objective was more than achievable and that this time next week they would be standing on Sky Zone One and issuing their demands to the United Continents and the world.

'How can we be confident that we can overcome the security forces on Sky Zone One, it would be full of Commando Elite soldiers,' came a question from the group.

'From our intelligence, we estimate approximately one thousand soldiers and security staff on board. This means that we will be less in number although our previous planning and sleeper cells mean that we will have the upper hand when it comes to it. In addition to this, we also have an exceptional trick up our sleeve which will ultimately be the deciding factor in this battle.'

Looks of confusion passed across many of the faces in the audience, clearly they were not aware of what Gabriel referred to.

Gabriel let their confusion last just a little longer, more for his entertainment than anything else, 'We have been harbouring a secret, a secret that has not even been privy to you.'

He eyed the crowd as he felt their interest spike, 'Our attack force will be supplemented by super soldiers. These soldiers will be the difference between success and failure,' he said, finally settling their curiosity.

There was a wave of hushed voices around the room as the audience took in what was being said to them, apart from Boris and Teresa who were already aware of this information.

'What do you mean super soldiers?' enquired Constantin, clearly also unaware of this last minute detail.

CHAPTER 16

'They are genetically enhanced soldiers from a secret project within the United Continents, shut down many years ago. However, through our allies we have acquired these soldiers for our own needs and they will join us for the final attack of Sky Zone One.'

The silence in the room was deafening as everyone tried to compute the information they had just been told.

'This is why the forces on Sky Zone One will be no match for us. This is why we will be successful in our objective.'

The rest of the briefing continued and covered every detail that needed to be discussed. By the end of the briefing, no stone would be left unturned. It was now 1:00 am, and they had been going for four hours with very few breaks, Gabriel was confident that they had covered as much as they could in that time. They still had time to conduct further rehearsals and orders before the attack scheduled for next week, anticipation ran through his veins now, and his sole focus was on the mission ahead.

Now that he was confident that he had all the intelligence he needed, he had one more task to do before the night was finished. He arrived at the holding cell where Karl Roberts was being held, once the guard had let him in, he could see the Sky Zone engineer asleep on the single bed in the corner of the room.

'Karl, its time to wake up,' spoke Gabriel loud enough to make the person in front of him stir.

'What time is it?' came the simple reply.

'It's time for you to go, get dressed.'

'What? I'm leaving. You're letting me go?'

Gabriel didn't give a direct response, 'Get dressed, I will wait outside.'

Karl Roberts couldn't quite grasp what was just said to him, he had been captive for days, brutally tortured and then questioned non-stop for hours and now they were just letting him go. His mind swam as he hastily got dressed, putting on the basic clothes that had been provided to him by the nurse earlier in the day.

Gabriel waited outside the room on his own; he had relieved the guard that was in place as he felt there was no need anymore. Not long after he had left the makeshift cell, the door burst open, and Karl Roberts exited.

'You're letting me go?'

Gabriel didn't respond and instead started walking towards one of the exits that led to the main courtyard, 'Follow me.'

Karl followed him, 'Where are we going?'

The night was still when they entered the courtyard, the silence only broken by the variety of wildlife that came alive as darkness set in. The stars were in abundance in the clear night sky, the moon was full and covered the landscape in an eery light. As he walked, Gabriel looked up at the sky and thought about Sky Zone One and their mission.

'I want to thank you for your part in all this and helping us to make our dreams become a reality. You have provided us with vital information, and I know this was difficult for you as it meant putting your friends and colleague in jeopardy.'

Karl Roberts was limping behind him now, clearly struggling due to his wounds, wounds that Gabriel had inflicted on him.

'Ok, so are you letting me go then?' came the strained voice.

'I would love to let you go to be with your wife and child. Would you keep all of this a secret if I let you walk away into the night, or would you raise the alarm the first opportunity

CHAPTER 16

you got?'

'You can trust me, I just want to go home,' there was uncertainty in his voice now.

Gabriel had led them to the tree line beyond the buildings, 'I want to believe you, I do,' Gabriel turned to Karl and removed a handgun from below his jacket.

'No, No, No, you don't have to do this,' Karl Roberts could feel the colour draining from his face, his stomach twisted in knots. He could feel any hope that he may have had slipping away, he thought of his family in that instant, and an immense sadness hit him like a sledgehammer.

Gabriel raised the handgun and fired a single shot into the forehead of Karl Roberts.

Chapter 17

Rye sat in the debriefing room back at the United Continents main offices in London, he and Si Morgan had arrived earlier after a previous meeting at ArmorCorp with Felix Danner. It had been seventy-two hours since they had returned from the recent mission in Riyadh and both men had been on a multitude of debriefings already.

Sylvia DeMarco had been transported back to London and was currently in a coma within a secure medical facility, and it was unlikely that she was going to recover. The mission hadn't gone as planned, and they had encountered a series of events which had changed the situation on the ground. These included the unknown men in Sylvia's apartment and then the rooftop attack as the teams attempted to exit the area.

'It's been nearly three days, and they are still going over the same ground,' said Rye as he looked over to where Si Morgan sat.

'They think we are withholding something,' Si replied, staring back at Rye.

'Well, we're not so this is pointless.'

Rye knew precisely what they were after, whatever Sylvia DeMarco has told him before she had fallen into the coma that was causing the United Continents senior ranks some curiosity.

Rye also knew that he couldn't tell them what she had said, firstly as this would cause severe issues for him and secondly because this was the first piece of information he had about who he was and what was happening to him. He was going to follow up on this lead, and there was no better place than the very building he now found himself in.

'I need to stretch my legs,' stated Rye as he stood and walked towards the briefing room door.

He had met quite a few United Continents staff during his time in the military and ArmorCorp, and he knew exactly who to find. Dylan White was a top-class analyst who had worked for the United Continents for many years, and Rye had worked alongside him on numerous tasks.

Rye headed down the corridor until he came to a room on the left which was signposted administration manager, this would help him find Dylan White.

'Afternoon,' Rye said as entered the room.

'Good afternoon,' came the curt reply from the middle-aged man sat behind one of the two desks in the room.

'I need to find an old friend who works in the building.'

'And you are?'

Rye passed over his identity card to the man sat down, who held it up to examine it. His eyes scanned over the details that were displayed on the card, and he quickly handed the identity card back to Rye.

'Thank you, Mr Braden,' said the man with a friendlier tone in his voice.

He could see that Rye had the highest level of clearance and what his role was, which had made the man slightly nervous and more than helpful from this point. Rye had experienced this type of behaviour before when people had realised who, and what he was, a wry smile crept into the corner of his mouth.

The man expertly manipulated the screen with both his hands and found the information he was looking for after Rye had given him the name of the person.

'Officer White can be found on the sixth floor, but you won't have access to this floor regardless of your clearance level,' spoke the man not willing to meet Rye's gaze.

'Ok, send a message to him to meet me on the rooftop,' came the response from Rye as he turned and headed out of the office. Rye took one of the four glass cylindrical lifts to the rooftop, as the elevator swiftly ascended he looked down into the central courtyard of the building and watched the people milling about getting smaller and smaller.

The elevator came to a quick but smooth stop, and as the doors opened the fresh warm air met him as he stepped out of the elevator, the sun was still shining so he chose a table sat in the shade and waited for his friend to arrive.

As he waited, he thought about the events over the last seventy-two hours and especially the capture mission of Sylvia DeMarco, he remembered the words she had spoken just before falling into the coma.

'They are coming... for you.'

'Eden... Everson... You are different!'

He still did not understand what she meant, although he was going to find out, and he was going to ask his friend Dylan White to help him. He had to find Rupert Everson and ask him questions directly, and he was going to get the answers he wanted about why he was so different.

'Rye Braden, you old dog,' came the dulcet tones of Dylan

CHAPTER 17

White.

Rye looked up and smiled as he stood to greet his friend, 'It's been too long.'

'Far too long,' came the simple reply.

They sat down, and Rye thought to himself that he was glad he had thought of Dylan to help him find answers, as he knew he could trust Dylan to find answers where no one else could.

'So, old friend. What do I owe the pleasure of this visit?' spoke the Cambridge educated intelligence officer.

'Just a social visit,' replied Rye.

'Really, that's nice of you although I know you too well Rye and you are always too busy for social calls!'

Rye smiled at the directness of the man sat opposite him, he was of similar age to Rye although the years had been much kinder to him compared to Rye. Dylan White was of average height and mixed race, his father originally hailing from Syria and moving to the United Kingdom after the Syria conflict in 2020.

'I need to locate someone, and I also need background information on this person,' Rye informed him.

'Ok, that sounds straight forward.'

'Maybe not, as the person in question is called Rupert Everson.'

At the mention of that name, Dylan looked directly at Rye.

'Yes, that may complicate things somewhat,' replied Dylan.

'But can you help? I wouldn't ask if it wasn't important.'

'The person is on our radar due to his seniority within the far-right group called Deliberate Action and associations with the Faction Against Continent Rule, he is also a past officer of the United Continents, but I believe you already know this?' Dylan now spoke with a hushed tone.

Rye knew both groups his friend referred to and that they were well known for terrorist activities, he also knew that they could be a handful.

'Is this an official request?'

'No, I need answers for myself, strictly off the file on this one.'

Rye hoped that his friend would operate under the radar on this as he needed answers without drawing attention to himself.

'Ok, leave it with me, and I will see what I can find,' Dylan said as he stood up.

Rye stood and thanked his friend. He knew that Dylan would do all he could, and it was just a waiting game now. They travelled down in the same elevator chatting about their previous encounters until the elevator reached level six.

As Dylan stepped out of the elevator, he turned back to Rye, 'I will be in contact.'

Rye headed back to the debriefing room where he found Si Morgan still sat there nursing a cup of coffee. There was nothing more that could be done for now, so both men headed down to the main foyer of the building before going their separate ways.

As Rye headed back to his apartment, he thought about contacting Ruby but suddenly thought against it. There was no need to involve her in any of this right now. When it had all calmed down a little, then he would find her and tell her how he felt.

Rye never felt comfortable wasting precious time; he always needed to be doing something pro-active. He decided to do some open-source research on Rupert Everson and the group Deliberate Action. He did not hold much hope of finding

CHAPTER 17

anything of worth, but at least it would allow him to build a picture of this person and how they were linked.

Rye had been researching for a couple of hours when his mobile device started ringing, he looked at the screen and saw that it was Dylan White.

'Dylan, I didn't expect you to get back to me so quickly,' said Rye as he answered the call.

'Is your line secure?' responded Dylan, not beating around the bush.

'Yes.'

'Ok, well the bare bones of it is that most of the files I have come across have been locked by someone at the very top of the United Continents. I say this as there are very few people that have higher security clearance than myself.'

'So, what does that mean?'

'It means that he may be protected from above, or that he is under investigation by an organisation I haven't even heard of?'

'What about Eden?' Rye said, hoping for anything now.

'Well that's another story as nothing of that nature is held on any government database, there's nothing at all.'

Rye gritted his teeth as he knew it would near impossible for anyone else to find anything if Dylan wasn't able to.

'Rye, there is nothing stored electronically, but I do know that Rupert Everson may be at a conference this Friday in London,' said Dylan with some shred of hope.

That's better than nothing thought Rye and meant that he could ask questions directly to Rupert Everson although not in a conventional face to face manner. Rye thanked his friend for his immediate assistance, although he asked him to keep trying where possible.

He knew that he had to start planning now if he wanted to get close to Rupert Everson as he assumed he would be heavily protected by bodyguards and internal security that would be securing the conference. He would need to identify a place where he could disable any bodyguards accompanying Everson. Alternatively, he could wait until the conference had finished and then follow Everson to wherever he was going. However, this heightened the chances of losing Everson or even worse being compromised before he had got anywhere near him.

Rye thought about who he could ask to help him although he didn't want to put anyone at risk and he didn't know what he was going to uncover. He had worked alone on missions before in some of the most hostile places on the planet, the only difference this time was that there would be absolutely no support of any kind to help him out if he got into trouble. He had two days to plan this personal mission, so he got straight into it. When he was focused, then nothing got in his way.

Rye started planning straight away, identifying the location where he would kidnap Rupert Everson and then exploring every micro detail regarding that location from floor plans, access points, security systems and so on. His experience and training had taught him to examine every detail of a mission and never to leave anything to chance. This methodology had probably been one of the main things to keep him alive so long when others in his line of work had died so young.

Rye worked through the night oblivious to his hunger or tiredness; he was a man on a mission. He had settled on targeting Everson and his security team once they were inside the venue where the conference was taking place, this being the Millennial Foundation building situated in Westminster.

CHAPTER 17

Anyone else would think this plan was madness, but Rye knew exactly what he was doing and what he wanted to achieve, he did not need to remove Everson from the building to get answers from him. Rye planned to pretend to be one of the conference members of staff and lure Everson and his security team to a private corridor where a disused office would be from where he could get the answers to the questions he had. Rye estimated that inside the conference building, Rupert Everson would have one or two security officers with him, and his plan would only work if there were a maximum of two protection officers.

Firstly he had to find a way to get into the building without being compromised. He knew there would be a lot of security although he had experience dealing with these such situations. A disguise was needed so that he wouldn't compromise himself in the future as security cameras and other biometric security systems would cover the building. His plan was daring although this excited Rye in a way, this line of work was what he was good at and what he was known for back in the Pathfinder Patrols.

Once he had finished his planning, he decided it was best to conduct a physical reconnaissance of the location to make sure that the building plans he had used were still relevant and that nothing had changed. It was now 9:00 am, and the conference started the next morning, so he had twenty-four hours to conduct the recce, pick up the required equipment and implement his plan.

The next morning Rye had managed to bypass any security at the Millennial Foundation building and was now inside one of the wings waiting for guests to arrive, his disguise included longer hair, beard and brown colour eye contacts, finished off with a black suit as worn by the conference staff working in the building. Intelligence passed on by Dylan White had the main guests arriving around 10:30 am, and this would include Rupert Everson, Rye looked at his watch and noted it was 9:45 am so he waited patiently. He had installed a small covert camera in the foyer area, which had facial recognition; this would allow him to quickly identify his intended target without exposing himself for too long.

Rye watched and waited, he could feel the swell of adrenalin associated with operations like this, although he controlled it well and stopped the effects getting the better of him. Suddenly the screen on his handheld monitoring screen flashed red. It had picked up a confirmed match for Rupert Everson. He scanned around the area to assess the proximity of other people around Everson. Fortunately, there was a big gap between Everson and the guests arriving behind him, and that would work in his favour. More importantly, Everson only had one security officer with him, which provided a brilliant opportunity for Rye to execute his plan.

'Excuse me, sir,' Rye spoke as he walked from the entranceway to the right of Rupert Everson, timing his approach just right and stopping Everson and his security officer in their tracks.

True to his role, the lone security officer stepped in front of his client to act as a buffer between him and the potential threat approaching.

'That's close enough,' said the security officer with an authoritative tone.

Rye raised his arms as if to inform the two men that he was no threat to them.

'Apologies sir, the main foyer entrance is becoming blocked

CHAPTER 17

with so many people,' Rye lied as he looked the two men in the eyes.

'We have opened the East wing entrance to speed up the seating process if you can come this way please.'

Rye watched as the security officer registered a flicker of uncertainty before looking at his client, for a second Rye didn't think they would go for the ploy.

'Sir, we need to get you seated as soon as possible,' Rye said to try and push the duo into following him.

At the same time, Rye spun on his heel and headed for the entrance he had just come from, hoping that the two would follow him.

'Let's go with this man,' spoke Rupert Everson for the first time.

'Yes sir,' came the swift reply.

Rye felt relief wash over him as heard the two men follow behind him. The door was open although Rye had rigged it so that he could close the door remotely to stop any other guests following them. Once the door had closed behind the group, the corridor continued straight with secondary corridors coming off this main one. The room that Rye was using for as his makeshift interrogation room was down the first corridor on the left. As he rounded the corner, he slipped a small black device from his pocket and held it tightly in his right hand. He knew this would pack enough power to drop the security officer in a heartbeat using fifty thousand volts of electricity.

Rye heard the footsteps approach and as the security officer rounded the corner, he squared up to meet him, at the same time he grabbed the back of the officer's neck with his left arm and rammed the taser device into the man's neck. Rye felt the current passing through the man's body although managed to increase his grip on him even more. The security officer fell to the floor shuddering. Rye estimated he had seconds now to get hold of his real target Rupert Everson.

The entire event lasted seconds, and this meant that Everson was still trying to compute what was acting out in front of him, in those few seconds Rye smashed him in the face with his left fist. Blood splattering the man's face, and it was evident that Rupert Everson's nose had broken under the force. At the same time Rye flung him sideways through the open doorway into the disused office, Rupert Everson slid across the floor coming to a halt by the far wall.

Rye then dragged the motionless security officer into the room and closed the door to the office. The whole episode had taken seconds, but Rye had to work quickly now to extract the information he needed from Rupert Everson before any complications arose. Rye wasted no time in grabbing Everson and lifted him onto one of the two chairs in the room. He then quickly secured Everson's wrists and ankles to the chair before pulling up the second chair to sit directly opposite the man that he believed had the answers he wanted.

'What is Eden?' Rye wasted no time in informing the man in front of him what he was after.

Rupert Everson looked at him through glazed eyes. Blood was now smeared across his face where his nose had been broken.

'Who are you?'

'It does not matter who I am, what is Eden?' demanded Rye.

'I don't know what you are talking about,' came the muffled reply.

Rye knew he didn't have time to mess about, removing a

small blade from his inside jacket pocket, he flashed the knife in front of Everson.

'What are you going to do,' Everson said in an even voice.

'I'm going to get answers one way or another.'

Rye placed the blade on the floor before removing a small vile from the same pocket. He then put this on the floor next to the knife, making sure that Rupert Everson had time to take in what was about to happen to him.

'What is that?' Everson asked nervously.

'It is hydrochloric acid,' Rye said simply.

Rye then ripped open the trouser leg covering Everson's right thigh before asking him one more time what Eden was.

It was then that Rupert Everson started shouting for help, trying hard to remove himself from his restraints and makeshift prison.

'The room is soundproof, and there is no reason for anyone to enter this part of the building,' Rye said calmly, 'Shout and scream as much as you want albeit you will be screaming for a reason very soon if you don't answer my questions.'

With that, Rupert Everson was still.

'You're making a mistake,' Everson said.

Rye picked up the knife, and with one hand held Everson's leg down whilst cutting a six-inch cut in his leg, Rye then picked up the vial and poured some of the contents into the open wound. Rupert Everson bucked in pain, his tormented screams filling the room.

'What is Eden?' Rye spoke calmly.

'What the hell do you want?'

'I want to know what Eden is.'

Rye ripped a hole in the other leg of Rupert Everson's trousers ready to inflict the same pain.

'Stop, just stop,' Everson screamed, drool coming from his mouth as the acid ate away at his flesh.

Rye didn't stop, making the same cut in the exposed left leg.

'Please, stop,' pleaded Everson.

Rye picked up the vial and held it over the fresh wound.

'Project Eden was a test; it was closed down years ago.'

'Testing what?!'

'Human subjects for genetic manipulation, developing super soldiers, but the project was terminated.'

Rye stood now and paced back and forth, 'What human subjects?'

'Those that chose to be tested on, those already serving in the military.'

'Where are these test subjects now?' Rye now stood directly in front of the seated Rupert Everson.

Everson ignored the question and looked down at his wounds that were weeping blood. His right leg was foaming from the acid eating away at his flesh; the smell making him sick. 'Where are these test subjects now?'

Rye didn't have time to mess about as he poured acid on the second cut, then watched as Everson bucked back and forth in pain.

As the pain subsided slightly, Everson answered, 'Their memories were wiped, they know nothing of what happened to them.'

Maybe I was part of these tests. But how could they wipe my memories? Only one way to find out, Rye thought to himself before checking his watch, time was against him now, so he needed to act fast.

'Tell me who is behind Eden, and where can I find a list of who was tested on?' Rye spoke calmly although with a clear tone of authority.

'I have answered enough of your questions, now tell me who you are and what you want?' Rupert Everson was now clearly irritated by Rye's questioning.

'I was one of those test subjects,' Rye chanced his hand with the man sat in front of him.

Rupert Everson looked up at him. He stared at Rye as if trying to remember him.

'That's not possible,' Everson mumbled, 'There's no way you would remember.'

Rye's belief in his abilities had now soared as Everson had just confirmed why he was different, but he hadn't told him how he was different. With that, Rye grabbed the seated man by the throat and in one movement picked him and the chair he was sat on into the air.

Everson writhed and gurgled as he struggled to breathe, trying to free himself from the vice-like grip around his neck.

Rye surprised himself at his own strength, but he felt more confident now in the abilities that he knew he had, now there was no confusion or uncertainty.

'Tell me where the list of test subjects is, and I will let you live.'

Rye lowered Rupert Everson to the floor, and the man gasped for air, his face had gone completely red, and his eyes were bulging from the pressure that had been applied to his throat.

'Impossible, you don't know what you're getting involved with,' Rupert Everson stated through a strained voice.

'Then the cover-up will die here with you.'

'Who are you? I don't recognize you,' Everson said flatly.

'I'm one of your test subjects apparently, one of the ones

that you state volunteered for the Eden program. However, I don't remember volunteering for anything!'

'How do you know what you are, it's impossible.'

'I have an awareness of what I am capable of; that's all I know.'

'I can help you, help you to understand your capabilities,' Everson was now trying to barter for his life.

'Just tell me what happened to me inside the Eden project.'

Time was ticking away, and Rye was aware that he needed to wrap this up.

'You were enhanced, everything from your skeletal system through to your sensory inputs. You're faster, stronger and more aware than any other human being. We created super soldiers, that's all you will get out of me so either kill me or leave.'

Rye knew there wasn't much more he could get out of Rupert Everson at present so he would allow him to live and extract more information in the future if he needed it. At least he now knew that what he thought about himself was true, he was different, and he just needed to harness his talents now.

He grabbed Rupert Everson's hair and pulled his head to the side to expose his neck, he then removed a syringe from his pocket and injected the contents into his neck. The man's eyes widened in terror but then glazed over, and within seconds he was asleep, Rye then checked the security officer to make sure he was still unconscious before leaving the room and closing the door behind him.

Chapter 18

Major Khan looked out over the control room of Sky Zone One from his secure office. He wondered how the new guests were settling in and the fact that there would be an influx of new citizens within hours from now.

He decided to worry about more pressing matters and focused on the missing crew and the recent intelligence he received. The update was that they had found the body of the engineer Karl Roberts. His body had been found dumped in a landfill site by one of the workers, and his identity had been confirmed almost straight away. He had been tortured and then savagely shot in the head in what appeared to be an execution. This meant that it was highly likely that Sky Zone One had been severely compromised. He couldn't rely solely on the security systems deployed throughout the floating city, so he had to ensure that the soldiers on board worked in unison with the technical security.

Pressing the intercom on his desk, he informed his secretary that he wanted to speak with the security commander, Captain Mike Trainer immediately.

'Michael, you wanted to see me?' came the voice of Captain Mike Trainer as he stepped into the office.

Not many people called Major Khan by his first name, so it

was unusual to hear, but he had built a good friendship with his security commander, and so he didn't mind.

'Yes, I want you to step up the patrols and brief the force to report anything out of the ordinary,' said Major Khan, 'Between you and me, I'm not convinced that we are risk-free.'

'What about those persons still to board? Are we going to conduct further security checks when they arrive?'

'All new boarders are checked at ground level, so as long as we utilize the scanning equipment as they step off the shuttle, then we should be fine. It would be impossible for anyone to smuggle anything untoward on board.'

'Ok, I'll get on it straight away and report back if any of the patrols come across anything suspicious.'

Major Khan nodded at his counterpart and directed his attention back to the screen in front of him. He didn't like this at all. The entire build of Sky Zone One had been faultless up to this point.

Have I become complacent at some point to let this current situation happen, he thought to himself.

The transport shuttles were now in full swing with hundreds of people being transported to Sky Zone One by the hour. The onboarding process was working seamlessly, and individuals and families were finding their feet on their home for the foreseeable future. It was well known that those onboarding were the fortunate ones to have been able to leave the surface and create a better life for themselves.

The people arriving were a mixture of business owners, corporate powerhouses, celebrities, politicians and hose with no health issues and could afford the privilege. Those even more fortunate were the military and administration personnel that serviced Sky Zone One. These were the ones that would typically not have been able to be where they now were due to the costs involved. They were selected due to their skill and knowledge. More importantly, they had been chosen due to being single with no dependents. This meant that Sky Zone One's critical space was not wasted on family members of the staff and officers that kept the platform operational.

Phillipe Montreux and his wife Carolyn had just arrived at their accommodation suite. As they entered, the voice of the artificial assistant welcomed them to their new home. The central computer of Sky Zone One also acted as a communication system for all new people arriving. It would be critical to ensure that the new population understood what was going on and when. This level of overwatch was the pinnacle of the 'Big Brother' syndrome that had been active since the end of the twenty-first century.

'Well, here is our new home,' said Phillipe as he started to explore the suite of rooms.

Phillipe and his wife had no children, which was one of the main reasons they had been accepted on Sky Zone One and were able to finance the lifetime of their stay.

Carolyn followed him around the room silently, observing her surroundings with a keen eye. As her gaze settled on a wall-mounted control box, she placed her right hand on Phillipe's shoulder, and as he turned, she nodded towards the panel on the wall of the kitchen area. Without pausing any further, Phillipe nodded and continued to browse his surroundings, stopping every so often to investigate one part of the suite, of interest to him.

Once they were confident they had found what they were searching for, they went to their luggage and Carolyn opened her large handbag and pulled out what appeared to be her make-up bag. Emptying the contents on the table in the lounge diner, she moved the contents about until evenly spread across the table. She then picked up what appeared to be her lipstick and started to unscrew the base. Once complete, she then pulled apart her hairbrush to reveal what looked like a small fibre optic tree. The stem was approximately three inches long with numerous smaller branches protruding from the top of the main stem. These were much shorter and thinner than the main stem. She then took the base of the lipstick, which was circular at the bottom and around one inch in length, and started to screw the two together, once finished she placed it on the table and stood back. The ends of the smaller stems glowed green, and she smiled to herself and turned to her husband.

'The communication jammer is active so we can speak freely,' she said, still smiling.

'Great. Pass me the screwdriver so that I can deal with this control panel.'

Phillipe Montreux removed the control panel screen from the kitchen wall and passed it to her.

'Pass me the scalpel laser,' he said without looking back at her.

She reached into her pocket and pulled out a small cylindrical object and passed it to him.

'Once I have bypassed the system, we can move about freely and meet up with our counterparts,' he said, turning to her.

A smile erupted on her face as she thought about what was to come, the opportunity to hit back at the United Continents in the most spectacular way. For so many years, they had waited for an opportunity such as this, and now all their hard work was coming to fruition. They would make the United

CHAPTER 18

Continents pay for years of oppression and discrimination.

'Done,' said Phillipe as he stretched his neck, 'We are now hidden from the main computer, so we have the freedom to do what we want when we want. We need to find the rest of the team and set the wheels in motion.'

'I can't believe we have got to this point,' said Carolyn, 'I want everyone on this Sky Zone to feel what it's like to be the underdog.'

'They will soon. First, we must make contact with Michael and the others and make preparations.'

Michael Danson sat in his bunk after finishing a twelve-hour shift as one of Sky Zone One's leading communications team. His bunk was devoid of any personal items and generally bland, where other people had made sure that their cabins were as homely as possible. Due to being reserved, he also didn't have too many friends around him. He kept himself to himself where he could. This didn't bother him as he had always been a loner, and he preferred it that way. He laid on his bed, staring at the wall with his mind fully on the task ahead. At that very moment, he felt a vibration in his trouser pocket, and he pulled out a small messaging device, he looked at the screen and entered his unique password before the device lit up to show him the message. The message read 'Stage two,' and that was it, but that was all Michael needed to know. He sat up and messaged with a simple response 'Confirmed.'

Michael Danson paced back and forth in his cabin while he thought through his next actions. He needed to meet up with Phillipe and Carolyn, although first, he had to stop by engineering to set some things in motion. The three saboteurs aimed to bring down Sky Zone One and take those on board hostage, this would require external help, but first, some of the security systems had to be shut down or destroyed, which was the role of Michael and his newfound team of saboteurs.

Major Khan sat in his office, trying to think if there was anything he had missed regarding the safety of Sky Zone One. He was also drilling through the multiple scenarios that could come from recent events. If only he knew who had kidnapped, tortured, and murdered Karl Roberts, then that would be a start. He was also concerned about the disappearance of his friend Nick Hughes who was still classed as absent without leave.

None of this added up, he mused to himself.

He headed to the main docking bay as he wanted a first-hand view of those boarding his ship. He would feel better being amongst the activity rather than concealed in his office. As he made his way to the docking bay, he passed many new faces, with most of them nodding with politeness, although some were ignorant of his presence. This was his ship in reality, and although he smiled with courtesy and respect, he believed he was currently more important than most if not all passengers onboard Sky Zone One. Anyway, he ignored his own pettiness and concentrated on the problem at hand, this being the possible threat against Sky Zone One and everyone on board. He passed numerous workers and soldiers with each one of them having a warm smile and salute for their superior officer, they all respected Major Khan, and he had a healthy respect for them too.

'Good afternoon sir,' said one of the soldiers as he passed.

'Afternoon Corporal.'

Many more soldiers were now on board as supplied by his senior officer and he had tasked Captain Mike Trainer and his team to ensure they were briefed. The threat was real,

CHAPTER 18

and Major Khan understood this, so he was adamant that he would make sure everyone else did, or at least those that needed to know. He arrived at the main docking bay to find a hive of activity. Shuttles were landing, and people were being registered and provided with their new accommodation details and then directed to a member of staff that would escort them to their new home.

'Seems like it's all under control,' Major Khan said to one of the soldiers on the periphery of the organized chaos.

'Yes sir, the entire process is swift and efficient,' came the reply, 'So many new faces though, each of them with a look of excitement and hope.'

Major Khan observed the activity in front of him. How could anyone conduct a hostile takeover of Sky Zone One, it was nigh on impossible, he thought to himself. He watched as his staff tendered to the needs of the newcomers.

Phillipe and Carolyn had now secured their new residence from being observed and listened to by overriding the cabin monitoring systems using counter-surveillance equipment they had smuggled on board.

They were now stripping the other items they had brought with them, which they managed to get through the embarkation's intense security. The level of equipment they had managed to secret in their personal belongings was surprising, including portable communication devices and signal jammers. Suddenly, there was an alert that someone was at their door. They stared at each other for an instant before Phillipe approached the door to their cabin.

'It must be Michael,' he said to Carolyn. If it wasn't, then they would have problems.

'Michael, come in please,' said Phillipe as he opened the door to their cabin.

Michael was dressed in his United Continents uniform. As he entered, he nodded slightly at both Phillipe and Carolyn.

'All ok,' he spoke as he observed the array of items on the table in front of him, 'You have all the equipment you need?'

'All is fine, and we are in a secure environment,' Phillipe replied as he waved his right arm around the room, gesturing all was secure, 'However, we do need weapons as we couldn't smuggle these aboard.'

'I can provide weapons, so not a problem.'

'We also need mapping for the locations where we can place the signal jammers. It would help if you had an idea of these locations,' spoke Carolyn.

'Of course, I do,' he said scornfully, not entertaining her authoritative tone.

'Good, as we need to move fast before the assault teams arrive from the surface. We don't have time to relax and must be ready for the final attack; this means we have less than forty-eight hours to make sure all is in order.'

She walked over to him as he removed a tablet from his bag and laid it on the table, he pressed a few buttons and the display projected into the air above the tablet. As Michael manipulated the virtual map of Sky Zone One, he identified several flashing beacons as the locations Carolyn mentioned, which would be for the jammers' placement points that they would be leaving around the station. These jammers would block the signals of many of Sky Zone One's functions, including communications, access control, and even life systems monitoring.

'Ok, so that's forty jamming devices to be deployed, each with an approximate jamming range of one kilometre. We best get to work,' said Phillipe as he looked over the mapping being projected from the tablet on the table.

'I will take twenty with me now and leave you two to identify the rest using the map. I will take care of all those marked red,' said Michael as he removed twenty jamming devices from the black holdall he had brought with him and placed them on the table, he then closed the bag and lifted the holdall with the remaining twenty jammers on to his shoulder and walked toward the door.

'Here, you need to take this too,' said Carolyn as she passed him a small computer drive.

'This is the malicious code for the Sky Zone defences?'

'Yes, you need to insert as close to the core system as possible. This will then spread through the system and disable the Sky Zone defences.'

'Understood. Good luck, and I will get in touch once I have completed my task,' he then left the cabin.

Major Khan left the main docking bay and wandered around Sky Zone One, visiting areas that he had not been to for some time. He marvelled at the engineering and design that had gone into this mammoth project; it had cost billions to construct and would continue to cost the taxpayer for its entirety. This was where the divide between rich and poor had finally become an infinite crevasse that could no longer be sewn back together. He had come from an average background, so he could appreciate why so many of the population were against the United Continents and Sky Zone One. If he wasn't an officer within the United Continents, then he doubted that he would even be on board now. He continued around the ship nodding in acknowledgement to all the new faces that were now present. Before now, it had all been engineers, soldiers, and other United Continents employees and contractors. He walked past one of the green spaces and was still in awe of the ship's beauty and serenity. All made to mirror the epic natural landscapes that had been found on the surface some years ago.

'Sir, we have some signal discrepancies on the mainframe,' came the voice over Major Khan's communications earpiece.

'Signal discrepancies?' Major Khan inquired sternly.

'Yes sir, enough to cause minor concern.'

'Ok, I'm on my way,' Major Khan informed the controller and set off in the direction of the main control room.

Major Khan arrived back at the control room in no time at all. As soon as he entered the bustling room, he made his way directly to the person that had just relayed the message to him via his communication system.

'Corporal Roberts, please show me these discrepancies.'

'Yes, sir,' the corporal replied as he manipulated the screen until an image showed of a graph showing various lines which in the main were horizontally equal except at one point where a red coloured line had flared upwards.

'Here we have a spike which cannot be explained. It seems like an external source has caused this discrepancy,' spoke the Corporal as he continued to navigate the screen, 'It was only brief, but there was some form of a surge.'

'We don't know what caused this? How can we find out?' queried the Major.

'The only real way is to conduct a technical sweep of the ship, using far-field and near field scans. We could run the far-field scan from here and then send teams out with technical countermeasures equipment to manually scan the ship. This would be the best option in my view.'

CHAPTER 18

'Agreed, make it happen, and let me know the outcome as soon as you know.'

This was starting to become a problem now, Major Khan thought to himself. First, we have glitches, then two main personnel go missing, and one turns up tortured and dead, and now we have abnormalities with the main system. Something wasn't right, and he needed to find out what.

Chapter 19

The morning was fresh and wet with a drizzle that hadn't let up for the last two days. The sun was rising, albeit covered by the clouded sky. The two men had left their billet and stood by the vehicle planning the day's activity.

'Ok, today we have house clearing drills on the FIBUA village,' said Si Morgan as he placed the last of the bags in the rear of the 4x4 vehicle.

The FIBUA village was a specially made village used for military training, FIBUA standing for Fighting in Built-Up Areas. This type of facility had been used by various military units since the 1960s and was an effective training ground where soldiers could hone their skills within urban environments.

'Sounds good!' Rye replied as he climbed into the passenger seat of the vehicle.

Rye, Si, and a couple of other faces from their ArmorCorp team had been training at one of the covert training areas owned and used by the United Continents. This location was a past training camp of many military units, law enforcement, and private military contractors.

They were both sat in the vehicle now, and as Si started the electric engine, he turned to his friend, 'Remember, we're not going to make this easy for you.'

It had been a busy time operationally with missions for Rye and his team members, so training had been neglected. With Rye now understanding more about his capabilities, he had asked his friend Si Morgan and a couple of other trusted operatives to accompany him to the training area. He planned to train and, more importantly, try and push himself to his limits to see exactly how different he was. Rye believed that he had only just scratched the surface of his actual capabilities.

'Since when have you ever made it easy for me!' laughed Rye, 'Anyway, I don't want you to take it easy on me. I want you to push me harder than you ever have.'

The day before, they had spent testing and zeroing their weapons to make sure that they were as accurate as they could be. Rye had overshadowed even the best marksman in their group and had achieved pinpoint accuracy on every shoot. Today they would be testing their Close Quarter Battle skills, or at least Rye would be as he would attempt to clear the village on his own using speed and controlled aggression. They made their way to the undisclosed location and exited the vehicle. Rye instantly picked up how quiet it was, although he knew that the silence would be broken very soon.

'Ok, you go and get prepared while we set up,' Si said to Rye as he opened the rear of the vehicle and started removing various sizes of kit bags. Guy helped him then carry the bags to one of the buildings before all three men disappeared inside.

Rye walked over to what he knew to be the preparation area where soldiers visiting the village would get their weapons and equipment ready before starting their CQB exercise. On the wall in front of him was a map of the village. Rye didn't need the map as he had been here many times before. Although on this occasion he did scan over it to make sure that he hadn't missed anything or that the village hadn't changed since his last visit. The map showed three main roads, which led north to south. These roads were joined at parts by smaller streets travelling east to west. This provided several routes that someone on foot or in a vehicle could manoeuvre around the pretend village. Today, Rye would be on foot clearing the village building by building. Numerous one and two-storey buildings were lining each of the roads and streets in the village. These represented shops, bars, and some residential houses, all designed to give the sense that it was a real town. They even had a traffic system with traffic lights and street lighting, but the part that Rye thought was exceptional was the integrated target system. This system consisted of lifelike targets being strategically placed around the village and linked to a rather impressive control and communication system, which, dependant on what program was initiated, then could end up being all-out war on the streets. He instinctively knew that Si Morgan was going to pull out all the stops on this one and have a few other tricks up his sleeve. Usually, an area of this size would be patrolled by a section or a platoon, not one operator.

Rye's communication device kicked into life, 'Rye, are you ready to commence?'

Rye clicked the button on the device, 'I was born ready!'

'Ok, the range is open. Good luck!' came the simple instruction from Si.

Rye was carrying his trusty Sig C20 sidearm on his hip and placed the butt of his G12 sonic rifle in his shoulder. Now he was ready to wage war. It didn't matter which way you went around the village, although Rye's training had taught him to be systematic when clearing buildings and compounds. Rye knew that his senses were much more acute now since opening his mind to the fact that he may have been genetically modified. He hadn't found out the true depths of his capabilities, although that was why he was here, to push himself and find out precisely what he could do through a range of tests.

He crossed the road, and as he did so, he scanned every building, every window, and every access point for any movement. The first building he came to consisted of two stories, with a café on the ground floor and possibly apartments on the second floor. Rye would need to enter the ground floor and clear every room before progressing to the upper floor. At this point, he was up close against the front of the building, using the building as cover. His eyes scanned all threat areas around him, including the buildings and windows across the road. On this occasion, due to being a lone operator, he wouldn't have any support, so he had to be even more tactical when clearing each room of each building, so he decided to enter from the rear.

As he made his way to the rear of the building, he scanned the environment as he went. There was a six-foot wall and a single gate at the back. He checked behind before grabbing the top of the wall with his left hand. He then fluidly pulled himself onto the top of the wall and rested on his stomach. Once the area behind the wall was clear, he didn't hesitate and rolled over the wall, landing stealthily on his feet. He immediately dropped to one knee and listened carefully for any sign of movement.

Once he was happy, he moved towards the rear door holding his rifle in his shoulder, scanning the ground in front of him.

With his back against the door, he tried it with his left hand to see if it was locked. The door was unlocked and creaked as he opened it slightly. Rye paused and visually checked around the door's frame for any wires or electronics that could mean the door has been tampered with. The last thing he needed was to walk straight into a booby trap on the first building.

He pushed the door open gently and stepped into what appeared to be a large commercial kitchen area. The units were made of stainless steel and hadn't been cleaned for some time; there were numerous utensils and pots littered around the kitchen. Rye systematically cleared each of the smaller rooms to the rear of the building before entering the café area. Three lines of four tables consumed most of the floor with walkways in between each of the tables. The blinds of the café were closed, so there was minimal light in the room, but this didn't seem to affect Rye as he took in the layout and contents of the room, constantly scanning and listening while doing so.

There was one staircase to the second floor, situated between the kitchen and the seating area. Rye took five steps, then paused. He could hear a mechanical whirring sound, albeit the sound was muffled. He took five more steps then paused again. He could hear the whirring sound better now, so prepared himself. As he reached the top step, he paused briefly before swinging his weapon left and then right down the hallway.

As he checked the right, he instinctively heard the movement before seeing the source of the noise. Seconds later, one of the range figures moved into the doorway at the end of the hall. Each figure was designed to be as realistic as possible; this one was approximately six feet tall with dark hair and

CHAPTER 19

dark clothing and holding a rifle that was pointing directly at him.

In a split second, before the dummy had even steadied itself in the doorway, Rye had knelt on one knee and released two shots into the head of the figure. As the shots made an impact, the figure exploded backward into the room. Before Rye could even lower his weapon, he heard footsteps behind him approaching fast. He spun around just in time to see a sizeable black-clad figure bearing down on him, swinging a baton in one hand. Rye didn't have time to draw his sidearm, so swung his rifle behind him on its sling and dived forwards, timing the movement between the swings of the baton. Rye knew this was of his colleagues as they were wearing a protective training suit; this meant he could go hard without causing any real damage to his colleague.

Rye smashed into the man coming toward him, with his momentum and speed forcing his assailant backward along the hallway passing another room on the left. Rye saw movement in his peripheral vision and braced for an attack from within the darkened room as they continued back. Another black-clad figure erupted from the room wearing a menacing protective suit, holding a stun baton delivering pulses of fifty thousand volts. Rye acted fast and lashed out with his right leg to the front, hitting the first assailant square in the chest. This additional force mixed with the momentum already in play ensured that the masked man landed hard on his back. Rye didn't even watch the figure hit the floor as he turned to meet the new threat; he only had time to deflect the baton as it came crashing towards his head. He didn't even flinch as he stalled the blow with his left forearm, not even registering the voltage emitting from the baton.

His right hand arced round and smashed the assailant in the side of the head. As soon as his fist made contact, Rye thought that without the protective layers, then the strike may have removed someone's head from their shoulders. The crunch echoed in the confined space, and this included the second crunch as the man's head ricocheted off the door frame.

Both assailants were down now and no longer a threat, so Rye took hold of his rifle and continued to clear the rest of the building. Eight minutes later, he was stood outside in the back alley scoping the windows and doors around him for any other threat before clearing the next building. He knew that the two assailants he had dropped would be back on their feet soon, ready for another scenario that Si Morgan would have planned for him. Although Rye knew that having a team would be better for safety and security, he felt empowered using his newfound skills. He was rapidly clearing the buildings, he had always been confident, but now he had something much more than confidence. He worked tirelessly but didn't even start feeling the effects of his actions, which he knew that others in his position would be feeling by now.

Rye made his way across the open ground, and as he did, his senses picked up slight movement at the end of the road where a large building was located. Instantly, Rye sprinted to a side street out of the line of sight from the window where he had seen a sniper. To confirm his heightened senses, just as he reached the side street, the tarmac around his feet erupted as high-velocity shots landed around him. If he had been a fraction of a second later, then the shots would have found their target.

It has to be Si, he thought to himself. He also knew that the sniper would have moved position by now, ready for finding

CHAPTER 19

their target again. This meant getting involved in a short game of cat and mouse. With that thought, he ran to the rear courtyard of the nearest building and with one swift leap, grabbed the top of the roof of the rear conservatory and pulled himself up. Without stopping and without hesitation, Rye leapt for the cast iron drain pipe and climbed briskly to the angled roof of the building, making sure to keep his head below the horizon. Keeping low, Rye moved to a spot where he thought he could get eyes on any further sniper threats, using his experience and knowledge from his days as an elite sniper. He knew that the sniper would have moved to a new firing position by now. This would complicate any attempt to locate where the next shot was coming from. Rye had to focus hard and rely on his heightened senses to best his opponent.

Rye waited and listened, making use of his enhanced hearing to pick up any movement in the buildings around him, eyes keenly scanning every window and doorway. He saw it before he heard it, the slightest indication that any other person, including a trained sniper, would probably have missed.

Got you, Rye thought to himself but remained static for a few more seconds to make sure it was his intended target.

His weapon was capable of delivering pinpoint accuracy at this distance, he looked through the weapon sight, and the digital range finder told him that there were eight hundred and twelve metres between him and the target. Rye steadied his breathing and on the exhale, paused before pulling the trigger, he watched as the window where he witnessed the movement imploded, and the figure behind it went crashing backward.

Rye immediately moved from his position, so he didn't become a target himself. As his feet touched the floor at ground level, he heard it. He had heard the sound many times before and instinctively knew it came from a drone, although this time it was multiple drones, three he guessed.

He watched as they cleared the top of the building across the road, three attack drones all in attack formation.

This will be interesting, he thought to himself.

As the drones identified him as hostile, they swooped down, firing non-lethal lasers at him.

Rye dived to his left and in one continuous movement, rolled forward and onto his feet, sprinting for the nearest cover. As he hunched behind a low wall, he saw and heard the drones rise and hover above him. Their rate of fire was alarming as shots rained down on him. He managed to move again but not before two shots hit him on the arm. Even though they were non-lethal shots, the pain was real.

As Rye ran for more cover, he turned and fired at one of the drones with his pistol. The drone moved with blistering speed and dodged the shot. Ahead of him, about ten metres away, was what appeared to be a residential house. He thought quickly and decided on his plan. He burst through the main door and directly up the stairs of the house to the first floor, he knew the drones would be repositioning ready for his exit and guessed one would cover the back while two covered the front of the building. Rye didn't even slow his pace as he continued running through to the main bedroom and then dived straight through the front bedroom window. As his momentum took him forward, he smashed directly into one of the drones grabbing it with both hands and pulling it apart as he fell back down to the floor. As he hit the floor hard, he rolled to his side and pulled his pistol. He then fired two rounds at the second drone, which was now turning on him.

CHAPTER 19

The shots hit the drone, and it fell to the ground in pieces.

'Endex, endex,' came the command from a strained voice, which he knew to be Si Morgan.

Rye guessed that he was recovering from the non-lethal shot that had hit him and didn't want to damage any more drones.

'Roger that,' Rye replied as he holstered his weapon and walked back to the main road.

Si was now in view at the end of the road walking towards him, and to the side, he saw two black-clad figures with their helmets removed, which he could now see was Guy and his second team-mate.

'How did I do?'

'Yes, I think you've proved yourself in this exercise!'

'Too easy,' Rye said.

'Very impressive indeed,' said Guy rubbing the back of his neck.

'These drones would have taken any normal person out in seconds, yet you destroyed two of them? Not to mention jumping from a first-floor window and using your body as the weapon!' Si said in awe.

Rye's performance had been on form as these were all experienced, highly skilled killers, and he had effectively taken them all out, all without breaking a sweat.

'Ok, time is ticking, and we still have a few more exercises for you to complete. In particular, we need to cover some reaction drills and strength tests.'

'Ready when you are, I want to learn how far I can be pushed and to what extent.'

There was a killing house on site that would help test Rye's reactions and capabilities, with mechanized targets that would spring up from different angles. This was standard training for most military units. However, he knew Si would turn it to the full difficulty to test him.

Throughout the day, Rye's abilities registered off the chart, and his fellow operatives found it hard to hide their awe of his capabilities. This was no mean feat as each of his fellow operatives was of the highest calibre themselves. They had worked tirelessly over the last few days, and even though Rye was still focused and on full steam, the rest of the team were starting to feel it now, the unrelenting testing and assessment of Rye's full potential.

'I think we are done here,' Si Morgan said as he removed his ballistic helmet and rubbed the dust from his face.

'You think,' Rye responded immediately.

'Yes, I think. We have conducted every test worth conducting, and it is clear that you have enhanced capabilities compared to a normal person and even compared to a Special Forces soldier. I don't know how or why, but it's incredible. Whoever has done this has created a super soldier, and I can only guess at who would benefit from this.'

'United Continents?'

'Yes, they would have the resources and motivation to attempt something like this, although we still don't know what the extent of the changes are to your body?'

'These last few days have helped me understand what I am capable of doing. It's as if my mind has now been fully opened. I've never felt anything like it. I can feel the capabilities surging through my veins,' Rye said as he looked down at his hands and clenched his fists.

His world was changing rapidly; his mind expanded beyond what he thought possible.

Who were the other Eden test subjects? Do they already

CHAPTER 19

know what they are? he thought to himself.

Chapter 20

Oliver overcame his amazement and walked around the room, taking in all the machines and equipment. It was a carbon copy of the laboratory he had been removed from twelve years previously. It was like he had been transported back to the time he had yearned for since being abruptly dismissed. He ran his hand across the many instruments laid out on metal trays, remembering the surgeries he had completed on the would be super soldiers.

'What do you think?' spoke Rupert Everson standing behind him.

'I think it's extraordinary. I feel like I'm home for the first time in many years.'

'Well, this is your new home, and I trust that you can continue where you left off when the United Continents took everything from you. Now you have the opportunity to take back what was yours and get revenge on those that took it away.'

'Revenge?'

'Yes, do you not want to make those that stole your life away feel the ramifications of that? We can help you fulfil your ambitions by completing your work and punishing those that took it away in the first place.'

CHAPTER 20

Oliver paused as he contemplated what he was hearing. Twelve years he had suffered when everything he had loved had been taken from him. Twelve years, he thought.

'Yes, I would like that. To make those people understand what they did that day.'

'Good, we shouldn't waste any more time then. As time is the one commodity, we don't have!'

Rupert Everson placed his arm around Oliver's shoulder and guided him to a second smaller room. The metal door slid open silently, and the two men stepped inside. Oliver could see that this was an operating theatre similar to the one they had many years ago, although he could see that the equipment was much more modern. There was one operating table in the centre of the room with high-performance surgical lighting on an extended arm hovering above the bed. To the side of the bed was the surgical machine, which consisted of the main control panel and robotic arms protruding from the rear. These would assist in microsurgery required for some of the surgery that Oliver and his team would be conducting.

'Very nice,' said Oliver.

'We have everything you need to continue and complete your work Oliver. If there is anything else you require, then all you have to do is ask.'

'How many subjects do you have?'

'We have twenty potentials, with fifteen of these being past candidates so only require their memories being restored, which we have started this process but will need you to reassess the modifications made. These fifteen are the only ones we found that were suitable for the project; many were not for various reasons. Then we have five that require a full overhaul by you and your team; these have already gone through the psychological assessments and are ready.'

'Who are the team you refer to?'

'Follow me,' Rupert said as he headed towards the door and back into the main room and then up a dozen metal steps into an observation room which looked out onto the main area through a large glass wall. Inside this room were seven people all wearing white clinical coats and all waiting for the arrival of Oliver Randall, the brilliant mind that had made more advancement in genetic manipulation than anyone before him.

'Oliver, please meet your team. Some of them you already know and some you may recognize from their exploits in various aspects of science.'

Oliver looked around at the faces before him. He recognized three from his last team, these he greeted first. The others introduced themselves, and more than once, his eyebrows raised as he realized who they were, experts in their fields, and welcome addition to his new team. Oliver took a mental note of each new scientist, and how they could assist in the program, his mind had already begun contemplating the work that needed doing as he didn't want to waste any time. He felt surges of passion return to him, and his mind was ablaze, unlike anything he had felt in the last twelve years.

'We have sleeping chambers in the building, so there is no need to leave this secret facility. We have high levels of security inside and out, and this is to stop people coming in or out,' spoke Rupert.

'I'm a prisoner?'

'Not at all. You are the lead scientist in the new Eden project. We are merely protecting you and your work.'

Once all the introductions had been made, and people were

aware of their roles, it was time to get to work.

They had five subjects to start on, and these would require immediate attention as they needed the most work, involving many surgical procedures, including brain surgery. The other fifteen were currently having their minds remapped to remember what had been done to them; more importantly, how to access their increased physical and mental capabilities. Once their minds had been restored, their biological upgrades needed to be reassessed.

He turned to one of the team members he knew well from the original Eden project, an older wiry framed man named Charles, 'Charles, you will work directly by my side.'

'Yes, whatever you need,' Charles replied as he knew that Oliver Randall was in charge as this had been made clear previously by those that were now in control of the project. They had instilled the importance of the project and that they would not take any time-wasting or mistakes.

'We need to prepare the five subjects for the initial tests before starting them on their surgery. You are still knowledgeable about the procedure?'

'Yes, we have all had refresher training in the past couple of weeks, although the knowledge never really left me anyway.'

'Good, I will leave the preparation work to you then. I have to speak with the rest of the team to make sure everyone is on the same page.'

Oliver left the room and went to find the others in his team, who would be responsible for various tasks. These included a clinical team that would help with the complicated surgeries involved with the genetic upgrades. They also had trained psychologists responsible for nurturing and mentoring the test subjects' minds through such drastic changes. A psychological evaluation would be a constant requirement throughout the project, firstly to ensure candidates themselves were coping with the demands placed on them. Secondly, to ensure that none of the candidates was becoming self-absorbed with their new capabilities and having ideas of grandeur.

Although all these people were under his leadership and were always at his beck and call, he was under no misconceptions that this was because they were ordered to be. He didn't for once think that any of them liked him as a person, and he didn't care to be honest. He was happy that he now had his work back. Life can be brutal, he thought, but then everything can change instantly.

After speaking individually to each team member, Oliver felt even more confident that they had the right people and that each person was a leader in their unique discipline.

His main priority was the task of turning the five slightly above average humans into super soldiers, having to manipulate muscle fibres to make them much stronger and faster than they were before. Then further manipulation to each of their skeletal system's using a solution called Xeren II. There was also a need for modification of their cerebellum, which was the receiver from the body's sensory system, the spinal cord, and other areas of the brain, in turn regulating the body's motor movements. The Eden project's final responsibility enhanced the sight and hearing of all those involved, ensuring that their sensory capability was sharper and more acute than any other person on the planet.

Rupert Everson had made all this happen without the United Continents, and this was impressive to Oliver. He pushed all unnecessary thoughts from his mind and concentrated on what was important, the task before him.

CHAPTER 20

The scientists worked around the clock, only returning to their modest internal quarters to catch up on sleep or feed themselves. Oliver himself was pushing nearly eighteen hours each day.

By the third day of the new Eden project starting, they were well on their way, with ten out of the fifteen having their memories restored and now undergoing familiarisation training. Oliver's team had been in surgery with the first of the test subjects bonding Xeren II to the subject's skeletal system to harden the bones and joints without limiting flexibility. Oliver himself had created the formula, so he took great pride in administering it to his patients.

'Ok, we can close the opening now and stitch it. The Xeren will take time to bond to the muscles, joints and bones. Place him in the recovery suite for the next seventy-two hours and prepare the next patient for Xeren implant.'

They worked tirelessly preparing each subject then undertaking surgical procedures twice a day, once in the morning and once in the afternoon. This meant it only took them a few days to complete the first stages of the manipulations on each of the five test subjects.

It had been a few days since Oliver had seen Rupert Everson and he had been too busy to notice anyway, now he was being called into the meeting room for an update. He cursed as he climbed the metal steps to where Rupert was waiting for him. He could do without this delay to his work, he thought to himself.

'Oliver, come in and take a seat,' Rupert spoke as he pulled out a chair for his lead scientist, 'How is everything going?'

'Fine, it is going fine,' replied Oliver, somewhat defensively.

Oliver knew that Rupert held all the control, but to him, it was his project, he was the one making it all happen, and he recognised that he was defensive when outsiders started to ask questions, even Rupert Everson.

'We are progressing faster than first imagined,' Oliver continued attempting to usher in a bit more respect into his responses.

'Good, so the new test subjects are responding well?'

'Yes, the Xeren II has taken well on all subjects with no side effects.'

'The previous test subjects have been revived without any issues?' said Rupert.

'All but one, that seems to have failed all the psychological evaluations and so would be a liability if deployed on operations.'

'Ok, so that means we will have nineteen ready to go soon?'

'Yes, I estimate another seven days, including final tests.'

Rupert Everson smiled inwardly, elated at the fact that they would have nineteen of the most advanced soldiers ready for the final attack of Sky Zone One. It was poetic justice that the fall of the United Continents would be by those that had been removed from the project initially.

'Good, seven days is fine. They should be ready to deploy on a mission in twelve days; this will be an important mission.'

'They will be ready; what is the mission?'

'This you do not need to know; your role is to get them ready.'

This annoyed Oliver as he wanted to know what his new super soldiers would be used for. He knew when the United Continents ran the project and that they were being used for specialist warfare on their enemies. But with this new secretive setup, he had no idea what Rupert Everson had planned.

'Will that be all?' said Oliver, etching to return to his work.

'Yes, thank you.'

Oliver left the room and walked across the main room, where some of his technicians were chatting.

'Oliver, can we have a word, please?'

'Yes, what is it?'

'Well, some of us are concerned about the project and the motivation behind it,' said one of the younger members, a tall ginger-haired female he knew as Erica.

'What concerns? Surely you understood what you were signing up for in the first place?'

'Well, yes, I suppose. But the more time that passes, the more concerned we are as to the real intentions. Has Rupert Everson told you anything?'

'We only get told what we need to know. If you have any issues with that, you should take it up with Rupert Everson,' replied Oliver. However, instantly he decided against that advice as he knew this would cause trouble for the confident yet quiet girl before him.

'It's Erica, right?'

'Yes.'

'If I were you, I would think hard about what you say to anyone. Do not ask questions and complete your work. If you then choose to walk away, then so be it, but keep your intentions to yourself.'

Oliver could see that his words had scared her, which he hadn't meant to do. He knew they all could be in a dangerous situation once the test subjects were operationally ready; he felt a nervousness in the pit of his stomach. Part of him did not care, as he was back doing what he was born to do, but he was aware of the risk involved.

He wandered over to the recovery suite, where the five newly transformed subjects were recuperating after their intensive upgrades.

My children, Oliver thought to himself, wherever you go, and whatever you do, I will be proud.

Chapter 21

Gabriel Durand stood in the cold night air, taking one last pull of the cigarette hanging from his lips before flicking it into the blackness surrounding him. He waited patiently for his guest to arrive who had flown in from London and then driven the sixty miles from Charles de Gaulle airport to the remote farmhouse, which was the Faction Against Continent Rule's current operating base.

As expected, Gabriel saw the vehicle lights approaching along the deserted road that led to the farm. As they neared, he stepped out onto the gravel road, and the car came to a gentle stop. The driver's window of the black SUV powered down, and a bearded male nodded to Gabriel along with, 'Bonjour.'

Gabriel returned the welcome and told the driver to follow him into the farmhouse's courtyard, which was surrounded on three sides by a large U-shaped building. The car silently drove over the gravel and came to a stop when Gabriel held out his hand, the metal access gate closing behind the vehicle.

As the back door of the SUV opened, Gabriel immediately recognised Rupert Everson and walked over to greet him. They embraced briefly and patted each other on the back as they walked towards the main building.

'It is great to see you, Rupert!'

'You too, Gabriel, you too.'

'You are limping?'

'Yes, it's nothing serious,' replied Rupert touching his thigh.

'How was your flight?'

'It was good, but I can never get used to all these remote locations you use, jumping from one to another all the time.'

Gabriel laughed, 'But this is how we keep safe by keeping one step ahead of our enemies.'

They continued through the main rooms and into one of the meeting rooms where Boris and Teresa waited for them. They both stood out of respect when Rupert Everson entered the room.

'Rupert, thank you for joining us,' said Boris, holding out his hand.

Rupert Everson took his hand with a tight two-handed grasp as he did for Teresa. He liked these people and what they stood for. It was the reason he was always defending them to the rest of the Elders. But this meeting was different. This was when they would put the final stamp of approval on the upcoming mission, a mission so extravagant that it would alter the course of history.

'It's good to see you all and especially under such circumstances,' Rupert removed his jacket and hung it on the back of the simple wooden chair.

'I feel like you have some good news for us?' said Gabriel.

'I do indeed, but I wanted to share it with you personally, so here I am!'

Boris upended another glass and filled it with whisky for their new guest, with Rupert taking it immediately and tasting the fine malt before continuing with his news.

'I am pleased to say that we have nineteen additions to our

CHAPTER 21

upcoming mission, all ready and waiting to fight for the cause.'

'Amazing!' replied Gabriel, 'Nothing can stop us now with that kind of force behind us.'

'These are the original Eden soldiers?' Boris asked.

'Most of them but with a few fresh faces added to the mix.'

'Well, it appears that we have a full fighting force ready to go then. Your super soldiers combined with our rebel fighters will prove a tough match for the United Continents. Especially with our agents already onboard Sky Zone One making preparations for our arrival.

'It seems you have been busy preparing, and your efforts are about to pay off. This is good as the Elders need some affirmation of your existence.'

'They do? What has been said?' Gabriel inquired.

'You know what they are like, they can be a little behind the times, but this mission will show them what the FACR is capable of and will be the making of your organisation.'

'Yes, it will be. It will be a message to the United Continents and the entire world; they will all sit up and take notice once we have finished.'

They spent the next hour or so going through parts of the plan. They discussed what was expected of each party. This was an FACR mission and would be carried out by them, albeit with the assistance of nineteen super soldiers provided by Rupert Everson and the Elders.

The team on Sky Zone One consisted of sympathisers working together to bring down the defences of the floating city. This was imperative for the ground teams to make it anywhere close to their target without being blown from the sky. With the nineteen Eden soldiers, they would have an attack force over two hundred with five shuttles to take them ten thousand metres above the earth to where Sky Zone One was floating. With their inside knowledge of the systems of Sky Zone One then they would have the upper hand in the attack, not to mention having more than a dozen primed super soldiers ripping through the Commando Elite. There was also the fact that the corridors on Sky Zone One would only allow a certain number of soldiers to engage in a firefight at any one time. So, although the United Continents force was numerically larger, it made no real difference within the ship's close confines.

Gabriel felt the confidence surge through his body. All the years of planning were coming to fruition. His patience had been justified waiting for this gift from Rupert and the Elders.

'Some disappointing news is that five hundred additional troops have been sent to Sky Zone One as it seems the missing crew members have caused some concern.'

Gabriel turned to Rupert, 'That is not good, but this will not deter us and proves that we must not wait too much longer until we attack.'

'The numbers of troops does not deter you?' asked Rupert.

'Not at all as once we are on the ship, then it is merely a case of capturing the hostages, and there will be plenty to choose. The United Continents are not going to put people's lives at risk. The area that concerns me is the approach; we are heavily reliant on our saboteurs doing their job and putting the defences out of action.'

'The entire plan was such bravado and daring,' Rupert thought to himself as he looked at the three people in front of him. But it was more than achievable, and that's why himself and the Elders had given their consent and support.

'Well, one thing is for sure. We will soon find out!' laughed

Rupert.

They continued to discuss the plans in detail, exploring the team's work on the ship already, and then the attack method from the ground. They would be using five shuttles with approximately forty fighters in each, with the Eden super soldiers being split into three teams of six and distributed between three of the attack shuttles. This was to ensure that if any of the shuttles were destroyed, then it hopefully wouldn't take out all of the Eden personnel in one go if they were on one shuttle. The final Eden soldier would be a personal bodyguard to Gabriel Durand, along with his most trusted rebel fighters.

The Eden soldiers' main task was to get to the control level of Sky Zone One and take it with any force necessary. This would likely be the most guarded area on the floating city and so needed experts in their craft. The rebel fighters would take various other targets, and this included finding and taking captive some of the most influential people residing on the ship. Once these people were hostages, then the entire operation would become much more comfortable as Gabriel, and his crew would have all the power, and the world would not take long to sit up and take note.

Gabriel raised his concerns over the Eden soldiers and their loyalty and obedience to take orders but was comforted when Rupert explained the process behind mind mapping them to the cause.

'They would be more obedient than the most faithful dog,' Rupert quipped.

As Sky Zone One was high above sea level, they could effectively launch the attack from many locations even though the ship was pretty much above the United Kingdom. They had identified an area just north of Amsterdam, which had been agreed would be the most successful launch for the attack. The area was quiet, with only small villages and towns scattered around the local vicinity. They had located an abandoned farm with various large outbuildings that could be used to hide the attack shuttles. Each shuttle had been transported separately by lorries over an extended period to avoid any undue interest from the locals. The land having been purchased with the assistance of the Elders and Sylvia DeMarco. The word spread around the local area that the new owners would start producing machinery parts for farming industries across the Netherlands. The story seemed to hold its weight.

The large but modest attack force was also making its way to the location, albeit separately, and with most doing it under cover of darkness, there were only so many of the two hundred or so fighters that could be passed off as workers.

'When will the Eden soldiers be transferred to the final attack point?' asked Boris, who had been relatively quiet up until this point, letting Gabriel take the lead in explaining the plan.

'They will be set to travel early next week. We will use a private jet to get them to a private airfield just outside Amsterdam, and then they will be transported by road to the farm.'

'Will they need any orientation training once they arrive as time will be short,' replied Boris.

'No, they won't, as we will have details of the plan, and these can be relayed to each of them before transportation.'

'Great, so they just turn up ready to start the mission. Makes life easier than trying to herd cats like the rest of the rebel fighters,' Gabriel mused with them.

'Teresa, would you like to talk to our guest through the summary of the attack?'

'Yes, certainly,' she said as she stood up and moved in front of them.

She tucked her hair behind her ear and started to describe the main parts of the plan, 'There are five stages, the first stage is nearly complete, and this consists of preparing the main attack force. The second stage is that we must wait for the saboteur team's signal onboard Sky Zone One, which will tell us that the Sky Zone defences are down. As you can appreciate, this will be the most important stage as if they fail, then we all fail, as we will not get close to the target. Once we have confirmation, we can activate the third stage, which is to initiate the attack, bearing in mind that we will already be in the air and approaching Sky Zone One by this point, so timing is critical. Once onboard, stage four is to take the main control room, which is your super soldiers' job. Finally, stage five is to capture the most notable residents on Sky Zone One and those that will give us the most leverage over our enemies.'

When she had finished, Rupert looked over at Gabriel, and a broad grin crept across his face.

'Fantastic, I feel more than confident with this approach. It feels like the plan cannot fail in my eyes, and once I get back to the Elders and inform them, then I am sure that they will feel the same.'

They all stood as Rupert stood, and they all felt the infectious excitement that was emanating from him. Even terrorists got excited, it seemed.

'I must leave soon as much to be done back in London. Final preparations of the Eden soldiers before they depart for the

Netherlands. Plus, I must also tie up some loose ends, it seems,' said Rupert.

'I will walk you to your vehicle,' replied Gabriel as the other two said their farewells.

As they walked back through the building and out into the early morning darkness, Gabriel turned towards Rupert before they reached the vehicle.

'If I don't see you again, take care, my friend. I know I have been rebellious towards the Elders, but I hope you know why and that it was necessary?'

'Gabriel, you don't need to apologise to me. You have done what you have needed to do and now look at the results, staggering. I wish you good luck, and I will see you on the other side, whether that is alive in victory or heaven through defeat.'

Gabriel smiled at this and opened the rear car door for Rupert. As Rupert settled into the back seat, he looked up, 'I look forward to the fireworks!'

Chapter 22

Rye had only been back for a few days from the intense battle training organised by his good friend Si Morgan. Sitting around in his apartment, he already felt twitchy. There were still so many questions to be answered, and now that he had more understanding of his capabilities, he thought that he was the best person to get these answers.

He paced back and forth, and every so often idly stared out the window into the city below, not focusing on any one thing. He was waiting for his friend Dylan White to get back to him as he had helped him once before finding Rupert Everson.

As if his wishes had been answered, his personal communications device burst into life. As he picked it up, he could see it was Dylan White calling.

'Dylan, hopefully, you have some good news?'

'Hello Rye, considering the limited intelligence we have on this person, then I believe I have good news.'

'Sounds promising,' Rye replied immediately.

'Well, we only have his current movements, and this means you will have a very narrow window to pick him up. So, you will have to do most of the groundwork if you want any chance of finding him. He certainly is a slippery character these days.'

'What can you tell me then?' Rye said, not wanting to waste

time.

'Well, I can tell you that he has recently flown to France then Moscow although we do not know where he went to in either country as like I say he is a slippery character! I assume he will return to the United Kingdom through the same airport, so I suggest you use your legendary surveillance skills and pick him up when he comes back through.'

'He could come back at any time though?' It was more of a statement than a question from Rye.

'Yes, he could indeed. As I said, you will have to do some work to locate him.'

Dylan White continued giving Rye as much information as possible, and even though Rye knew it wasn't perfect, he was still grateful to his friend for pulling it out of the bag again.

Once they had finished speaking, Rye wasted no time in making plans as he knew that Rupert Everson could return at any time from Moscow. He called Si Morgan and hoped he would help as he believed he might be running out of favours with those closest to him.

'Si, Everson is out of the country but should be coming back soon,' Rye said as he continued to get his gear together to leave for the airport that Dylan had identified.

'Ok, do you have any timings?'

'Unfortunately not. I'm heading to the private airfield now. If I send the location, can you meet me there?'

'I can if you tell me what you have planned in that crazy head of yours!' replied Si wanting to get some idea of what his friend had planned.

'Surveillance, just surveillance for now. Then when the time is right, I would like to finish my chat with this guy.'

Si Morgan didn't like it, but he couldn't let Rye deal with

CHAPTER 22

this on his own, however good he was.

'Ok, send me the details, and I will confirm once I'm in position.'

'I appreciate it, Si, I really do, and I only need you for the surveillance part. Nothing more, I promise.'

'Ha, how many times have I heard something similar!' Si laughed as he ended the call.

In no time at all, Rye was out of his apartment and already stepping into the building lift, which had him down at ground level in seconds. He wasn't sure what else he would get out of Rupert Everson, although he did have more questions. The main burning question that had been grinding away at the back of his mind was one of the most fundamental questions that had ever been asked by any human... 'Why?!'

Everson had told him that he and the other test subjects had their minds wiped when project Eden had been closed down, so Rye had no idea why he had volunteered for the project or whether he had volunteered at all. He didn't like the hidden parts of this ongoing mystery, and there were just a few more loose ends to tie up.

Dylan had informed Rye that Rupert Everson flew out of a small private airstrip just west of London. Dylan knew this as the United Continents intelligence sector had carefully watched the airstrip for a couple of years after being identified as a hot spot for illegal activity of varying sorts. There was no reason why Rye's target wouldn't be flying back into this airfield at some point. They didn't know when but it was the best lead that Rye had and possibly would have.

Rye reached the garage below his apartment and pressed the button on the key fob in his pocket. The garage door opened, and his electric motorcycle rolled out silently due to its electric motor, coming to a halt next to where he now stood. Rye climbed on the sleek self-balancing motorcycle and put on his protective glasses that had been clamped to the motorcycle. He would use this means of transport to get to Northolt, where he had arranged to pick up one of the ArmorCorp duty vehicles. Even though this was a personal mission, no one would question the use of the vehicle. The benefit of using one of the ArmorCorp vehicles was that it would contain most of the kit that he would need to observe the airfield, including a range of covert surveillance equipment from drones to long-range camera systems. He had to monitor the airport without being compromised. He knew that Rupert Everson would be conducting some form of anti-surveillance to identify and deny any surveillance on himself.

Rye arrived at the nondescript location, which to anyone else would have appeared like an everyday industrial compound with two fabricated buildings. As Rye walked up to the compound gate, he scanned his retina against the discreet access point, and the metal pedestrian gate opened up for him to walk through. As Rye knew the location, he knew the level of security the site had hidden behind its bland appearance and quickly thought about the difficulty and danger someone would face if they attempted to breach the perimeter of the compound.

'Mr Braden, we have your vehicle ready,' spoke a thin, wiry man walking towards Rye.

'Thanks, I need to make it a quick turnaround, so can you confirm the kit I requested is packed?'

'It is, full surveillance pack in the boot,' came the simple reply.

Rye was shown to the waiting vehicle, which was a high

CHAPTER 22

powered estate wagon with 4x4 capability. This was a good choice for what Rye needed as the vehicle could blend in on motorway environments but could also travel off-road if required.

As Rye headed towards the target location, he called Si Morgan, 'How are you doing Si?'

'I've arrived and plotted up eight hundred metres to the north of the airfield, and I have a full view of any aircraft arriving. There are only two main vehicle routes in and out of the location, one to the north that I can cover and then one to the south-east, which I recommend you cover. Then we have the entire area covered when they land.'

'Sounds like a plan, and we can deploy the tracking drone once he is on the move, then follow at a safe distance behind. Send me the coordinates of the second exit point, and I will be in position in fifty minutes.'

'Roger that, details inbound. I will let you know if any movement.'

With that, Rye increased his speed as he wanted to be there before Rupert Everson arrived so that he wasn't spending the rest of the day catching up. However, he had the impression they could be waiting a while as they had no real idea when and if their person of interest would be returning. Rye hoped it was a short trip to Russia.

Forty minutes later, Rye approached the private airfield and found a suitable plotting up position just off the main access route, with enough of a view of the airport to see any aircraft landing. He knew Si had the entire place covered, so he felt at ease. He also had two drones that could be deployed to provide an aerial perspective of the airfield. He would use one drone to hover around a thousand metres above the airport, which could send live video directly to his portable monitor, each drone having a flight time of six hours. The second drone would be kept for when the target landed, and then the drone could follow any targeted assets from above, reducing the chance of the two-person surveillance team being compromised.

With everything set, all they could do now was wait. Having both served in the military, they had the experience so nestled down patiently. It was coming up to 7:00 pm, and the sun was beginning to set. There had been no movement for the last four hours, and Rye was starting to wonder if Rupert Everson would even arrive today. Even though Rye was impatient to get answers, he knew that any surveillance mission could involve plenty of inactivity, and he had plenty to occupy his mind.

He was now lying up in thick overgrowth, camouflaged from anyone passing through the area. He had left most of the equipment in the vehicle, which had been pulled off the road to hide it from prying eyes. For now, he would rely on his long-range spotting scope and one of the surveillance drones. He was wearing his covert earpiece, so he had direct communication to Si Morgan, situated approximately three kilometres from his position.

The plan was to observe Rupert Everson landing and then identify the vehicle he would be using to get to his next location, wherever that was. Depending on the situation on the ground decided on when Rye would attempt the snatch, he had no idea of whether Everson would have a security team, if so, how many would be in that protective detail.

Just before midnight, Rye heard it before he could see any sign of it. A slight whir of an aircraft heading towards them from the south, the sound was difficult to pinpoint in the night due to the hydrogen fuel cell-powered motors now used across aviation.

Rye got straight on the radio to confirm that Si could also hear the aircraft. He didn't!

'Ok, it's coming in from the south, sounds like a twin-engine aircraft,' Rye informed him.

'Ok, still can't hear it, but I'm ready either way.'

'Once it lands, I will send the tracking drone up, so there's no delay, imagery and GPS will be shared to your vehicle console.'

'Roger that, let's hope it is him.'

Rye watched the distant sky, and within minutes he could make out a twin-engine aircraft travelling relatively low and heading directly for them. As he expected, the aircraft had no lights meaning it would have been difficult for any person to make out the grey silhouette against the blackness of the night.

The small aircraft touched down in relative silence and reduced speed. It then expertly manoeuvred to one of the small hangars. Luckily for Rye, it parked just outside so they could see anyone disembarking.

Rye wasted no time and started to unfold the four rotor arms of the tracking drone and powered it up. As this was a covert drone, there were no fancy lights or start-up noises as with recreational drones. To avoid any compromise, he set it off in the direction away from the airfield until it had gained height, and then he would navigate it back to hover well above the airfield. Once they had observed Rupert Everson exiting the aircraft and get into a vehicle, then that vehicle could be targeted, meaning the tracking drone would follow that vehicle until it ran out of power.

The small jet had powered down now, although no movement outside the aircraft.

What are you waiting for? Rye thought to himself.

'Si, the drone is up and relaying video as we speak.'

'Received.'

Ten minutes had passed with no movement, and then Si Morgan's voice came on the secure radio, 'I have one vehicle approaching my location heading to the north entrance to the airfield.'

'Confirmed,' Rye replied briefly to allow Si Morgan to provide a running commentary on the activity unfolding in front of them.

'Vehicle is now at the access gate to the airfield. Black SUV with blacked-out windows. The vehicle is through the access gates of the airfield and travelling at speed towards aircraft.'

This type of commentary was vital for Rye to build a picture of what was occurring, although now the drone had an aerial visual on the vehicle, and Rye could also see using the high powered spotting scope he had set up.

'I now have eyes on,' Rye said.

They both observed as the vehicle came to a sudden halt close to the aircraft. One male exited the vehicle from the front passenger side and had a good look around his new environment. Rye then observed the man's lips moving before the door to the aircraft opened, and a set of steps lowered automatically to the ground.

Here we go, thought Rye. He could feel his heart rate elevate and felt like sprinting over there now, taking out the security team and grabbing Rupert Everson.

As he watched, he saw Rupert Everson exit the aircraft

before being greeted by the lone figure stood on the tarmac, who immediately opened the rear door of the SUV for Rupert. In that instant, Rye instructed the drone high above them to target that specific vehicle, so this meant they would have complete eyes on Rupert Everson without any chance of a compromise or a loss.

Once the tracking drone had been activated to track the target vehicle, it was time to get into his vehicle, ready for the follow. The target vehicle was already in motion when Rye had reached his car, but there was no panic at this stage as they had continuous surveillance of the target vehicle from above.

'Si, the target is heading back to the north access point. I will let you take the lead although hang back and trust the drone.'

'Roger that, now back in the vehicle and awaiting target vehicle to pass my location.'

'I will head back to your location and follow from behind,' said Rye as he started the engine of his high powered estate car, and the GPS information from the drone instantly synced with the vehicles centre console.

'Nowhere for you to hide now,' Rye mumbled to himself.

Both Rye and his counterpart Si Morgan were actively following the black SUV as it headed back towards London, the vehicle opted to take minor roads instead of the motorway. Rye thought it would be best to snatch Rupert Everson before he got to his next location. This was due to the time of night and the isolated nature of backcountry roads, as Rye didn't know the level of security that would be waiting for them at the final destination. He had to make a decision, and he had to make it now.

'Si, you copy?'

'Yes, go ahead.'

'I want to take him soon while we are on these types of roads.'

'Makes sense,' Si agreed.

'Ok, but I will need your help after all,' Rye said after previously only needing his colleague for the actual surveillance part of the mission.

'Ha, I wasn't going anywhere anyway!'

'Thanks, I appreciate it. Time is of the essence; we will need to hit them before they reach any major road. I have an idea of what routes they will take, so I need to leapfrog them and set up a road-block. It will be tight, but more than possible.'

The two surveillance vehicles were linked through GPS. In addition to this, the live camera feed being fed to them by the tracking drone meant that each operator could see precisely where the other was. All Rye had to do was drive at speed to get ahead of the target vehicle, and he wasted no time in putting his foot down. In conjunction with the advanced driving skills that every operator of his calibre had, the sheer power of the car should be enough to get him ahead.

Rye had to add extra distance to leapfrog the target vehicle, and everything that wasn't in his forward vision just blurred into blackness as he reached over two hundred and fifty kilometres per hour. He knew exactly where he needed to get to, and that's all he focused on for now. He knew that his plan would be simple as he only needed to stop the target vehicle, and he could use his vehicle to assist with that.

It took Rye eight minutes to get ahead of the other two vehicles, 'Si, I'm coming up on a junction where I will use the immobiliser.'

CHAPTER 22

The immobiliser would release a high energy beam, and if directed at a vehicle, it would completely shut down the vehicle's power. This would immobilise the vehicle and leave Rupert Everson and his security vulnerable.

'Ok, I'm closing up to the target vehicle now. Approximately two kilometres back,' Si explained.

Rye made it to the junction and, using the drone's live footage, waited in cover for the target vehicle to approach him. There were no other vehicles on the road due to the time of night, so the risks of targeting the wrong vehicle were low.

His wait didn't last long as he observed the target vehicle on his handheld monitor, with Si Morgan not far behind. As the vehicle lights bathed the area around him, he took a step forward out of his concealed location and fired the burst of energy at the vehicle. The effect was relatively undramatic as the vehicle instantly slowed and rolled to a standstill. He assumed the vehicle would be armoured, so he readied a small explosive entry device to breach the vehicle door.

As Rye had envisaged, the vehicle came to a halt a few metres from where he was waiting. As it did, Rye sprinted over and attached the explosive entry device to the front passenger door as he knew this was where the most significant threat was with the bodyguard of Rupert Everson. He instinctively stood at the back of the vehicle as the small charge initiated blowing the door open. Rye instantly moved back to the front side of the car, aiming his weapon at the open door. At the same time, Si Morgan screeched to a halt behind the SUV and jumped from the vehicle providing Rye with much-needed cover.

'Out of the vehicle!' Rye shouted as he rounded on the bodyguard in the passenger seat, although he quickly saw that the bodyguard was bent forward, blood pouring for the side of his head. Due to his training, Rye knew not to take any chances and shot two paralyzing stun shots into the man before aiming his weapon at the driver. The driver had both hands in the air and verbally agreeing to comply with Rye.

'Unlock the doors now!' Rye shouted.

The driver tentatively moved his right hand to the door unlock button, and as soon as he heard the click, Si Morgan ripped the rear passenger door open and aimed his weapon at Rupert Everson, who had a look of shock spread across his face.

The entire attack from the vehicle being immobilised to them having control over all occupants was less than ninety seconds. That meant that it would have been unlikely for any person to take in what was happening around them.

Si Morgan roughly grabbed Rupert Everson by the arm and dragged him from the vehicle, half dragging and half pushing him towards his own vehicle. Rye aimed his weapon at the driver and loosed one disabling shot. This meant both the driver and the bodyguard would not be able to raise the alarm any time soon.

Si reached his vehicle and pushed Rupert Everson face-first up against the side of the car, grabbing at his hands and in a menacing tone telling Rupert to put his hands behind his back. Rupert did as he was asked without hesitation. Once the restraints were on, Si opened the rear door and shoved Rupert into the back seat. By this time, Rye had pulled up next to him, his driver's window fully open, 'Follow me,' were his only instructions.

Rye led both vehicles at speed from the scene of the snatch, trying to get as much distance between them and the badly

CHAPTER 22

damaged SUV as possible and in as little time as possible. Rye took them along the quieter back roads until they reached the location Rye had been searching for. It was a disused farm just outside Watford. The farm had been a busy pastoral farm for many generations until the early 2030s where like many similar farms, it had proven too difficult to make a profit and so had shut down. What was left was a series of dishevelled outbuildings and an even worse looking main farmhouse, ideal for questioning someone without being disturbed.

The two vehicles pulled up in front of the old farmhouse, their headlights peering through the darkness of the early morning casting eery shadows against the old brick building. Rye exited his vehicle and conducted a quick recce of the immediate area. He then reprogrammed the drone to hover at a set height above the farm to have a birds-eye view of any hostile approaches.

Once Rye was happy that the site was secure, he signalled for Si Morgan to exit his vehicle with their hostage Rupert Everson. The front door to the old farmhouse was locked. Although it only took Rye one attempt to shoulder barge the door open, a haze of dust surrounded the now accessible entrance after being disturbed from its resting place.

'There, secure him to the kitchen chair,' Rye told Si as their flashlights scanned the open-plan room.

Rupert Everson hadn't muttered a word since being removed from his vehicle. He had merely followed the instructions from his captors and provided no fight towards them. He had already come across Rye before, so he knew what could happen if he started playing up.

Once Si had secured him to the robust steel-framed chair, he took up a position by the front door, half monitoring the live feed from the drone and half using his night sight to observe outside the front of the building through the partly open damaged front door.

'Rupert, we meet again,' Rye said as he stood in front of Rupert Everson.

The only light in the room was from Rye's flashlight, which had been stood on its end and was now acting as a mini lamp, spreading just enough light into the open space so both men could see each other's faces.

'I didn't expect to see you again. I hoped not to see you again!' replied Rupert avoiding the man's stern gaze stood in front of him.

'I need more information. I have realised my potential, which has brought me more questions that need answering. Unfortunately, you are the only one I know of that can provide answers to these questions. Hopefully, you will give me these answers, and we can all go on our way.'

Chapter 23

Gabriel Durand left the farmhouse and walked over to the large outbuilding with its grey brick exterior walls and corrugated iron roof. It looked flimsy and decrepit even though it had been standing for more years than Gabriel had walked the earth. He opened one of the large steel doors enough to squeeze through and into the large open space. Compared to the outside, the inside was a hive of activity with people moving around the space with a purpose. In the centre of the room were five transport shuttles all stood in line. Engineers were making final checks on the shuttles to ensure that they were ready for their next flight, which could be their last ever flight, depending on Sky Zone One's defence systems being disabled.

'Evening Gabriel,' said Teresa as she walked from behind the first shuttle.

'Good evening, couldn't help to get your hands dirty, hey Teresa?!'

'You know me, Gabriel, as much as I have faith in the engineers, I also want to make sure everything has been double-checked,' she said with a broad smile spreading across her oil-smeared face.

'Yes, I do know you, and I'm glad you are around to do that.'

He placed his hand on her shoulder as he continued walking. He knew his team would do everything correctly, but he felt more at ease, watching it being done.

It was 8:56 pm, they only had just over six hours before the final inspection of the fleet and the fighters. Everything and everyone had to be ready by 3:00 am, ready for lift off at 4:00 am the next morning. Most of the attack force had made their way to the derelict farm over the last few days under darkness and then had secreted themselves within the buildings that made up the isolated farm. From the outside, no one could have known that this non-descript location was now housing an attack force that would, if successful, change the course of history.

Gabriel exited the large outbuilding through a back exit and crossed a short expanse to where a smaller building was found, made up of similar materials to the one he just left. The single door was locked, so Gabriel knocked and waited, he heard two large bolts being drawn back, and the door opened slightly. As soon as the person saw it was Gabriel, he opened the door fully and let him enter.

There was a large corridor with five doors peeling off it, two on each side of the corridor, and a final door at the end. The guard sat back down on his chair by the main entrance to the building. In his lap, he held one of the largest weapons Gabriel had ever seen. Each room was being used as a mission room for each of the groups. This meant that each mission was kept secret, and only those on that particular team would ever know the full orders for that specific mission. Except those such as Gabriel, who knew every aspect of the mission.

Gabriel knew that the super soldiers were located in the room at the very end of the corridor. He also knew that they had been briefed back at the secret location used by Rupert Everson and his scientists. He thought of entering the room but faltered at the last minute. Even he didn't know what to make of these biologically enhanced individuals as he hadn't even been introduced properly. They belonged to Rupert Everson and the Elders. He just had to take Rupert's word that these soldiers would fall into line with the rest of the mission. Deep down, he wondered whether the Elders had their own objectives. He pushed the thoughts from his mind and entered the first room on the left.

He found one of his trusted comrades stood in front of a crammed room going over the details of this group's specific responsibility. As Gabriel entered, the man named Zak stopped and greeted Gabriel.

'Please, carry on,' Gabriel said as he waved his hand in the air dismissively.

With that, Zak continued his briefing, 'Once we have landed on docking bay three alpha, which is one of the main docking bays, we will break into five teams. Three teams, including Echo three, four, and five, will head directly for the communications room found on Level Two. They will then breach this room and hold it. It is vital to breach the room quickly so that we can limit the number of messages being sent to the surface once they know we are coming.'

Zak looked at the faces of concentration around the room, each with their reasons for being there. Some had been affected by the United Continents first hand while others just wanted an end to United Continent tyrannical rule.

'The next two teams consisting of Echo one and two will head to the main engineering deck, where they will contain all personnel until further notice and also make sure that all systems continue to operate.'

'I will co-ordinate your movements from the docking bay where myself and the other team leaders will be positioned. Any questions?' he added as he looked at each of them in turn.

Gabriel noticed that all of their faces were like stone, he knew they were scared, but he also knew they were committed. Gabriel had chosen each one of them, mainly for their unique skillset and their belief in this mission. They had all worked hard for this mission, and although not all of them had military experience, they had received military tactics and weapons training from the more experienced members.

'Right, final weapons check at 11:00 pm. Then rest up until we board the shuttles.'

At this point, Gabriel nodded at Zak, then left the room. As he closed the door behind himself, he leaned back on it and exhaled.

Did everyone in that room know that they may not survive the day, he thought to himself.

His curiosity pushed him to open the door at the end of the corridor, but he stopped himself again and instead knocked twice on another door. This time the room was a lot less serious, with many of the occupants smiling. He instantly knew why as his close comrade Teresa was stood at the front, beaming down at the volunteers sat in front of her.

'Teresa,' Gabriel said as he smiled at her, 'I see you can always find a place for humour!'

She laughed, and he couldn't trace an ounce of fear in her, just like a typical day speaking with some colleagues. He envied her for that.

'We were just discussing the shock on the faces of the privileged once they see us waving weapons in their faces!'

CHAPTER 23

'Yes, their faces will be a picture for sure,' Gabriel replied simply.

'How is everything else? Going to plan?'

'Yes, like clockwork,' he replied, being careful not to say too much in front of the volunteers.

'Good! Well, I think we are all done here. Did you want to say anything to the group?'

Gabriel didn't, but he knew that he should, he knew they looked to him for encouragement. He walked to the front of the group and started speaking.

'I know each of you has a reason for being here. We have all been touched in one way or another by the tyranny of the United Continents. No longer will we stand back in the shadows and oppose this unrelenting force. It is our time to step forward and make our actions count,' heads started nodding, and people agreed with him verbally.

'This mission is dangerous, far more dangerous than anything we have attempted before. I know this, and you know this, but if we keep to the plan and work together, I am confident that we will have our day and bring Sky Zone One under our control. Once we do that, we can start to make the changes needed. People and governments will sit up and listen!'

There were more shouts of approval now as people stood up clapping. The energy in the room became electrified as he spoke. It made him feel more confident, every word boosting his belief in himself and the mission.

'It is not every day we get an opportunity like this, an opportunity to strike at the heart of the United Continents, and dare I say it, an opportunity to change the course of history. I want you to all fight like you're possessed tomorrow.

Keep battling until we have achieved our mission. Stay focused, and we will be victorious!'

The entire room was now on their feet, and Teresa slapped her friend on the back, 'Well done, Gabriel, well done indeed.'

Now the preparation was over. Everyone dispersed either into groups or on their own. Some grabbed sleep or at least attempted to, while others whispered between themselves in small groups. All team leaders had completed their briefings, weapons had been checked, and the shuttles were ready for the final attack. There was an air of calmness about the place. Although beneath that calmness was an energy loitering just below the surface. This would be unleashed as soon as they boarded the shuttles ready for the approach.

There was a heavy reliance on the FACR members onboard Sky Zone One as if they didn't complete their mission, then none of the surface team would make it anywhere near their intended target.

It was time for Gabriel to communicate with the team on board and receive an update; he had to know that everything was going to plan on their end. He made his way to his private area, one of the bedrooms in the main farmhouse. Sat on the desk was a small communication system that Gabriel had been using to communicate with the Sky Zone One team.

The saboteur team onboard Sky Zone One was headed up by Phillipe Montreux, who was on board as a resident with his wife Carolyn, albeit these names being aliases. In reality, they were both undercover agents of the FACR and who had been purposefully kept distant from the organization from the outset, for this very purpose. Their purpose was to be accepted as Sky Zone residents. This involved intense security vetting of all residents. There had been no links to terrorism for them, as they had been strategically removed from any interaction with the FACR.

Along with the genetically mutated super soldiers, these saboteurs on board Sky Zone One were the reason they would be successful in their plight against the United Continents.

He switched the device on and waited for the lights to change green, which told him he had a connection. Phillipe should be ready for this call as they had scheduled their communication with each other. It would be the last time that they spoke before the assault began, a final check that Phillipe and his colleagues were in a position to take down the defences of Sky Zone One. If they weren't, then the entire mission would be a non-starter as there would be no way for them to break through the defences, it was just impossible.

Gabriel entered his security code and selected the only contact in the communication device, Phillipe Montreux. Phillipe answered almost immediately.

'How is the schedule?' Gabriel said simply, they never used names when communicating and always kept the communication as brief as possible to avoid the signal being tracked.

'All is well. We have control of the systems and will activate power down at the agreed time.'

'Excellent, we are ready for visiting, and our arrival is the same as planned,' even though the communication was secure, Gabriel didn't want to take chances, so any communication was verbally low key as not to highlight any specific information.

'Good luck, my friend, we will catch up when you arrive!'

Gabriel knew his friend was referring to the slim chance that they had not considered all the defences, the slight chance where the weapons of Sky Zone One could obliterate all their shuttles.

'Good luck to you too, we will meet again soon, one way or the other.'

Gabriel shut down the communication link and packed the device into a nearby rucksack. That was it then. Everything that could be done had been done. All that was left was to board the shuttles and initiate the attack, Gabriel thought.

He heard footsteps behind him. He turned round to see Teresa stood there, holding a half-full bottle of whisky.

'Fancy one last drink before we go to battle?' she said, passing him the bottle.

'Don't mind if I do!'

They both sat down on the dusty floor, sharing the bottle of fine whisky in silence; neither of them had to say anything as they both understood the gravity of the situation. Gabriel enjoyed the silence, it felt like the calm before the storm, and he would enjoy every second of it.

They sat there for thirty minutes, enjoying the tranquillity of the moment before Gabriel got to his feet and brushed the dust off his tactical trousers before handing the bottle back to Teresa.

'Well, I suppose it's about that time,' he said casually.

'Yes, I suppose it is,' Teresa replied as she stood up and screwed the lid back on the whisky bottle.

They both left the bedroom and headed for the main staging area where the shuttles were located. The place was now becoming a hive of activity as the time grew closer to 3:00 am. Gabriel and Teresa were on different shuttles, so they said their goodbyes there and then and wished each other good luck. They both knew that it could be the last time they ever saw each other.

CHAPTER 23

Gabriel approached his shuttle, a large yet simple transport carrier covered in small dents and scratches. The hydrogen fuel cell engines were good as had been newly fitted. The structure of the shuttle was sound if a little battered in places. Only primitive weapons had been fitted on each of the shuttles as they needed to keep weight down. They had discussed attaching larger cannons to the craft, although even with weapons, they would have little effect against the Sky Zone's defences or any other United Continents military aircraft.

Gabriel's team were starting to arrive, and he verbally acknowledged each of them. He didn't need to say much more to them as he knew they had been briefed on the mission and their responsibilities. The pilot was a woman called Sandy, who had been a long-haul airline pilot before accepting to pilot one of the shuttles, she had supported any cause against the United Continents for many years. When she had found out about the FACR, she had made it her mission to get involved wherever she could. Ultimately this attitude had led to her piloting one of the final attack shuttles in what could only be described as the event of the century.

Did she know what she was doing, did she hate the United Continents that much that she would potentially give her life for the cause, Gabriel thought to himself before giving her a welcoming smile.

'Right, everyone board the shuttle if you are ready,' Gabriel said. He looked around the large room to see that other team leaders were instructing their teams to board the shuttles.

Once everyone was accounted for, Gabriel took Sandy to the side for some last-minute words, 'When we get the green light, I don't want you to hesitate, full speed towards the target location. We will know soon enough if some of the defences are still in action, but by that time, it will be too late anyway. I want you to quell that fear inside and push through. God speed be with us.'

'I understand. You can count on me,' she replied.

Gabriel situated himself just behind Sandy and placed the communications headset on, giving him a communication link to all the pilots and team leaders.

'Power up your engines, prepare for lift-off,' he commanded over the radio.

As Sandy started the engine, the shuttle began to vibrate. A distinctive humming sound spread out around the shuttle interior. Gabriel looked around to see the different reactions from those sat aboard as the realization started to hit home. Some lowered their heads, others closed their eyes in prayer, and a few just stared forward blankly. These were the more experienced fighters Gabriel assumed.

Gabriel checked his watch, 2:59 am, he waited, time slowed as he stared at the digital display, 3:00 am, 'All shuttles, advance to target.'

With that simple order, all shuttles began to rise from the floor and smashed through the decrepit roof of the large farm building before thrusting off into the darkness of the night. Five shuttles burned through the night, leaving the disused farm building in Amsterdam far behind, all on a course to change history.

The shuttle creaked and rattled as its high powered engines thrust it forward. Gabriel could see the digital altimeter on the cockpit, one thousand metres, one thousand five hundred metres, increasing in height rapidly. He knew that the Sky Zone One defences would activate at around nine thousand metres from their planning, he watched intently as they approached that altitude at speed. He knew Sandy was also aware of the target altitude of the defence systems, and as they approached that target limit, he felt Sandy come off the power slightly. He leaned forward and placed his hand on her shoulder. As he did, he felt the power increase slightly, and as they hit nine thousand metres, he felt himself squeezing her shoulder in anticipation.

Nothing happened. He looked through the front screen of the shuttle, half expecting missiles to be bearing down on them. All he saw was a blanket of stars in a peaceful night sky. Phillipe and his team had done it. They had disabled the defences of Sky Zone One. The only barrier now was the United Continents Air Guard's attack fighters. As the thought entered his mind, Sandy's voice came over the communication system, 'Attack fighters inbound!'

Chapter 24

Rupert Everson struggled in the chair, trying to free his hands whilst trying not to alert the two men talking in the next room. Rupert wasted his efforts as Rye Braden had secured him too well. He stopped trying and tried to listen to what they were saying, trying to establish what was going to be his fate.

'This is crazy Rye, what do you expect to be the outcome of all this?'

'I need to know more, but yes I'm sorry for dragging you into this mate. You should go.'

'Bit late for that isn't it!' Si said sarcastically.

Deep down, Si Morgan wanted answers as much as his friend. Rye had now dragged him into this mystery that was Rye's life, and to be honest, he was just as curious as Rye was.

'I'm here now so will stay until the end, plus I want to make sure you don't do anything stupid!'

'Thanks, Si, I do appreciate it,' Rye replied earnestly.

Rye walked back into the room where they had Rupert Everson strapped to the chair, Si Morgan followed closely behind.

'Are you ready to tell me more about the Eden project,' Rye said, although it wasn't a question, more of a statement.

'I've told you everything I know!'

CHAPTER 24

'Well I need to know more, I want detailed information about why and how I am different,' Rye quickly replied.

'There is nothing more to tell you if there was then I would.'

'Rubbish, you have a lot more information, and before you leave this building, you are going to tell me.'

Rye pulled up a chair and placed it down in front of his captive, before sitting down slowly. Si Morgan leant against a wall behind Rye, observing the questioning as it unfolded.

'I want to know how many others there are and where they are now?'

Rupert Everson didn't speak; he was too busy trying to figure out what to do. Like the last time Rye had him pinned to a chair, there wasn't much he could do, except tell Rye what he wanted to know. The only real difference was that he knew his captor had a lot more time this time around, as there was no chance of anyone walking in or disturbing them. This thought made him sick, so he decided to tell Rye what he wanted to know and hope that he kept his life by the end of it.

'Initially, there were thirty test subjects for the Eden project,' Rupert said with a defeated tone.

'Go on,' Rye said simply.

'They... You, all volunteered for the project. You may not remember, but you did, you all had your reasons for signing up.'

'How did we know what we were signing up for?'

'We advertised the project to all military personnel; we signposted it as 'Special Duties'. We gave it a very brief summary and then as people came forward we conducted initial assessments, those that passed were then told of the exact details of the project that they would be signing up for.'

Rupert looked to Rye but could instantly tell he wanted him

to continue by the lack of emotion on his stern face.

'We had hundreds come forward, but only a handful were appropriate emotionally and physically. Nothing of this nature had ever been contemplated before, let alone attempted. We knew that the psychological and physiological strains would be extreme, so this meant only a certain type of person could be considered. Once we had whittled it down further, we ended up with yourself and twenty-nine others. Then we asked them to sign a consent form which removed all liability from us. This means you gave yourself to us and believe it or not you fully consented to what was done to you.'

He looked towards Rye again, trying to evaluate what he was thinking. Rye portrayed no reaction to what Rupert was telling him.

'It took twelve months of intense surgery in addition to constant psychological assessments until we were confident that we had mastered the genetic manipulation. Until we had successfully turned you into the deadliest humanized weapons that the human race had ever seen, it was a masterclass in science.'

Rupert Everson had started to forget his predicament and was now recounting the success they had achieved; he even started to mimic the pride that came from this pioneering project.

'Why do I feel like I have lost part of my life then, the memories, even the fact that I have no recollection of volunteering for this?' Rye's tone was far from friendly as he was starting to get annoyed by the fact that Rupert Everson was revelling in his recount of the project.

Rupert lowered his head away from the intense gaze of Rye and continued a little less enthusiastically.

CHAPTER 24

'At the critical time within the project, we were shut down by certain factions within the United Continents. They gave orders that every test subject would have their minds suppressed about their abilities and the project itself. This is why you can't recollect anything; your capabilities were hidden from you. But somehow you have regained an understanding of your abilities and become aware of your enhanced characteristics. Once you are aware, then your mind can access your true physical capability, with further training, then you could reach your full potential.'

'I already know my full potential!' Rye retorted standing up.

'You think you do, but I doubt you know.'

'Really! What more do I need to know!'

'The others have been reprogrammed... I mean...' Rupert stuttered as he realised he had just said too much.

'The others? What do you mean?'

'Nothing, I meant the others could have been reprogrammed to unleash their true potential.' Rupert tried backtracking now.

'You're lying, there's something you're not telling me, and so you are now going to tell me,' Rye approached him now standing over him menacingly.

'It was a slip of the tongue.'

With that, Rye gripped the man's face hard and forced him to look up at him, fury blazed in his eyes as he looked down at his captive. Rupert tried to move his head, but the iron-like grip kept his head steady, he grimaced with pain as Rye's grip tightened.

'What do you mean the others, what have you done with them?'

Rupert struggled in the chair now as Rye's grip felt like it would crush his jaw, his eyes full of panic and shock like a wild animal caught in a snare.

Rye sensed Rupert wanted to say something, so he let go harshly, pushing Rupert's face to the side.

'What is it?' Rye said scornfully.

'You think you are hard done by, you act like you don't care, but you have a gift,' Rupert had a surprising amount of bravado in his voice despite his situation and nearly having his face crushed to a pulp.

Rye just stared at him, tilting his head slightly like a dog does when it's trying to understand what it was being told. Fury rose inside him. How dare this man push this back on me, he thought to himself.

Rupert continued to speak, 'You have the strength, speed and senses of a god. You don't deserve this gift. I should have it!'

Was this man feeling jealous of Rye, he wanted to be like the thing that he had created.

'It's only your word that I asked for this, where is the proof!'

'There is no proof. Everything was destroyed,' Rupert replied.

'Tell me about the others, you have found them and reprogrammed them haven't you?' Rye knew this was what Rupert Everson had meant when he slipped up.

Rupert didn't answer; he just stared down at the ground.

Rye went over to a small bag that he had brought in with him, he unzipped it and pulled a syringe and small vial of dark liquid. He plunged the needle into the vial and drew out 1cc of fluid. He then flicked the syringe before turning back to Rupert Everson.

'Do you know what this is? It's a mixture of Thiopental and

other substances, it's a rudimental concoction to inflict pain but at the same time ensure that you speak the truth.'

Rupert didn't like what Rye had just said. He looked past Rye to Si Morgan stood at the back of the room.

'You have to stop him, please.'

Si Morgan didn't even flinch, as a tier one soldier for many years, he had seen far worse, and he backed his friend with this approach, regardless of how painful it would be for their guest.

'Wait!!' cried Rupert as Rye levelled the syringe with his neck.

Rye stopped although didn't withdraw the syringe from its position, 'You have something to say?'

'We have them, the other test subjects,' Rupert said simply.

'You have them for what?' Si Morgan had stepped forward now listening intently.

Rupert didn't say anything, and he just stared down at the ground. Rye grabbed his hair and yanked his head back, at the same time breaking the skin with the syringe.

'I'm losing patience with you.'

Rupert knew he had little choice other than tell the two men in front of him what they wanted to know.

'We searched for the other test subjects, the ones that went through the project with yourself. We found most of them, but it took years, we reprogrammed them, so they are fully aware of the abilities. We also started a new project with fresh subjects using a new laboratory. We didn't think it would work until we tracked down the original scientist.'

Rye and Si Morgan were listening intently now, Rye had released his grip on Rupert and took a few steps back.

'Why have you done this, why now?' Rye asked with a little

less anger in his voice.

'Because we needed their skill set.'

Rye started to feel uneasy now as he knew what he was capable of, so only imagined what many super soldiers could be capable of.'

'Stop talking in riddles and tell me what you have done. Otherwise, I will jam this syringe in your eye and watch you die a slow, painful death!' Rye took a step forward now.

Rupert flinched at the words, his hands were numb due to the restraints he had on them, and his whole body was burning with pain from being in a seated position for so long.

'We needed them to bolster a small army raised by the FACR, an attack force so to speak. We wouldn't be able to execute the mission without them, each one of them is worth ten normal soldiers, you should know that by now.'

'An attack force for what,' Si Morgan interjected.

'An attack force to strike at the heart of the United Continents, for years of oppression and lawless rule. Many are not prepared to sit back anymore and watch the United Continents continue their bias rule. I have seen it from the inside and know exactly what they are all about, so myself and the Elders support the FACR against United Continent rule.'

Rye looked over at Si Morgan and knew he was thinking the same, that they had one of the Elders captive in front of them. For years people had been chasing the myth that was the Elders organization, and now they had a direct route to them, especially as he knew Rupert Everson couldn't resist much interrogation.

'What is the target of the attack Rupert?' Si said.

Rupert Everson looked up at them both. The defiance back in his eyes, 'Sky Zone One!'

CHAPTER 24

Rye knew that Sky Zone One had just been completed and that nearly two million citizens would be populating it. He also knew that it was one of the most heavily secured places on the planet. Rupert had to be bluffing as no one could even get close to it due to the security defences in place, he had learnt from colleagues of the next generation weapons that were used on Sky Zone One.

'That's impossible,' Rye said simply, almost mockingly.

Rupert just grinned at him, 'Nothing is impossible, look at you for instance.'

'The Sky Zones are floating fortresses, nothing can get close to them,' Si added.

'Yet we have found a way to penetrate it, and once aboard we will take control of Sky Zone One, and the world will be at our control!'

Rye thought Rupert was starting to go crazy as his story sounded ridiculous, but if they had found a way, then that would be a disaster.

'If what you are saying is true, then when are you planning this attack?'

Regardless of how crazy Rupert sounded, Rye wasn't one to take chances and discount information, especially on this occasion due to the person that was telling them.

'This is why I can tell you about the mission, as there is absolutely nothing you can do about it now. Even as you've had me strapped to this chair, wasting time questioning me, our attack is in progress. You are too late. Once we have control of Sky Zone One then we have won, the world will bend to our requests and the United Continents will be held accountable for everything they have done.'

It was just after 3:00 am so an ideal time for an attack, neither

Rye nor Si Morgan had their communications switched on so were in the dark with regards to any messages from ArmorCorp.

'Si, check your communication system for any information on an attack,' Rye said, trying to verify what Rupert had just told him.

Si Morgan left the room rapidly to ensure he had the best signal when he switched on his personal communications device.

'If you are telling the truth, then we will hear about it very soon.'

As the words left his mouth, Si came running back into the room, 'Rye, it's happening, its true. Reports are coming in of unknown shuttles breaching the secure air space around Sky Zone One. There is no communication with Sky Zone One either!'

Rye physically felt his heart stop for a second. How is this happening, he thought to himself.

He turned to Rupert and with an ice-cold stare, 'What have you done?'

Chapter 25

Gabriel's eyes darted from left to right, trying to identify the attack aircraft in the sky, his gaze diverted to the small radar screen on the dashboard of the cockpit where he saw six dots racing towards them.

'We've made it this far, we just need to get past these fighters now,' he said to Sandy.

The dots suddenly broke into pairs so they could attack more of the shuttles at once, thinking that the shuttles threatening their air space were defenceless. We just need to get as many shuttles to Sky Zone One, Gabriel thought to himself.

They were less than a thousand metres from their intended destination, so close yet now so far with the threat of the attack aircraft on them. Some of the best fighter pilots in the world would be piloting the attack fighters the United Continents had, all with the latest weapons systems onboard. Compared to the volunteer pilots they had with their passenger shuttles having rudimentary weapons attached to the outside, it equated to a band of outlaws against one of the finest fighting forces the world had seen.

Gabriel hoped all the pilots had remembered the actions on for this type of scenario, although they probably hadn't been listening at this point as many believed they wouldn't even break through the Sky Zone One defence. But they had, they had escaped the onslaught and certainty of destruction from the primary defence systems of the floating city.

'Initiate defence positions,' Gabriel shouted over the communication system to all pilots.

To his amazement, he could see their shuttles changing position, three shuttles including his own positioned themselves in line with the last two shuttles behind them and slightly above. In his line of shuttles, the outer two had weapons covering the side approach whilst Sandy aimed her guns to the front. Their priority was to hold off the attack fighters as long as they could until they reached Sky Zone One. The other two shuttles would engage any attack fighters that came from the rear and those that approached from difficult angles, even if it meant probable destruction for them.

Gabriel could see the attack fighters now, two of the pairs were coming directly at them from the front, he cursed to himself as he knew their weapons would have more range than his own.

'Where are the other two,' he said out loud, more to himself than anyone else.

'They are flying around and look like they will be attacking from the rear', Sandy said, her eyes now intently focusing on the two pairs of attack ships rapidly approaching from the front.

'All shuttles, listen in. When I give the command, I want the front three ships to climb hard with the two end shuttles banking left and right respectively. The rear shuttles I want you to drop height and do the same, banking left and right. They are going to hit us hard. Hopefully, we can manoeuvre to

CHAPTER 25

respond to the attack, giving us more time to get to Sky Zone One,' Gabriel was sweating profusely now, and his mouth was dry as sand.

The attack fighters to the front were less than two hundred metres from them now. The pair at the rear had positioned themselves for an attack run from behind. Gabriel's timing had to be spot on if any of them were going to survive this, deep down he knew they would take casualties, his primary focus now was to ensure that none of this was in vain.

'Steady… Steady… Execute!' Gabriel commanded.

As he gave the command missile warnings sounded throughout the shuttle as the attack fighters from the front fired their missiles, red lights flashed as the missile lock was identified.

'Bank faster Sandy. Come on, don't let me down now!'

Sandy fought with the controls of the not so responsive shuttle, forcing upwards and to the left. Once the manoeuvre had been completed, Gabriel looked across to see where the other shuttles were. As he caught sight of the nearest shuttle to his right, he also saw the heat signature of the missile fired from the enemy and watched as it smashed into the side of the shuttle. There was no noise, just an explosion of light as the rocket found its target, both Gabriel and Sandy turned away as the light burned their eyes. Lights and sirens were still wailing on the control panel, Gabriel hoped that one of the missiles wasn't going to be their imminent future. No explosion came for them.

'All shuttles, send SITREP,' Gabriel had regained focus now and wanted a situation report from all shuttles.

'Shuttle two still here.'

'Shuttle four still here.'

'Shuttle five still here.'

That meant there were still four of them surviving. They had nearly made it to Sky Zone One, so close but Gabriel knew the attack fighters would be repositioning themselves for another attack run.

'All shuttles, this is Gabriel. You all need to do whatever you can to get your shuttle to Sky Zone One. God speed be with you.'

With that, each shuttle focused on straight-line speed to Sky Zone One, once docked then they would be safe from the attack fighters. Gabriel could see from the radar screen that all shuttles were now pretty much side by side heading directly for the Sky Zone, their entire mission now relied on four little dots on a screen.

More missiles were picked up by the radar, four in total, enough to destroy all the remaining shuttles.

'Sandy, you know what to do. Keep us alive!'

Sandy did know. She dived hard in an attempt to evade the missile targeted on their shuttle. Gabriel lurched forward at the sudden movement and hoped that the creaking and yawning from the shuttle didn't mean that it was breaking apart under the force of the manoeuvre. Sandy continued to carry out evasive manoeuvres, hoping that the missile lock on their shuttle would disappear and it did.

We were lucky that time, Gabriel thought.

In that instant, Gabriel watched in disbelief as a shuttle came into view firing down on the attack fighter that was targeting them. However, the shots were having a limited impact against the superior aircraft. Gabriel continued to watch, waiting for the attack fighter to release its weapons on his shuttle again, ending his and the forty other passenger's mission there and then.

What he saw felt like a dream as he watched the same shuttle head directly for the attack fighter, then he heard a familiar voice come on the communication system, 'Make them pay Gabriel.'

It was Teresa in shuttle five. She must have known that Gabriel's shuttle was about to be blown from the sky and had made the command decision to give her own life to save his. His stomach sank as he watched forty of his comrades explode into a flash of light, along with the attack fighter.

'Make them pay, yes indeed he would make them pay,' he said to himself.

They were so close now that he could see the docking bay ahead, inviting them into safety.

'Get us there now,' he shouted at Sandy, not with compassion but with authority born from the pain of losing so many close friends.

Sandy pushed the shuttle to full throttle, ignoring the sounds emanating from the hull. There was no thought for any other missiles, if any were coming then it was down to fate now whether they were blown into a million pieces or managed to find their way into the docking bay of Sky Zone One.

Mini explosions rocked the shuttle as rounds exploded around them from the cannons of the attack fighters, the shuttle rocked from side to side from the effects. Gabriel couldn't help but think that the metal frame of the shuttle was about to split in half, leaving them all to fall to their deaths from ten thousand metres. He grabbed on to whatever he could and could see that the rest of the passengers were doing the same; all they could do was pray and hope that Sandy could finish the job.

Gabriel could see intricate details inside the docking bay;

he even thought he saw someone running from one side to the other shouting something. He gave a thought for the lives on the other shuttles although the only thing that mattered now was what was happening to their shuttle, all forty souls weighed in the balance as the attack fighters maintained their pursuit of the jittery shuttle.

'Everyone brace,' came the nervous shout from Sandy.

Gabriel pulled his seat belt tight and held fast to whatever he could, as he looked up through the front screen of the shuttle he saw that they were heading directly for the opening of the docking bay at full speed. Explosions erupted around the entrance as cannon rounds missed their shuttle and smashed into Sky Zone One.

At the very last moment, Sandy knocked off the power for the shuttle spinning it one hundred and eighty degrees as they passed through the opening of the docking bay. As the shuttle faced the opposite direction, she pushed on the power abruptly causing a massive change in direction within a split second. Gabriel felt like his insides were going to physically force themselves out of his body; his neck was lucky to not break under the strain. One of the other passengers was not so fortunate and hadn't heard the brace command in time. The man was flung forward from his seat when Sandy had cut the power but then had been slung to the back of the shuttle once power had been restored. There was a sickening crunch as his body smashed into the back of the shuttle before he slid to the floor, dead.

'Get the doors open now,' screamed Gabriel as he released his safety harness and moved to the shuttle door.

The door hissed as the locks were released and started to lower to the floor of the docking bay.

CHAPTER 25

'Ready your weapons; this is it!'

Even before the shuttle door reached the floor, the occupants poured out and instinctively took up the position of cover as the first wave of incoming rounds ripped up the docking bay around them. The Commando Elite had already taken up their positions ready to kill those that threatened Sky Zone One, Gabriel saw at least three people drop to the floor as they left the safety of the shuttle.

Trying to gather his mind, Gabriel dived behind a large transport crate and turned, so his back was up against it, this allowed him to see what shuttles had made it and which had been blown from the sky by the attacked fighters. He could see three shuttles in the docking area, all with various damage, his shuttle had lost most of its undercarriage due to the extreme manoeuvre pulled off by Sandy.

He could see Zak engaged in a ferocious firefight and it looked like he had most of his team with him. He could also see the super soldiers at the far end of the hangar as they were wearing all black combat fatigues and state of the art personal body armour. Just by the way they moved he could tell they were going to cause some damage to the ranks of the Commando Elite, he thanked the gods they were on his side.

Gabriel got on his communication device and tried to speak with Zak, who was in a firefight with a large squad of Commando Elite soldiers.

'Echo One, do you copy?' Gabriel shouted over the maelstrom of noise.

'Echo One, come in,' he tried again.

'This is Echo One, what is it?!' came the blunt reply from Zak.

'If you fall back behind the Eden soldiers and let them take the brunt of the attack, you can then split your team off to get to communications and engineering. That's where we need you most.'

'Roger that,' came the response from Zak.

Gabriel could see Zak indicating to the Eden soldiers to push forward in a counter-attack, allowing Zak and his team a better opportunity to break away from the firefight and get to their intended destinations.

'We're wasting too much time being pinned down,' Gabriel muttered to himself.

He looked around the vast docking bay for options, but it was clear the only options were to make use of the super soldiers that were supporting them. As he flipped back around to assess the size of the force pinning his group down, a bullet smashed into the corner of the transport crate. Splinters from the metal crate ripped into the side of his face. He cursed in agony as he moved back down into cover.

'We're through to one of the main corridors,' came the positive response from Zak over the communication system.

The Eden soldiers had managed to push the attacking forces back enough so that Zak and his team could access one of the corridors. From there, they could split into groups, and each get to their primary objective, that was to secure the communications room and engineering department.

'Confirmed, good luck,' Gabriel replied through gritted teeth due to the pain of the shrapnel in his face.

The Eden soldiers were now in four teams, Gabriel needed to get two of those teams over to his side of the hangar if he was ever going to make some ground.

'Eden One and Two, make your way to my location now!'

Immediately, he saw two of the Eden soldiers look over

at him from the other side of the docking bay. Initially, he thought they were going to ignore the command although he watched as they both instructed their teams to move.

He watched in awe as they moved efficiently and with purpose, one team giving covering fire whilst the other moved with speed and grace. Gabriel also noticed that their shots hit every target. Their input was what was starting to win the firefight for them, even though they were heavily outnumbered. The Eden soldiers made it to where he was sat with his back up against the transport crate; they hardly acknowledged him and kept their focus on the battle in front of them.

'Fall in behind us, we move now,' said the closest Eden soldier to him, a large, heavily built black man with a shaved head. Gabriel could see dark red blood pooling from below the man's body armour, although there was no reaction or recognition of the wound from the soldier.

Gabriel counted approximately ten Eden soldiers and thirty of his party, still enough of a force to get the job done. He didn't know how many fighters Zak had with him, hopefully, a similar number of FACR fighters and maybe a handful of the Eden soldiers.

The Eden soldiers began their advance towards the Commando Elite that had them pinned down, half providing covering fire whilst the other half moved with lightning speed. Gabriel and his fighters closed in behind them although letting the Eden soldiers take the brunt of the returning fire, he aimed to keep himself and as many of his FACR fighters alive whilst completing their mission.

Just then he saw a flash of movement out of the corner of his eye, too late to stop the butt of the rifle smashing in the side of the head as one of the Commando Elite soldiers led a small group from behind. Gabriel fell to the floor hard, his vision clouded, and he struggled to keep control of his body. He could hear shouting and what looked like people struggling in hand to hand combat, although his vision was heavily blurred due to being struck down violently. He was being trampled under the feet of those that seemed to be entangled in the violent brawl.

'Get up!' came a voice out of the confusion.

'Gabriel, get up now!'

Gabriel thought he recognized the voice, but the pain emanating from his head was making it difficult to think straight, he touched the side of his head and felt blood.

'Get up now or you are going to die here!' came the ever-increasing menace in the voice.

He felt hands pick him up roughly from the ground. His legs felt weak as he tried to stand. He became aware of stepping over bodies on the floor as someone half marched and half-carried him away from where he had fallen.

'What happened?' Gabriel said shakily.

'You were hit from behind by a small group of Commando Elite soldiers. You lost a few men, unfortunately.'

'Phillipe?' Gabriel enquired.

'Yes, my friend, it is me. You must keep moving until we have reached safety.'

'Where is Carolyn?'

'She is waiting for us in a secure location; she will then help us breach the main control room. They have a large security force in that area, so we need your super soldiers to overcome them.'

'We need to access that control room; otherwise it's all been

CHAPTER 25

pointless,' Gabriel verbally confirmed what they both knew.

Gabriel was able to walk unattended now. He watched as the Eden soldiers ahead of them fought through the defensive lines of the Commando Elite using sheer power, motivation and speed. He watched as one of the female Eden soldiers sprinted forward into the ranks of the opposing soldiers. She ducked an extending arm which was swinging a large combat knife towards her throat. In an instant, she was back up and forcefully extending her palm into the tactical visor covering the soldier's face. The soldiers head snapped back as the visor shattered into pieces. Before the head had even returned to its neutral position she had span round lunging her elbow into the now exposed throat of the Commando Elite soldier, Gabriel even heard the gurgling eruption as she crushed the windpipe. The soldier crumpled to the floor as the female Eden soldier moved on to her next victim.

They battled through the main corridors of Sky Zone until they reached the inner zone marked Alpha One, from the plans Gabriel knew this was the last security point before entering the corridor leading to the main control room of Sky Zone One. They had taken many casualties, but once they had secured their position, Gabriel could make a more precise assessment of their group.

'Gabriel, thank god you made it!' came the voice from behind him.

Gabriel spun round to see a tall, dark-haired woman dressed in black combat trousers and body armour worn over a short-sleeved white t-shirt, she held an attack rifle in her right hand.

'Carolyn, it's so good to see you,' Gabriel said with evident joy in his voice.

'Great to see you too. Our dream is finally coming to

fruition,' she replied.

As he wrapped his arms around her, there was an eruption of gunfire from one of the interconnecting corridors. He felt it before he saw it, as he felt her entire body shudder from the impact of the high velocity round and the warmth of her blood covering his face. Seconds later, her body gave way, and he struggled to hold her weight. He looked down as her body sagged in his arms. He could see where the round had entered the side of her head and removed most of the back of it. He stared in horror at the bloody mess in his arms, the deadweight dragging at his arms.

'Where did that come from?' he mouthed to himself in shock.

Just then more rounds exploded around him, sending sparks flying as bullets connected with the metal walls of the corridor.

'Take cover,' one of the Eden soldiers growled as he returned fire in the direction of the new attack.

'They must have been waiting for us, an ambush,' Phillipe said.

'What about Carolyn?' replied Gabriel.

'She's gone, focus on us staying alive and then we will mourn her!'

Gabriel was shocked by the bluntness of Phillipe's response. She had been his lover, yet still, he focused on the mission in hand. That was enough to kickstart Gabriel back into the present, raising his rifle and replying to the attack with a ferocious volley of shots.

The brutal onslaught from the Commando Elite subsided, and a voice echoed around them.

'This is Major Khan, put your weapons down and surrender. You have no way out of this situation, put your weapons down, and you will live. If you refuse, then you will all die!'

Chapter 26

Rye turned to Si Morgan, shocked at the news he had just learned from Rupert Everson.

'We need to report this in and get up there,' Rye said.

'Sky Zone One?' Si replied quizzically.

'Yes, and we need to leave now!'

'What about him?' Si said gesturing towards Rupert Everson still strapped to the chair.

'Leave him for now and call it in, someone will pick him up.'

Rye looked over at Rupert Everson, but he didn't have time to worry about him now, he had just heard that Sky Zone One was under attack, more importantly, that the very thing he was trying to understand was behind the attack.

'Si, we need to go now,' Rye said, heading for the door of the old farm building.

Si muttered something under his breath, took one last look at Rupert Everson before following Rye through the main door of the building.

As soon as Rye was in his vehicle, he was calling Felix Danner personally, as he needed to find the quickest way to get up to Sky Zone One. Felix answered almost immediately.

'Rye, I know what you are going to request, and I have already sent orders to Si Morgan,' said Felix before Rye could say anything.

Rye looked over at his friend to get confirmation, Si checked his communications device and as promised their orders had just landed in his inbox.

'We have them,' Si said, scrolling through the newly received instructions.

'Felix, let me call you back once we have gone through the orders. I trust we are going up to Sky Zone One immediately?'

'Ok, and yes you are deploying so digest the orders and get to your nearest base asap!' Felix replied as he hung up.

Rye pushed his foot to the floor and felt the vehicle accelerate with ease, it was early morning now, and the sun had just risen in the sky, spreading a warm glow over the land.

'The report is stating that five unknown shuttles made their way to Sky Zone One and that the air defences had been neutralized internally?' Si Morgan said as he rapidly went through the orders sent from Felix Danner.

'How is that even possible?' replied Rye.

'I don't know, but it states that most of the shuttles made it onto Sky Zone One, they have limited intelligence after that as communications seem to be down.'

'So, we have unknown shuttles landing on Sky Zone One with an unknown attack force. In addition to that, we have information that whoever is behind the attack has an army of super soldiers?'

'Yep, that's about it!' replied Si.

'Have you told Felix what Rupert Everson told us?'

'Yes, I've uploaded the intelligence report. We need to get to base and meet up with the rest of the force. They want us up there as soon as possible. They want Sky Zone One back at all costs.'

The base they were headed for wasn't far, and they arrived in no time, it seemed that everyone had been called in for this exceptional mission. Rye knew that the United Continents would throw everything it could at the problem, the main concern was when the terrorists started taking hostages if they hadn't already.

'We're over there,' Si Said as he pointed Rye towards a sleek looking aircraft.

As Sky Zone One was so high, they needed something that could get them there quickly and safely, and the K120 stealth cruiser was the aircraft to do that. Its sleek lines were difficult to make out against the matt black colour of the outer shell. Even though it was designed for stealth missions, it was a capable troop carrier and could carry twenty heavily laden soldiers, which was enough for Rye and his team.

'We have twelve of us from our group within ArmorCorp and three from the United Continents, so we need to board and get going immediately,' Si said as grabbed his kit and headed for the rear ramp of the aircraft.

Rye grabbed his weapons from the rear of the vehicle and followed Si to the aircraft. He had enough equipment for the mission at hand, which would be a rapid assault of Sky Zone One.

'Ok, were up in five!' Si Morgan said to the pilot as he arrived at the aircraft.

Without any fuss, the pilot nodded and went back to his pre-flight activities. Rye could see the seriousness of the mission etched across the pilot's face.

'That's it. Everyone is aboard so time to go,' Si said.

'Roger that,' Rye replied simply.

Within minutes they were off the ground and travelling at

speed towards Sky Zone One, multiple aircraft all heading for the same destination. There had been no planning or rehearsals for this mission, but the objective was simple, take back Sky Zone One.

'What about the Sky Zone defences, have the terrorists taken control of them?' Rye asked.

'Apparently not, the United Continents were wise enough to protect against that by having a kill code which disables the defences. They never wanted the Sky Zone defences to be used against them, small mercy really,' Si replied.

'I'm getting updates, and the Commando Elite have managed to secure some of the docking bays. It seems the attackers are making their way through Sky Zone One. The Commando Elite are finding it hard to slow them down.'

It must be the super soldiers making it so difficult, Rye thought to himself.

As their aircraft neared Sky Zone One, Si delivered a concise and accurate intelligence report to all those on board so that they knew what would be welcoming them as they left the aircraft.

Gabriel ran through his options, which he knew were currently limited. They needed to get to the control room if they had any chance of taking control of Sky Zone One. He had one ace up his sleeve, and now it was time to show his cards.

'Major Khan, I know about your wife and child. How they were mercilessly killed by the Rebel Alliance, the day you lost everything,' Gabriel shouted and then waited for a response, but none came.

'If it wasn't bad enough to lose everything, you are then lied to for years by the United Continents and forced to live and breathe close to the person that killed your family!' Gabriel continued, hoping to get a reaction from Major Khan.

The corridor was deathly quiet as the two groups held their fire, all listening to the lead terrorist Gabriel.

'I will not repeat it, put your weapons down and surrender,' shouted Major Khan.

As the words left his lips, he struggled with what the terrorist in front of him had just said. What did he mean, close to the person that killed his family?

'You're a fool, Major Khan. If only you knew the truth!' Gabriel repeated.

'I am not interested in your games, surrender now or face the consequences.'

'What about one of the Unicoms, you must have some form of recognition?'

Major Khan furrowed his brow at this statement, as he did feel that he recognized one particular Unicom.

At this point one of the Commando Elite soldiers began firing at the attackers, losing patience with the mini cease-fire.

'Stop firing!' Major Khan yelled at him through an icy glare that would have made any person comply.

Gabriel knew the seed had now been planted, so he continued with the manipulation of his foe, Major Khan.

'You have spent all these years being the focus of a lie. Now you need to know the truth. Unicom's are those individuals that wanted a second chance at life, that wanted to start again with no complications and no memory of their past. The United Continents thought it would be wise to even include criminals and terrorists in the Unicom program; they believed a criminal mind was more creative, and so was a better match

CHAPTER 26

for the Unicom program.'

Major Khans interest had peaked now, 'What are you saying?'

'I am saying that one of the Unicom's was the same person that planted the terrorist bomb all those years ago, the bomb that killed your wife and daughter!' said Gabriel, confident that he had challenged everything that Major Khan had believed in.

As the K120 aircraft landed in the docking bay, the occupants wasted no time in exiting the craft and taking up tactical positions around the bay. The scene was chaotic with damage everywhere. Small fires were emanating from the crashed shuttles lining the docking bay area. Sparks fell from the damaged ceiling where after the ferocious firefights had taken place.

'The terrorists have broken down into groups, some heading for the residents whilst others head for engineering and the main control centre. We are heading to the control room, to stop them taking full control,' Si said.

'Confirmed, let's get going,' Rye said hastily. Secretly, he wanted to meet one of these other super soldiers, although deep down, he knew that there would be carnage from such a meeting.

They took an extra ten of the Commando Elite soldiers, as these would provide detailed knowledge of Sky Zone One. They set off towards the main control room with an emphasis on speed although ready to engage any hostiles that they came across. As they travelled through the various corridors, they passed a mixture of dead terrorists and United Continents personnel.

'Looks like all hell broke loose,' Rye said as he scanned the area in front of him.

They stopped as they reached an intersection of corridors, they could hear shouting and firing coming from the left although they were informed that the control room was straight ahead.

'You lot follow that corridor and support whoever is under fire down there,' Si said to a small group of their party.

The main group continued towards where the control room was located, not knowing what they would find.

Major Khan couldn't think straight; deep down, he knew what he was being told was true; he had recognized something familiar about one of the Unicoms.

'Sir, what are we doing?' came the voice of one of Commando Elite hunched next to him.

Major Khan was lost, his mind reeling. What was going on, he thought to himself.

Out of nowhere, he heard a familiar voice, 'Major, everything ok?'

Major Khan looked back to see Senator Bob Mills stood there holding an assault rifle.

'Senator, what are you doing here?!'

'I'm not one to shy away from a fight!' the Senator said.

'Sir, we need to advance. What are we waiting for?' repeated the soldier.

Major Khan's mind was jumping back to the fateful day of the bombing, seeing his wife and daughter motionless. He was trying to make sense of what he had just been told. If it was true then he had been made a mockery of for all these years, he thought.

All of a sudden shots rang out as the Commando Elite soldiers started firing at the terrorists to win back the momentum. Major Khan didn't move; he couldn't engage himself as all he could think about was the Unicom.

Rye picked up the pace as he heard shouting in front of him, unsure who the voices belonged to but eager to find out. As he turned the corner, he saw them, a group of five men dressed in black from head to toe. He knew they weren't Commando Elite soldiers as they were laid on the floor around the black clad figures feet, blood soaking their uniforms. They saw him instantly, and all looked over to him at the same time, a bloodthirst clear in their eyes. Rye had moved faster than the rest of his team so he was on his own now, against five of the enemy and he instinctively knew that these were the super soldiers he was so keen to meet.

He didn't hesitate and stood his ground as they fanned out in front of him, he felt his heartbeat quicken and the surge of adrenalin course through his body. He knew violence was imminent and he was ready, even though his body was readying itself for action he felt a strange calmness coming over him.

The first opponent approached with the confidence of someone that knew they were stronger and faster than the average person, not knowing that the lone figure in front of him wasn't an average person. The soldier arrogantly threw a punch at Ryes head, thinking that it would take his head off. In a split instant, Rye caught the mans fist in the air, twisted and pulled down in one clean movement, the man's shoulder pooped with a disheartening sound. Rye then instinctively kicked out to the front and sent the man flying onto his back, with a grimace of pain and shock on his face.

'You must be Rye Braden,' said one of the aggressors.

'My reputation precedes me, I see,' replied Rye.

'It does, and we were briefed about you, and that's why some of us received some additional upgrades to deal with you!'

Rye faulted for a nanosecond before he launched himself at the person speaking, grabbing the mans face to disorientate him. At the same time bringing his knee into the man's groin, but his opponent was fast and stepped sideways before the knee made contact. The aggressor looped his arm around Rye's in an arm lock and applied pressure. Rye thought his arm was going to snap under the sheer strength of his opponent. The man smiled as he manoeuvred Rye round to face the rest of them, instantly the closest super soldier took one step forward and punched Rye directly in the centre of the chest, on impact the wind was forced from Ryes body, and he felt immense pain. Even before he could try and take a breath in, the man punched again in the same place. Rye's chest exploded in pain, but he couldn't move due to the arm lock the first super soldier had him in. Rye focused all his strength on the arm lock, and with one fluid movement, he managed to loosen the hold enough to twist around and face the man holding him. Rye smiled briefly and in that instant, thrust his head forward into the man's face, blood erupting from the man's nose.

'You weren't expecting that hey!' Rye said, now free from the mans hold.

Rye bent down and swivelled full circle whilst one leg was outstretched, knocking the bloodied nosed man from his feet with a ferocious leg sweep.

At that moment, Si Morgan and the rest of Rye's unit came flooding into the area. Without hesitation, they fired upon the remaining standing super soldiers, taking one out instantly although the other two standing were able to take cover and

CHAPTER 26

retreat from the immediate area.

'Friends of yours?' Si said as he scanned the immediate area for any further threats.

'Not particularly,' Rye replied.

'Good,' Si said as he shot the two super soldiers that Rye had put on the floor.

'Find the other two now! The more of these super soldiers dead, the better!' Si commanded.

Gabriel knew that Major Khan was now out of the fight, his mind would be all over the place, hearing what he had just heard about the Unicom. The hidden gem of information about Major Khan and the Unicom had come from Rupert Everson. It had delivered the expected results, knocking the fight from the primary motivating force on Sky Zone One, Major Khan.

'Let's take the fight back to them,' Gabriel said to the fighters around him.

Gabriel stood from his cover, weapon in his shoulder and started his advance towards the defenders in front of him. He had nothing left to lose now and had to reach the main control room. He fired at will and ignored the return fire exploding around him, his group of fighters following him towards the objective. A figure beside him took a shot to the face and dropped to the floor instantly. Another was hit in the chest but managed to remain on their feet, at least until another shot smashed into their stomach, then they were still.

Shots were fired from both sides as Gabriel, and his fighters moved forward, casualties were taken on both sides, yet Gabriel didn't skip a step, his mind focused on the prize. With the speed and aggression of the remaining super soldiers, they made good ground and started to push the Commando Elite backwards.

'We've worked too hard to be stopped at the final hurdle,' Gabriel said to himself.

Just then, a bullet hit him in the shoulder, the pain shooting through his arm and chest. He fell to one knee and cursed to himself. He cleared his mind and stood, returning a lethal shot at the man that had shot him. The man was much older than the rest, and Gabriels shot hit him in the side of the neck, blood ejected from the wound, and it was clear that an artery had been hit, the older man stumbled forward before collapsing to the floor, dark red blood pumping from the wound.

Major Khan looked up just as Senator Bob Mills stumbled forward, blood pumping from his neck. He looked in horror as the older man fell forward and was still, except for the blood pumping from his neck.

He saw his men falling around him, the enemy force cutting through them with unrivalled speed and aggression. He was still hunched in a doorway which was now giving him minimal cover as the terrorists pushed forward, his mind still reeling from the words of the leader of the fighters.

One of the Unicorns killed my family, he thought to himself.

'Sir, we need to retreat now!' shouted one of the Commando Elite stood over him, fear evident in his voice.

As Major Khan looked up, the man's temple exploded as a bullet found its mark. The man's body gave way, and he crumpled to the floor next to Major Khan.

'This is it, I'm going to die here,' Major Khan mouthed, but deep down he didn't feel afraid, he didn't feel anything at that particular moment in time.

He was on his own now as the last of his men were killed, he closed his eyes and thought of his family.

CHAPTER 26

Rye and his group made their way with haste, trying to reach the main control room before the terrorists.

'It's just down this corridor,' commented one of the Commando Elite soldiers with them.

As they turned the corner, they saw more bodies, this time belonging to the terrorists, further long they saw even more bodies belonging to the Commando Elite. Whatever had gone down here, it had been ferocious and nothing less than a blood bath.

They then saw a group about a hundred metres away, making their way through one of the final security doors before the control room; it was clear that they were the terrorists. Just as they were about to fire on them, the same Commando Elite soldier shouted out.

'That's Major Khan. They have Major Khan with them.'

Rye could see a man dressed in United Continents uniform being manhandled by the group. He then watched as one of the group grabbed Major Khan by his hair and held his face against a control panel on the other side of the large opening.

'They are going to close the security door. If that happens, we won't get through,' said the soldier.

Rye didn't hesitate and set off at a sprint towards the security door. He felt the bullets pass by as the others tried to cut down the group in a hail of bullets. But Rye could see that only those at the back were in the line of fire, acting as a shield for the rest.

Rye watched as the security door started to lower, he forced himself forward at a speed that even belied his recent understanding of his capabilities.

Ten more steps, he thought to himself, willing himself on.

At the last second, he dived forward and slid the remainder

of the distance through the closing security door, hearing it thump shut behind him.

Chapter 27

Rye was quickly on his feet; he could see that he was in the final area before entering the main control room. He knew this area had a high level of security, although they did have Major Khan, meaning they could bypass the security measures. The corridor itself was about ten metres in diameter, and he could see Major Khan and the group of five that held him at the far end of the corridor. The length of the corridor was approximately fifty metres, and he knew he could cover that ground in no time at all.

One of the black clad figures had his weapon pointed at the head of Major Khan, and this made it difficult for Rye to use his own weapon. They had one more access point to get through, and they would have control of Sky Zone One. The only thing able to stop them now was Rye Braden.

'You've lost,' said Rye stepping forward towards the group holding Major Khan.

'On the contrary, Mr Braden. We are just beginning, one more step and we have control of the first Sky Zone in the world. There's never been anything like this before,' spoke a tall, shaven headed man which Rye knew to be Gabriel Durand.

'You were deluded ever to think you could pull this off,' Rye replied.

'How can I be deluded when we have achieved our mission?'

'But you haven't achieved it have you. You still need to get past me!'

With that, the man speaking made a gesture and said something to the group. The man holding the gun to Major Khan's head remained where he was, whilst three others raised their weapons at Rye. Rye noted two of them were dressed in the black assault gear, whilst the third wore older military-type clothing.

Two more super soldiers and one terrorist, Rye thought to himself as he prepared for the attack.

Rye calmed himself and focused on the capabilities he had; he knew he was faster and stronger than any average person. He needed those attributes now if he was going to survive these next few moments. He took a deep breath in and looked up at the three men readying their weapons on him.

He heard the tension on the trigger from the first weapon to fire. He felt the surge as the bullet left the barrel of the weapon. In that instant, he leapt to the left. He heard the bullet smash into the door behind him, at that moment he heard another shot being loosed by the second aggressor. He turned sideways and simultaneously dropped to one knee, hoping the bullet would be aimed at his centre of body. He was lucky, as the bullet grazed his shoulder as it missed its intended part of the body. With no time to waste Rye was up on his feet and charging towards his enemies, knowing that further shots were imminent. A third round was loosed, but this time there was no way of escaping the bullet, it entered his body just below the rib cage. Pain seared through his body and his pace slowed, although only briefly, he knew he had to reach the group if he had any chance of staying alive.

He was within a few metres of the closest person, who was one of the two super soldiers dressed in black assault gear. The super soldier was taller than Rye and more heavy set, but this didn't cause him to hesitate. The super soldier dropped his primary weapon freeing both his hands. He then lunged at Rye, grabbing him by the neck and stopping him in his tracks. Instantly, Rye lifted both his arms above his head and brought them down on the outstretched arms of the aggressor with every fibre of strength. The first impact had little effect on the larger man, so Rye raised his arms again and hit down in the same place, he felt the man's arms buckle slightly. That was all he needed, he grabbed the man wrists and pulled apart with all his might, trying to prize the man's grip from his throat. He felt his muscles burn as he slowly forced the opposing super soldier's arms apart, making him lose the grip on his throat. As soon as the man's grip had been released, Rye kicked out to the front sending the man sprawling back into the rest of the group.

'Kill him now', shrilled Gabriel, his voice echoing the fear that his plan could fail at the last hurdle.

The terrorist dressed in military clothing pulled a large combat knife from a sheath attached to his leg, he brandished the knife in front of him and started towards Rye. The man looked awkward, holding the blade, and Rye knew he didn't have time to waste. As the man slashed downwards trying to slice Rye from head to stomach, Rye blocked the man's arm and pulled him close, twisted him around and in one clean movement snapped the man's neck.

Rye grabbed the blade from the falling dead man's grasp and turned on the group. The two black clad super soldiers circled him readying for unarmed combat. Rye could feel the blood seeping from the bullet wound, and he knew he was losing strength rapidly, he needed to finish this now.

Rye waited for them to attack and they did, both at once. Rye held the knife at eye level in front of him, he forced the knife forward at the first person, but his target was exceptionally fast and managed to evade the blade. The second super soldier grabbed Rye from behind in a bear hug style hold, instinctively Rye flipped his head back into the face of the man holding him, he heard his nose crack, but the hold didn't falter. The first super soldier wasted no time in attacking again, smashing his fist into the bloodied area where the bullet had entered Ryes body.

Rye dropped the knife to the floor as the pain thrashed through him like rage, although this had an opposite effect to the one Rye's attacker wanted. Rye felt his strength swell as the pain touched every part of his body, his desperation further enhancing his strength. Rye unleashed his head again into the face of the man holding him from behind, again he heard bone crunch as the back of his head made impact. Rye felt the hold on him falter and used his newfound strength to break free from the hold. As soon as he was released, he smashed his fist into the face of the man in front of him. The two men went head to head punching wildly at each other, trying to use brute force to win the fight. Rye felt the presence of the man behind him and let out a ferocious back kick, striking the man in the throat with his foot. The kick disabled the rear attacker although faltered his ability to fend off the punches raining down on him from the front attacker. Rye took multiple blows to the head, which had the desired effect on him. He stumbled under the blazing attack allowing his attacker to grapple him to the floor, ending up on top of him.

'Do it now!' Gabriel bellowed at the super soldier holding the gun to Major Khans head.

The soldier dressed in black assault gear grabbed Major Khan's hair with his free hand and forced his face against the access control point of the final security door, for the system to authenticate access.

Rye was in trouble now, losing strength from the bullet wound in his stomach and having two of the super soldiers to deal with. He heard the final access door start to open and knew that he was losing his grasp on the situation. He looked over to see the door nearly open, ready for Gabriel Durand and his captive to reach their intended destination.

Rye focused his attention back to the attacker on top of him; he raised his hips off the ground as much as could. This provided just enough room for Rye to manoeuvre his body from underneath the bigger man. His timing was impeccable as he saw the second attacker coming towards him after recovering from the devastating kick to the throat. Rye had now reversed the situation and was above and behind the first attacker. Rye placed his arm around the man's neck and put him in a chokehold, as he did this, he felt the second attacker grab hold of his assault vest in an attempt to pull him off. Rye could only now deal with one attacker at a time, but at that moment, he heard a familiar voice.

'Rye, move away!' came the shout from Si Morgan.

Si and the rest of the group had managed to bypass the security measures on the first door and gain access to the final corridor.

Rye released the chokehold and moved to the side, as he did a hail of bullets slammed into the two super soldiers.

'Rye, the door!' Si shouted from the far end of the corridor.

Rye looked away from the super soldiers as they took round after round and looked towards the security door that Gabriel had gone through. It was closing rapidly.

If I lose them now then they will have control of Sky Zone One, Rye thought to himself.

He looked at Si Morgan and then back at the door, 'Here goes nothing,' he mouthed to himself.

Rye ran towards the closing security door, knowing that Si and his team would once again be stuck on the wrong side of the door and delayed trying to bypass the security.

'You're too late, there's nothing you can do,' spoke Gabriel as Rye ran into the control room.

Rye could see that the room was heavily populated with Sky Zone staff; most were sat at their desks with a mixture of shock and fear etched on their faces.

'Come any closer, and I will start killing people, starting with Major Khan here,' Gabriel continued.

Rye looked at Major Khan, the man looked defeated, and his eyes showed that he had no fight in him. The last super soldier still held a gun to Major Khans head, he had a wicked grin on his face, and Rye knew he was itching to pull the trigger.

'Major Khan, look at me,' Rye said.

But Major Khan didn't, he just looked down at the floor, totally unresponsive.

'Get on your knees,' commanded Gabriel taking a step towards Rye.

Rye hesitated, trying to figure out his next move. Whatever he was going to do, people would die, starting with Major Khan. As his mind raced, he saw movement behind Gabriel and the super soldier. He watched as a young female with shoulder-length blonde hair hesitantly approached the super soldier holding Major Khan captive.

Don't do it; Rye thought to himself as he watched her pick up a long metallic object from behind one of the control desks. He watched in slow motion as she swung the metal object at the back of the super soldier's head, listened as metal made contact with bone, watched as blood spurted from the area of impact. He then watched as the confused look on the soldier's face turned to rage, watched as the super soldier released his grip on Major Khan and focused his attention on the pretty blonde haired Sky Zone crew member. This was Ryes chance, probably his only chance. He sprinted towards Gabriel with blistering speed, ignoring the burning pain and blood still seeping from the wound in his stomach.

In the time that it took to reach his intended target, Rye watched as the last remaining super soldier grabbed hold of his female attacker, pulled her head back and fired one lethal shot up into her chin. Her body fell back with the impact of the shot, the top of her head falling away and outwards, a grisly look of shock on the pretty face as her body hit the floor.

Rye reached Gabriel before he could even think about drawing his weapon; Rye was able to grab hold of Gabriel's pistol in his thigh holster. He pulled the gun and placed it against Gabriel's head, positioning himself behind Gabriel as he knew he might need his body as cover from the last super soldier.

'Everybody remain still. If I see any further movement then I will shoot that person,' Rye shouted as he needed to ensure he now remained in control of this situation.

'Especially you, I don't need much to finish you off,' Rye

whispered with a menacing tone into the ear of Gabriel.

Once the super soldier had finished with Private Sarah Ashford, he turned his attention back to Rye, who was now holding Gabriel Durand hostage. The look in the super soldier's eyes was a mixture of excitement and bloodlust, which made Rye think that not only was this a super soldier but a crazy one at that.

The super soldier started walking towards Rye, his gun raised at Rye's head. His steps were slow and purposeful.

After five steps, an almighty noise stopped him in his tracks. A sound none of them were expecting, a sound born from unbearable loss.

'No, No, No,' came the strangled words from Major Khan.

The super soldier had turned now and was looking down at Major Khan who was on the floor cradling what remained of Private Sarah Ashford's head.

'You've killed them all, everyone I ever loved! Everything I have worked for and dedicated my life too, and for what? To be taken for a fool, to have the one thing I believe in to be ripped away from me.'

Major Khan was rocking back and forth now, stroking the bloodied head of his partner for the last year, the one person that had given him the will to carry on after the loss of his wife and daughter some years earlier.

'You will not get away with this any longer,' Major Khan was on his feet now, fists clenched, his eyes burning into the super soldier facing him.

With a roar that shook the room, Major Khan sprinted towards the super soldier. It only took a dozen steps until he reached him, grabbing for his throat. Major Khan wasn't a weak man, quite the opposite although against this super

CHAPTER 27

soldier then there was no competition. The super soldier dropped his weapon and grabbed Major Khan by the head, placing his thumbs into his eye sockets. Major Khan's roar instantly changed into a high pitched scream as the super soldier raised the Major from the floor and pushed his eyeballs inside his skull.

Rye watched as blood oozed from where the eyes had once been. The Major's body went into spasms before falling still, hanging lifeless in the grip of the super soldier. Rye took this opportunity, aiming his gun at the back of the super soldier's head and fired, one shot after another smashing into the back of the head of the last threat. The super soldier dropped Major Khan's lifeless body to the floor, then stumbled around to face the attack, but it was too late, his head was destroyed with brain matter pulping out of what was left of the man's skull, and he merely fell forward and was still.

Rye still had hold of Gabriel around the neck.

'You can't do this. You can't stop me. This is my destiny!' Gabriel said in a hushed angry tone.

'I have stopped you. It is over Gabriel.'

'It will never be over while the United Continents rule this planet. Don't you see what you've done, you haven't saved anyone! We will all be hostages to them, the rich prosper whilst we all suffer under their tyrannical rule. You are blind to their real intentions. What do you think they will do with you now, you think they will just let you walk out of here knowing what you are?'

'I will take that risk,' Rye replied.

Rye looked around the room at the carnage laid out in front of him.

'Open the door,' Rye said to the closest operator.

At that moment, Gabriel reached into one of his pockets and pulled out a small explosive device. Rye saw it instantly and released his hold on Gabriel, at the same time shoving him forward.

'Don't do it, Gabriel,' Rye shouted.

Rye watched in slow motion as Gabriel turned towards him and raised his arm holding the device, as his thumb began to move towards the top of the device. With lightning speed, Rye fired two shots. One aimed at the face of Gabriel and the other at his arm, both shots found their mark. Gabriel's head erupted in a shower of blood, at the same time his arm ripped away from his body at the elbow. Gabriel's body fell limp to the ground with the explosive device clattering to the floor at the same time, still held in the lifeless hand of Gabriel's severed arm.

As the door of the main control room opened, Si Morgan and his team entered the room.

'Looks like a butcher's shop in here!'

'We lost Major Khan and one other. Do we know what's happening on the rest of Sky Zone One?' said Rye.

'The latest updates suggest that all hostiles have been killed or detained, not without major casualties on both sides though. The Eden soldiers were a formidable weapon.'

The adrenalin was ebbing away now, and Rye started to feel the pain of his bullet wound, he touched the area and could see that he had lost a lot of blood.

'We need to get you checked over Rye.'

'I'll be fine,' replied Rye.

'You may be superhuman, but you still need blood and looks like you've lost a lot, so get yourself checked out asap. That's an order!'

CHAPTER 27

With that, Rye started to leave the control room.

'Rye, well done. You've saved a lot of people today,' Si said as Rye left the room.

They had stopped the Faction Against Continent Rule from taking over Sky Zone One and by doing so had saved many lives, more importantly, they had prevented terrorists from gaining the upper hand over the United Continents. A terrorist organisation having that level of control would have been disastrous for the planet and didn't even bear thinking about. Gabriel Durand and most of the super soldiers were dead, those that were still alive would be charged with the various crimes they had committed, and Rye knew they would never see daylight again. They had also found out more about the secretive organisation named the Elders, meaning that further investigations would be conducted. Especially now that they had something to work with, that something being a self-confessed Elder by the name of Rupert Everson.

As Rye walked, he thought about the long journey he had undertaken. His questions about who he was had taken him far beyond anything he had imagined. He still had answers, but these could wait for another day. Whatever the future held for him, he would deal with it the way he had always dealt with life. For now, he just wanted to get back to the surface and find Ruby Monroe.

Printed in Great Britain
by Amazon